• BALDWIN'S LEGACY BOOK FIVE •
LINEAGE

NATHAN HYSTAD

Copyright © 2020 Nathan Hystad

All rights reserved.

No part of this publication may be reproduced, distributed, or transmitted in any form or by any means, including photocopying, recording, or other electronic or mechanical methods, without the prior written permission of the publisher, except in the case of brief quotations embodied in critical reviews and certain other non-commercial uses permitted by copyright law.

This is a work of fiction. All of the characters, names, incidents, organizations, and dialogue in this novel are either products of the author's imagination or are used fictitiously.

Cover art: Tom Edwards Design
Edited by: Scarlett R Algee
Proofed and Formatted by: BZ Hercules

ISBN-13: 9798666306406

Also By Nathan Hystad

The Survivors Series
The Event
New Threat
New World
The Ancients
The Theos
Old Enemy
New Alliance
The Gatekeepers
New Horizon
The Academy
Old World
New Discovery
Old Secrets
The Deities

The Resistance
Rift
Return
Revenge

Baldwin's Legacy
Confrontation
Unification
Culmination
Hierarchy
Lineage
Legacy

Red Creek
Return to Red Creek
Lights Over Cloud Lake
The Manuscript

PROLOGUE

The alarm chimed softly through the office, drawing Brandon's gaze off his work. "Computer, what tripped the sensors?"

"*Movement in quadrant zero point seven, sir,*" the computer's feminine voice told him.

"Zero point seven…" Brandon found the referenced region on his console and put his hands behind his head as he watched the feeds. "Damn it." He kicked away from the desk, rolling across the floor to the transmitter. He quickly pressed the blue button, trying to reach the others. "Guys, we have a code nine."

He waited for the response. When none came within a minute, he tapped it again. "Quit messing around. We have a code nine. They're coming."

Still nothing.

Brandon rose, rubbing sweaty palms on his gray jumpsuit. He saw the patches in his reflection but ignored the symbol that used to mean so much to him. He should have ripped them off by now.

"Where are they?" he muttered to himself, leaning over his screen. He linked to the camp drones, sending one high above the Martian surface. The camp was spread out below, and he was proud of what they'd accomplished in a decade. Ten years of blood, sweat, and tears. This was their home.

Brandon tried not to think about the brother he'd left behind, or any of the countless others that had been lost since their escape, but he couldn't help it. Clark would be so proud of him. But if President Basher discovered them, it was over.

The camp was spread out across two square kilometers, with seven habitats interconnected by long underground tunnels, and the drone hovered over the first dome. Behind the clear glass was a humid garden, and Brandon smiled at the greenery amongst the red dust and rock. The juxtaposition wasn't lost on him.

The next two domes contained the majority of their population: seventy people sleeping in close quarters. It wasn't ideal, but they'd managed to make do. Brandon slept in his command center most nights, so it didn't really bother him.

When the drone hovered over the fifth dome, half a kilometer from the first, his breath caught in his chest. Someone was there. He saw the glint of metal where it shouldn't be and lowered the drone toward the anomaly. Two of his people were standing outside the habitat, but from this distance, he couldn't identify them.

The rover was approaching, and he noticed the gun in one of the colonist's hands. This wasn't good. He ran to the edge of the office, ignoring the alarm from the distant ship's presence. "Computer, has anything landed nearby in the last day?"

"No detection of orbital breach, sir."

"Then how the hell is a rover heading for our camp as we speak?" Brandon asked.

"That seems unlikely."

"Never mind. Send a red alert. We have company. Direct them to the tunnels and make them seal themselves

Lineage

in," he said, slipping into his EVA.

"*Sir, most of the...*"

"Just do it, computer!" he shouted. He heard the beginnings of her calm message pouring through the console speakers, and he was about to proceed to the airlock when he remembered the gun. Brandon tested his EVA's functions, and when he had the green light, he jogged behind his desk, using his verbal password to open the black safe. He pulled the modified weapon from its case and pressed the power button on the side. It whined as the bars filled along its barrel.

Brandon darted from the office, sealing the airlock first, and exited his command center. It was the only building on their colony to not be connected to the others. He'd wanted to have a space far enough from camp to keep watch, and it doubled as a safe zone should trouble come their way. The airlock hatch was built into the sharp cliff of the crater, and he walked out of it, heading for his own rover.

The solar panels showed he had three quarters of a charge, and he turned the unit on. It had four waist-high tires, with space to carry four comfortably in their EVAs, along with a truck bed to hold supplies. It was empty now, and he clicked the vehicle into drive, sending dust behind him.

The idea of an alien rover on their planet was difficult to fathom. They had securities in place to prevent this exact thing, but somehow they'd been breached. First, he needed to mitigate any danger, and secondly, he had to ensure this wasn't repeated.

The rover was a couple of kilometers from the fifth dome, which they'd dubbed "The Island." It housed their main facilities: gym, mess hall, kitchens. The dome over was their storage facility, and where they initiated construction on each additional tunnel and structure. Already two more domes were underway, but they were waiting for another supply shipment to arrive. He hoped that was what had set the alarms off. Unfortunately, that wasn't the path the traders were supposed to take from Earth.

Brandon slowed as he approached the Island and drove around the far edge, glancing at the sky. It was littered with stars, and his hand settled over the gun sitting on the seat beside him. He wasn't going to let anyone ruin what they'd created.

When he was sure he'd be exposed if he continued, Brandon parked the rover, turning it off, and hopped out, his boots landing softly on the surface. The gun felt unusual in his grip for a second, but the memories of the civil war flooded into his mind. His spine went rigid, and he could almost smell the battlefields inside his EVA. "Not now," he mumbled to himself.

Hugging the dome, he moved toward its entrance, which faced the expanse of Noachis Terra. Brandon preferred night on Mars. If he closed his eyes while indoors, he could almost pretend he was in a place more habitable, somewhere that the world wasn't trying to harm him at every bend. This desolate landscape had killed twelve of them over the last decade, and there were days he thought that number was a blessing.

He stopped when he spotted the other rover, this model unfamiliar. Someone stood in front of it. He pulled free the digital binoculars strapped to his belt and peered through them. Not a someone; a some*thing*. Brandon had seen androids like this near the end of the war, but this one looked far more advanced. His silver hands gave him away, and the fact that he didn't wear an EVA made it even more obvious.

Brandon assumed the android was speaking to them,

linking to their EVA headsets, but he wasn't close enough to hear the conversation. He continued forward, recognizing his friends. Carl was at the lead, Jun beside him. Brandon hoped her reckless behavior was on pause today. He wished she'd stayed inside.

They were still a hundred meters from his position, when the android's transmission relayed into his headset too, and he slowed, trying to make out the choppy words. He stepped closer, finally receiving a clear feed.

"*You do not seem to comprehend my message. You are to stand down and await the arrival of our team. You will be kept alive if you cooperate,*" the robot told them with a neutral tone.

"And you listen here, you bucket of bolts…" Jun started to say, but Carl raised a hand, silencing her.

"How did you reach the surface?" Carl asked it.

Brandon noted the gun on the robot's arm. It was built into its forearm, and the android was likely extremely quick on the draw.

"*That is none of your concern. This colony is hereby unsanctioned by President Gordon Basher on behalf of Earth and its residents. You have been labeled insurgents and will be treated as such,*" the android said.

"Look, we only left to escape his tyranny. We aren't harming anyone," Carl pleaded, and the robot stepped closer.

"*You have misspoken of our leader and will be brought to justice.*" The bot's arm lifted, and Brandon made his move. He bounded across the empty space between them, using his years of training to pass the distance in seconds. The android turned to face him, sending a blast. Brandon jumped, using the low gravity to his advantage, and spun in the air, rolling forward as he struck the ground. His weapons tracked on the android, firing twice. The first blast missed the target, but the second struck the android in the leg, damaging its knee.

Brandon didn't relent. He kept moving, making himself more difficult to pursue, and shot another volley of blasts, this time striking the robot a few more times.

"*You will regret this, insurgents.*"

Brandon heard its voice in his headset, but it only fueled his anger. "You came to us, uninvited, interrupting our chance at a fresh start. All we ask is to be free. Send that to your leader." He pointed the weapon at the robot, who was lying on its back over the red dusty ground. It was dark, but the stars cast a dim glow over the ominous landscape. Their time had come to an end. All this effort. For nothing.

"*You will cease fire and do as order…*" Brandon fired from close range as it attempted to sit up, and the blast hit the target on the smooth-featured metallic face. It fell, circuits exposed with flashing arcs, quickly dying.

Jun raced to his side, and she kicked the metal device with her EVA boot. "Damn it! What are we going to do?" She turned to Brandon, her eyes glowing with the soft green reflection of her helmet's HUD.

"We're going to do what we've always done," Brandon told her.

Carl walked over, staring at the ruined android. "That's correct. Prepare to fight."

ONE

*A*dmiral Thomas Baldwin exited the elevator on the top floor of the Concord's administrative headquarters in the center of Ridele, the capital city of Nolix. Everything was so pristine: the floors stark white, the walls glass, the lighting glittering and opulent. The style somewhat matched the fleet ships like *Constantine*, but that was where the parallels ended.

Thomas had been coming to this office for the last couple of months nearly every day, and he still hadn't grown used to it. Walking into the space felt like he was a stranger in his own clothing. The sounds were unfamiliar. He heard them now: the shuffling of the breakfast delivery man's feet, the chatter at the reception desk, the muffled voices speaking behind closed doors as he made his way toward his own office.

There were currently ten admirals. After the debacle with the Statu had revealed the old regime's lies and cover-ups, the entire organization had been reset, with Admiral Jalin Benitor, the Callalay leader, at the helm.

Tom strode past Prime Xune's office, which usually sat empty unless he was in town. For most of Tom's first two months, the Prime had been traveling throughout Concord space, meeting with each partner, giving rallying speeches, and encouraging transparency. Tom didn't have much of a stomach for politics, but even he could see that Xune, previously a Zilph'i advisor, was the right man for the job.

Xune was bringing the partners together like never before, and his passion was paying off, according to Benitor. The Concord had been in shambles only a year or so ago, but their foundation had been rebuilt, and Tom was proud to be part of the reason.

He stopped in front of Admiral Benitor's office, which was right beside Xune's, and poked his head in, seeing she was scrolling through messages on her projected screen.

"Any news for me?" he asked. They'd been waiting for a message from Elder Fayle, but she'd been circumspect on the details of what exactly occurred when the Vusuls attacked Driun F49. Reeve Daak had been a witness, along with Ven Ittix, and they'd reported the events.

"Still no sign of Keen. I want you on this, Thomas. He was your capture, and…" Benitor didn't even glance up from her screen as she spoke to him.

"Don't go there. I wasn't the one who freed him from the prison. You'd do well to remember that," he told her.

She finally broke her stare from her work and met his gaze. "Thomas, just locate him. You know where he's going. How difficult can this be?"

"I have eyes on them, but this isn't going to be as simple as standing in the bushes waiting for Keen to appear at his wife's house. He's not that impulsive," Tom told her.

"Fine." She seemed ready to return to her work, but she paused, waving him inside her office. He did so, and the door slid closed behind him. Tom looked past her, at the marvelous view of the city. The panoramic floor-to-ceiling windows gave one of the best angles of Ridele. Even though he didn't love being in a city, there was no denying it held some sort of magical beauty he rarely saw elsewhere.

Lineage

Dozens of large transport vessels moved between the giant sky-piercing towers, carrying the locals from one section of the city to another. Ridele was spread across a hundred kilometers, but this quadrant, the core of Nolix, was the most impressive. Millions of lives, so close to one another. Tom shuddered to think of how much devastation could result from an attack, and blinked away his gawking stare, settling it on Benitor.

"I hear you've been doing some digging, Baldwin," she whispered.

"Is that so? Do you see a shovel in my hand?" he asked, and from her reaction, she wasn't pleased with his flippant remark.

Benitor rose, her chair squeaking slightly at the reprieve. She turned around, staring at the view like he'd been doing. "This is the pride of the Concord, Tom. Nolix. Do you know why?"

"The Tekol are a great people. They're a Founder, and the location was ideal for an information and supply hub. From Nolix, you can reach almost every corner of the Concord within three weeks," he told her.

She shook her head. "The Callalay were the first to conceive of this partnership. Aruto is majestic. Have you ever visited it?"

"No, I haven't." Tom had always wanted to, but his grandfather hadn't brought Tom along when he'd traveled there. "I hear it's wonderful." This was the truth.

"Aruto is. But there's a reason we haven't been such a central focus as Earon, Leria, or Nolix." Benitor turned to face him, and for the first time in his memory, he saw that she was upset. Emotional.

"What is it?"

"Stop digging, Thomas. The Ugna were welcomed into the Concord with open arms. The Prime has asked me to ensure that they stay happy, and that was part of the reason you joined our ranks," she told him.

He understood this already, but there was something she wasn't saying. "And you want me to passively sit around, waiting at Fayle's beck and call?"

Her misty eyes hardened as she frowned at him. "No. I want you to do your job. Find Keen. While you're doing that, you'll be the Founders' liaison—not to Elder Fayle, but to the Ugna. She respects you, and you have befriended Ven Ittix. You were the perfect man for the job. Don't make me regret bringing you into the fold."

He wanted to counter, to say that he might be the one full of regret. Two months. Already he felt different, changed, from being grounded on a planet. He missed *Constantine,* both the ship and his grandfather's AI. He'd bonded with the crew—from Brax to Reeve to Ven, and certainly with Treena Starling. She was the most capable officer he'd ever worked with, and he was positive she would be an astounding captain, but a huge part of him wished he was still behind the helm.

"You didn't tell me what happened with Aruto," he said.

"You'll find out soon enough. I'm sending you to meet with President Bertol." The elderly Callalay admiral smiled, years slipping off her face with the gesture.

"You are?"

"That's right. Elder Fayle will also be going. It was her request," Benitor said.

"I thought you said I didn't work for her," Tom reminded her.

"That's right. You work for me, and for the Prime, but most importantly, for the Concord," she said, taking her seat once again.

"When do I leave?"

Lineage

"In two days. I've asked the crew of *Shu* to accompany you."

Tom had been hoping *Constantine* would have taken him, but it was probably for the best. They had their own imperative mission on hand, and as much as he wished he could join them, it wasn't to be. He'd accepted this role, and he wasn't going to start to complain about his choices now. "Very well."

Admiral Benitor returned to her inbox, scrolling through messages as they emerged on her projected screen, and he let himself out without another word.

He entered his own office, which held the same impressive sight of the city below—only with windows half as wide—and took a seat at his desk. It was uncluttered. He looked around at the walls, seeing that they were bare. There were no plants, no personal mementos. He realized it felt like the office was empty, like no one would notice if he walked away at this very moment.

"Can I get you anything, sir?" a young Tekol man asked, waiting outside Tom's door.

"Can you help him track down Lark Keen?" another voice asked from out of view, and Tom bristled.

"Uhm, sir, I don't think..." the assistant stuttered.

"It's okay, Gill. I'll have a cup of Raca, please, and feel free to ignore Admiral West. He probably forgot to eat his morning snack," Tom said. The young man rushed the steaming beverage inside and continued on, pushing the hovering food cart.

"Oh, Baldwin, I was only having some fun," West said.

At my expense, Tom thought. West was everything he despised in a coworker. There were three human admirals, and Tom wished Anthony West wasn't one of them. He was ten years older than Tom; his head was clean-shaven, but he sported a thick beard. It was more gray than brown, but it was obvious the man had undergone a lot of procedures to hide his age. He had that unnaturally smooth skin only modifications could create.

"If you don't mind, I have work to do," Tom told him, and West tapped his wrist tablet. The time projected above it.

"Interesting. The rest of us arrived an hour ago. I guess you don't need to put the work in," West goaded him, walking away.

Tom liked to give people the benefit of the doubt, but he truly despised the man. Being on a ship, he'd been in charge. Even when he wasn't the highest-ranking officer, others had looked to him to lead, had deferred to his judgment. Tom hadn't dealt with a workplace bully before, but he could tell that West was more bite than bark.

Tom sipped from his cup and reviewed his messages, hoping for a clue to Keen's whereabouts, and wondering how it was possible to have escaped from the transport in the first place.

"I can't do it," Treena said, trying to sit.

"Yes, you can." Conner Douglas was ten feet away, arms outstretched like a doting father waiting for his toddler to hobble over for the first time.

Treena wore robotic braces on her legs, which assisted the process, and she'd worked herself down to only using them at twenty percent power. It had been Conner's idea to try to walk without them, but she didn't think she was ready.

"Listen, how about we call it a day?" she asked, sweat dripping over her spine.

"No."

"It's my…"

"Just try it, Starling!" he shouted, catching her off-guard. "You've been pushing yourself so hard. Look at you! Did you think that after only two months you'd be almost walking? Your eyes are far better, your mobility is impressive." His voice lowered, along with his arms. "Do it. Not for me, but for you."

Treena took a deep breath, wobbling in her stance slightly. It was only ten feet. How tough could it be? She took a step, her knee wavering, but it held. Those exercises to build up her idle muscles were working. Compared to operating her android body, this felt like torture, but if she was ever going to be herself for good, she needed to push it. The next foot came down, and she smiled as it settled. "I'm doing it…" Her left knee caved, and she sprawled out on the ground, landing on her hands.

"Are you okay?" Conner rushed over, crouching near her. His touch was warm on her skin.

She laughed, rolling onto her side. "Am I okay? I'm great!" she exclaimed. "I walked by myself. Or I stepped, at least. I can't believe this is really happening."

Conner helped Treena to her seat, and she flicked the leg-assisting device on, settling it to fifty percent. She stood up unaided and saw her reflection in the gymnasium's mirror. She was used to seeing this version of herself on the bed, being plugged into the android, but here she was, moving about with the damaged and worn version of Treena Starling. Her hair had grown longer, and she'd left it. It was time for a change. Aimie Gaad had offered to remove the scarring, and Treena knew she might take her up on it one day, but for now, she didn't think it was necessary.

"What's next?" Treena asked.

Conner peered over at her, grinning. "I'm leaving in two days. I guess *Shu* is taking Baldwin and Fayle to Aruto."

Treena wondered if she heard that right. "Aruto?"

"Yeah. Have you been there before?" Conner asked.

"Never. It's rare for anyone to visit, isn't it?"

"I've seen it a couple of times. I don't know what all the fuss is about. It's a nice place, but the mere fact that one of our Founders—arguably, the *main* Founder—is reluctant to have others drop in has always struck me as a little cagey." Conner walked her to the edge of the gym, and she flipped the robot-assisted leg device to eighty percent before heading into the halls. This entire floor of the R-Emergence building was closed off for her use, and she had access to countless rehab specialists.

Today, she'd asked them to take the day off as Conner came to visit, which he'd done at least twice a week over the last couple of months. She stopped in the dim corridor, staring at the man she'd grown close to, and didn't have to squint to see him any longer. They'd completed the surgery on her retinas, and she could see as well as in her artificial body.

Conner seemed to feel her stare, and he stopped walking, turning to face her. "How about you? When do you leave?"

"A few days after you. We're going to stop by and pick up Ven, and I meet my new commander tomorrow," Treena said.

"I've only heard stories," Conner told her with another grin.

"I hope they've been embellished." Treena was upset they'd given her *Constantine* with the caveat of making her take on an ex-Concord captain to be her second-in-command. She'd been told it was only for this one mission. If

Lineage

it was up to her, she would have stolen someone like Conner and promoted Ven or Brax to commander. But she hadn't been given the choice, and Treena had a feeling that Benitor would continue to tug on her strings for her first few assignments. Tom had put up with a lot, but Treena wasn't Thomas Baldwin. She'd been through the wringer for the Concord, and after what R-Emergence had done to her, she deserved some compensation.

They entered the elevator, heading for the top floor, where their respective shuttles waited. The tower was one of the tallest in the city, and she felt a wave of vertigo she wouldn't have experienced in her artificial form. Conner rushed to her side, clutching her arm, steadying her. "You okay?"

"I'm fine. Just not used to this yet," she assured him. The city spread out in every direction as far as she could see. "I can't believe Baldwin took the role." She said this quietly, as if to herself, but Conner replied.

"I know. Rene was flabbergasted. She's also upset you were requested for the Earth mission instead of her," Conner admitted as he walked past the first five parked shuttles to the Concord-issued model. Hers was next, with the First Ship logo painted on the doors of the white vessels.

"You never told me that. Why?"

He shrugged. "She didn't want anyone to know, but it's you and me, right?"

Treena didn't respond at first, but the air was thick with tension. She took a step toward him, her entire body aching from today's efforts. She wasn't going to win any beauty contests with her ragged body, but she had to know. "What do you want?"

"Adventure, a good book, a nice glass of Vina," Conner said with a laugh.

She stood beside his shuttle, straight-faced. "That's not

what I meant. Why have you been visiting so often, pushing me?"

"Because you seemed like you could use a push. And a friend," he said softly. She got the sense there was more behind his words, but nothing else parted from his lips.

"Okay… good." She watched as he entered the shuttle, stopping to catch her eye.

"Keep in touch."

"Thanks for… coming," Treena told him, and the shuttle's door closed, leaving her alone on the top of the R-Emergence tower.

TWO

"It is a shame you have to depart soon," Hanli told him as they walked along the river's edge.

Ven Ittix basked in the sunlight, a rare thing for their people. He wore a protective layer of cream over his face, which would be beet red if not for the substance. The Ugna were powerful, but things like too much sun tended to alter their pale skin in minutes.

"Truth be told, I am excited for the mission," he said.

"Earth…" Hanli slowed, turning to stare at the water. "How is it no one knew the location of the humans' home world?"

"Technically, Celevon, the Pilia's planet, is their true home world," he told her. The Pilia had sent off five colony ships a million years prior. One had ended up becoming the Vusuls, who were the same race that had fought with the Minon only a few short weeks prior. They'd also been destroyed by the Ugna fleet with ease. The Minon and the Seeli were the other two races, aside from the colony ship where they'd discovered the pure Pilia girl, Eve, alive.

"Have you heard from Talepen recently?" Hanli asked him.

"Yes. The Minon have been successful in their efforts. They expect to begin implementing the DNA adjustments, allowing their race to breed and thrive once again. The Seeli managed a few pregnancies as a result of the testing," Ven told her.

"That *is* great news." Hanli moved toward a boulder and took a seat, leaving room for Ven. He'd thoroughly enjoyed his time on Driun F49, learning more about the Ugna this last while, but he longed for the comfort of his cabin on *Constantine*. With Baldwin gone, things would be different, but Ven was still excited at the prospect of traveling to Earth.

"Has your Doctor Nee returned?" she asked him.

"I think he will arrive at Nolix in time for the crew's introduction to the new commander." Ven wished he could be present, but he was being picked up on the way out of Concord space.

"You should have been promoted. You are capable, and Ugna." She said that as if it should be enough to claim he'd make a competent commander, despite the fact that he had only a year of experience.

"My time will come. It is not yet. *Patience is a learned attribute. Faith in the Vastness is honed. Seek either too quickly and falter. Balance your mind and efforts, for the finish line is rarely when you expect it.*" He spoke the words with the respect they deserved, but Hanli broke into laughter.

"I am sorry, Ven. You are always so serious. I understand your point. Perhaps you are too inexperienced. I do wish you the best success on your venture. Will you return to Driun when you are able?" she asked, her short hair styled to the side, her soft pink eyes boring into his.

"I will return." He didn't know what else to say.

"Good. Were you aware that Elder Fayle is gone?" Hanli changed topics. She stood again, slowly walking in the direction of their village, which was becoming more of a city.

"I said goodbye to her last week." Since then, Ven had

spent a lot of time within the training structures, working on restoring his own faith. After learning how much had been kept from him over his life, he'd felt betrayed, but Fayle had assured him it was for his own protection. Before she'd departed, she'd issued an odd omen: a warning about High Elder Wylen. *Be cautious around him. Do not show your true strength. I fear he will use you.*

The rocky river's edge changed to paved walkways as they entered town, and Ven greeted a couple strolling by, boxes floating over their heads as they exited the storage warehouse with supplies. This city held somewhere around fifty thousand people, but it never felt crowded, despite the numbers. Many spent days, weeks even, training indoors. It was rare to see more than fifty people in the streets at the same time, and even the optional communal dining halls were never fully occupied.

The sky was growing dark as the sun began its daily routine, setting behind the mountain range they lived beside. For a moment, he forgot he was leaving soon, and relished his time spent with another of his kind. Hanli was the perfect partner, and Fayle had more than hinted at their coupling potential. He remained unsure, not wanting to create waves quite yet. The idea of being with Hanli so intimately sent a ripple of nerves through him.

"Do you want to eat?" she asked, but as much as Ven wanted to, he didn't think it was proper. Perhaps after their next mission.

"I should return to my quarters. I have an early morning," he told her.

She gave him a smile and touched his hand briefly. He felt her thoughts, her mood, her obvious interest in him. It was partly veiled with intrigue because of his notoriety, but not so much that it was disturbing. Hanli liked being around him, and she fed him those emotions. Ven stepped back, the onslaught of her intentions too much for him.

He didn't say a word, but only took off, leaving her alone in the middle of the walkway.

Ven's mind felt clouded. By the time he made it to the third resident tower, he'd stopped, making sure Hanli hadn't followed him. She was nowhere to be seen. He felt like a fool for storming off. She'd put herself out there, and he'd run from her like a child. Never had one of his own kind opened themselves up like that to him, and it had severely startled him.

"What has you so perturbed, my son?" a voice asked.

Ven spun to see High Elder Wylen lingering near the building's entrance. He was alone. Ven sensed others in their vicinity and scanned the promenade, recognizing the High Elder's personal guard watching over him from twenty yards behind. He counted four of them, which meant there were likely ten or so others in hiding at this moment.

"Nothing, High Elder. I'm only returning from a pleasant evening stroll," Ven told him.

The High Elder looked younger than he had the first time Ven had laid eyes on him, his eyes so dark and red, it was difficult not to stare into them. His head was bald, and he had once been very tall, but age had stooped his spine enough to cause a slight hunch in his posture. Wylen had scars on his cheeks, one on either side, and he guessed the cuts had been deep. He didn't ask about them. It felt like there would be a long and personal story attached to the injury, and it was none of Ven's business.

"An evening stroll. I once had time for such activities," Wylen said. He wore dark clothing, a long gray cloak draped over his shoulders. He was thin, as were most Ugna, but Ven saw something else in the High Elder. A sickness, perhaps. "Were you with First Officer Hanli?"

Lineage

The question sounded innocent enough, but Ven heard the accusation laced behind the words. Or was it something else? Was the High Elder the reason she'd been spending so much time with him?

"Yes, with the First Officer, but I assure you…"

High Elder Wylen shook his head, clicking his tongue onto the roof of his mouth. "You have no need for explanations. I was only curious. You two are well-suited. Tell me, Ven. When are you setting off?"

It was becoming a popular query, and the fact that Wylen had asked it made Ven want to leave Driun F49 even faster, especially after Fayle's warning. He undersold it. "In a few days. Not long."

"Good. You are doing a satisfactory job with the Concord. It's nice to have someone on the inside, if you will." Wylen had a different way about him, one that set him apart from the other Ugna, the Elders especially.

"I appreciate it, sir. I have enjoyed my time spent aboard…"

"Enjoyed? Are you not supposed to be training? Working on *Constantine*?" Wylen's expression shifted, and he frowned. His brows were wisps of white-blond hair.

"I am working, yes. I am an Executive Lieutenant…"

Wylen cut him off. "Yes, I am aware. I only meant that the reason you're there is not relevant to your amusement at the position."

Ven didn't move, the High Elder preventing him from entering the residential block. "I do not understand."

"Fayle told me you were aware of your role. Is this not the case?"

It was Ven's turn to frown. "I still…"

High Elder Wylen stepped closer, and Ven wanted to retreat the second he felt the intense vibrations emerging from the powerful man. Ven had seen what they were capable of, and it had taken some convincing from Fayle to not renounce his faith at their actions against the Vusuls.

"Listen closely, Ven Ittix. You are one of us. You belong to the Ugna, which means you"—he pushed a long, bent finger into Ven's chest—"belong to *me*. You will be my eyes and ears aboard *Constantine*, do you understand?"

Ven nodded, even though he would do no such thing. If he denied the man, he had the feeling he'd be killed on the spot, his body removed by Wylen's personal guards and buried somewhere no one would find him. "Of course, sir. I was hoping you would ask me this very same thing," he lied, struggling to force the words from his lips.

The man's mood changed in a flash, and he smiled, the sight disturbing. "Good. Let's not tell Elder Fayle, though, okay? She has plenty on her plate, and I know how much she cares about you and your position. I've programmed my personal communication details into your console upstairs."

Ven peered up the building's wall, wondering how long Wylen had been snooping through Ven's things up in his room. "Very well. I look forward to reporting to you."

Wylen walked away, the bottoms of his shoes scraping against the path as he entered a hovercar. The guards moved in after him, and Ven continued standing where he was until the vehicle was no longer visible. He exhaled and wondered how Fayle would react when he told her the news.

"You're really going to let Anthony West get the best of you? That guy has been a thorn in R-Emergence's side for years. He's constantly voting against every little ruling, each law that we've tried to pass. He's as far against cloning as you can be. A younger man with old-world ideologies," Aimie Gaad told Tom as she massaged his tense shoulders. Her apartment overlooked the ocean from the penthouse, which was impressive, since the water was at least ten kilometers from them.

The sun had set an hour ago, and he'd rushed over, using one of the personal robotic shuttles, where he was dropped off on the rooftop pad with two minutes to spare. He'd already been late for three dates over the last month, and he didn't want to get on her bad side.

"I agree with some of his reasoning, but I still hate the jerk," Tom told her.

"Are we going out or staying in?" Aimie asked, sitting on the couch beside him.

"I have to go," he told her.

"But you just arrived," she complained.

Tom laughed, rubbing his temples. It had been a long day. "No, that's not what I meant. Aruto. I'm going to Aruto."

"You have to be kidding me. What for?" she asked.

He was a little surprised by her reply. "Is it really that odd?" Tom tried to think about his previous posting and couldn't recall if Yin Shu, his previous captain, had mentioned the planet. They'd all studied the Founders in depth during their Academy days, and nothing had stood out as overly unique about Aruto to him.

"They never did allow us to put an R-Emergence research center there."

"So that's what this is about. You're upset? I thought you were going to retire anyway."

Aimie rolled her eyes at him, and he smiled, pulling her in for a kiss. "They're working at fixing their issues, and since the board has been removed, I think I can help steer the company in the right direction. With the Concord's approval, of course."

Prime Xune was disappointed in R-Emergence, and his actions had been fast and efficient. A deep dive into their politics and records had instantly gotten underway, and nearly a quarter of their staff had been removed. The company had a long way to go, but Tom agreed that they were on the right track. Each of their facilities had a Concord representative attached, and so far, the sites were playing along nicely.

"Back to Aruto," she told him. "What are you doing there?"

"That's Concord business, I'm afraid," he told her, without specific awareness of why he was being sent.

"I see. How long will you be gone?" she asked.

"I'm not sure."

"Wasn't part of the reason you took this promotion to work on this?" She wagged her finger between the two of them.

"It was… it is…"

"How can we do that if you're off on starship adventures?" Aimie smiled, but Tom felt her hesitancy at the news.

"It won't be long, and then we'll be together," he assured her.

"Until the next time," she whispered.

"Let's stay in tonight," he told her. She looked beautiful, and she'd obviously put a lot of effort into her appearance, but he needed to meet with the crew of *Constantine* in the morning, and then he'd be leaving with *Shu*.

"You read my mind," she said.

As much as Tom was enjoying her company, he was thrilled at the idea of departing Nolix and accompanying Captain Rene Bouchard and her crew into the unknown.

Lineage

But he couldn't tell Aimie that, not after their time together over the past few months. And he didn't want their relationship to end either. He wanted it all, but remembered his grandfather's words.

Tommy, there will be times when you need to decide what's truly important to you, because it's those choices that will lead your life's path. You may want everything to be exactly as you desire it, but it doesn't work like that. Choose wisely. And if you want my advice, choose selfishly.

Tom watched Aimie beside him and considered the old man's guidance.

They ordered in, discussed Treena's progress, and eventually, they ate, had some Vina, and lay in each other's arms. Tom stared at the ceiling, wondering which path he was going to take.

When he woke, Aimie had already gone to work, and he felt like an intruder inside her giant penthouse suite. Everything was practical, if not overly expensive, but he appreciated her taste. The bedding was from Gatiz, woven from a rare worm's silk. The kitchen table used an ancient stone from the pits of Tavu, covered with a thin sheet of blue-tinted glass, adding to the effect of the stone's coloring.

Tom used her steam shower and changed into his Concord admiral's uniform. It was similar to his captain's version, only with a gray collar instead of red. He shaved, combed his hair while staring into her fogless mirror, and for a brief moment, felt older than his age. He wasn't an old man, barely over forty, but the stressful adventures since he'd taken on *Constantine* had been enough to exhaust him.

With Aimie around, he was starting to take even better care of himself, not wanting to get out of shape like some of the others that sat behind their desks every day. As a crew member on a cruise ship, he'd always been on his feet, rushing from task to task, but once he'd settled into the flagship, the immense size of the vessels had meant that there were staff for every little thing.

Tom remembered what he was about to do and shook off the cobwebs of his daydreams. He hadn't stepped foot aboard *Constantine* since he'd made the decision, and he knew it was going to be a daunting task. Not the entering part; leaving after would be the real challenge.

After a light breakfast, Tom walked to the rooftop dock and waited for the shuttle to pick him up. It arrived right on time, and the robot-driven craft floated over Ridele, using the intricate system maps and roadways to avoid an accident before it began ascending into the atmosphere. Eventually, he came to one of the distant docking ports outside of Nolix.

The area was bustling with activity, the moon bases lined up with freighters, and Tom could only smile at how different this was than the Zilph'i world of Leria. Earon was busy like this, with the human space station taking the load of traffic from the planet, but what would it be like at Aruto?

Constantine appeared through the viewscreen, and he saw its twin, *Shu*, a few kilometers in the distance, waiting for him to arrive after his impending meeting. The shuttle moved into the hangar and Tom rose, stepping off the craft and onto his old ship as an admiral for the first time.

The clapping surprised him, and he glanced up to see the entire crew in straight lines, cheering for him as he entered their home. He smiled in shock and spotted Treena Starling front and center, her red collar crisp and bright. She was in her android form, not yet ready to live full-time with herself. Brax Daak was beside her, his big palms slapping together loudly. Reeve was the first to break formation and meet Tom halfway, nearly knocking him over as she jumped into a hug.

"I'm sorry, sir." She grinned sheepishly after releasing him. "It's just so great to see you again."

The cheering had subsided, and Tom looked at the full contingency of a couple of hundred crew members, plus all of the other staff. Many of their faces were familiar, and he'd worked relentlessly to memorize as many of their names as possible.

"Reeve, I'll let it go today." He smiled at the chief engineer as they stalked across the hangar, stopping near the new captain. "Captain Starling. It's good to see you."

"Likewise, Capt… *Admiral*," Treena corrected herself. She motioned to the crew, who were standing in anticipation of his arrival. "Do you mind saying something?"

Brax clapped him on the shoulder and passed him a device to amplify his voice. Tom clipped it to his own collar and turned his attention to the crew of *Constantine*. The ship's AI surfaced near Treena, and the young projection of his grandfather smiled at him in support. This was going to be more difficult than he'd expected.

"Hello, crew of *Constantine*." Tom hadn't prepared anything. He'd thought he was coming for a private meeting with the executive crew and their new commander, but he tried to speak from the heart, not wanting to mince words. "We didn't know each other long, but we've been through some serious conflicts together. I came to *Constantine* as an untested captain and left as a veteran and survivor of the Statu, not once, but twice. You did the same, and for that, you should be extremely proud.

"Our efforts, along with those of our allies, have allowed the people of the Concord to continue to live in a peaceful and prosperous time. We assisted the Ugna to their new home in an unprecedented offer to our newest

Concord partner, and I am confident that *Constantine* will continue to do remarkable and brilliant things under the guidance of your new captain, Treena Starling." Tom paused while everyone began applauding and hooting once again. He smiled, clapping along with them until the noise began to falter.

"Thank you, Admiral Baldwin," Starling said, and hearing his name used so formally with his title didn't feel quite right.

Another craft entered the hangar's energy field, and Tom recognized the older model of Concord shuttles. This was the new commander. Tom had met the man on many occasions and knew for a fact that Constantine Baldwin hadn't liked him. He used to mumble about Captain Pol Teller being an arrogant son of a bitch. Tom didn't want to prejudge the man, but he did find it an odd choice for Benitor to make.

The doors opened, and the ovation ceased as the old man stepped off with a young woman at his arm. The man was in his seventies, but most people that age were on extenders or used modifications to alter their appearance.

Pol Teller did neither of those things. "What, all this for me?" he asked in a gravelly voice.

THREE

"It was nice of you to make everyone greet me, Starling, but next time, you might not want to leave Engineering devoid of life. Something dire could have happened," Commander Pol Teller said the moment his bony butt sat down at the meeting room table.

Treena didn't like him, not from the moment she heard his first words. She had to be patient, and judging from the expression on Tom's face, he was trying to pass on the same warning.

Before Treena could reply, Reeve spoke up. "My second in command, Harry, was there to watch over things. Don't worry, we didn't break any protocols."

"Good." Pol's assistant stood behind him, her hands hovering near a duffel bag, as if he might ask for something at any second.

Treena glanced at the young woman and wondered what kind of terrible karma had caused her to have to cater to this cantankerous old man. She'd only been introduced as Missy, but Treena doubted that was the girl's name. She was short, with shoulder-length brown hair, and had blue eyes that darted around the room nervously.

Tom was on his feet near the end of the table, and Treena locked gazes with him. He seemed to understand it was now her seat and moved to sit beside Doctor Nee at the opposite end.

Treena remained standing as she took in the table's occupants. Ven's absence was noticeable, and she hoped to the Vastness that his loyalty was still with her and the crew. "On behalf of the Concord and the crew of *Constantine,* I welcome you, Commander Teller."

His face contorted in a grimace, and he smacked his dry-looking lips together. He was mostly bald, with a few sporadic white hairs along the sides of his head. His cheeks were covered in three-day-old rough stubble, like coming to this posting wasn't worthy of cleaning himself up. "It's going to take a while to grow used to that title, I have to be honest."

"How long has it been since you were on a posting?" Tom asked him innocently.

"Why isn't Benitor here?" Teller avoided answering.

"She thought it best to send me instead, considering I was the former captain—" Tom stopped as Teller raised a thin arm.

"No need to explain. We all know the story. You're the grandson of Constantine Baldwin, the biggest prick to ever fight against the Statu and the laziest admiral ever to sit in Ridele. You moved up quickly to captain, and here's another one, reaching the rank before she's ready. That's why I'm here. Got it? Good?" The old man sat forward, a vein throbbing in his thin-skinned forehead.

Treena stood silently. What was happening?

Tom only smiled, sloughing the insults off with more class than Treena could have managed. "Con," he said, and the AI appeared. "I assume you're familiar with the commander?"

Constantine's projection walked over to the elderly commander and grinned toward him. "If it isn't my old friend, Pol. I'm sorry about your wife."

Lineage

Pol paused, his eyes wide as he stared at Constantine's AI. He reached a finger out, the digit passing through Con's chest. "I'd heard about you but didn't believe the rumors. How have they managed to make you so realistic?"

Treena had seen some of the previous models of the projections, and they were clunky and unresponsive. The ones from Teller's era were downright archaic.

"The technology is new. Quite impressive, isn't it?" Reeve asked.

Teller barked a laugh and shook his head. "I assume there's an off switch? I don't want that... *thing* around me. Understood, Missy?" he asked, and the girl nodded absently.

"Constantine is a member of our crew, and..." Treena started to say, but Teller once again felt the need to interrupt someone else.

"It's no member of *my* team," he said, his bushy brows furrowed deeply.

"Enough small talk." Treena said, taking control of the reins. "I can see you're going to have some adjustments to make for your role reprisal, and I can allow some leeway given your previous rank and experience, but this is my ship, *Commander*. If you don't feel like shaping up and giving me the respect of my title, feel free to stay on Nolix."

Teller acted shocked, and his mouth opened and then closed again, as if he'd forgotten what he was going to say. "Finally. Some balls from someone." He slapped a palm onto the table, making a loud banging sound. Missy hopped in surprise behind him.

Treena could already tell this wasn't going to work. "Admiral, can I have a word with you?" she asked, pointing to the door.

"Was it something I said?" Teller asked, but she ignored him as she entered the hallway with Tom.

"You can't be serious," she told him. "Is this a prank? A haze for the new captain?"

"I'm afraid not. Benitor wanted someone experienced, and he had the most logged hours as a captain over anyone left alive." Tom paced in a circle. "He's the worst, though. I'm beginning to understand why Constantine loathed him."

"There has to be another solution. Earth is three months away, and that's with the newly upgraded Nek converters. I won't be able to keep the crew from tossing him into the airlock for more than a week," Treena said, not wanting to come off as whiny. She crossed her arms and let out a sigh. "I have to do this, don't I?"

Tom took her by the shoulders, staring at her. "You're going to investigate the biggest mystery in humanity's past. Our origin. This information has been lost to us over the years, and we have evidence that we originated from a world named Earth. With the new Nek drive alterations, you'll be able to travel a distance that would have taken us years to navigate. There's another reason Benitor chose Teller too."

"What is it? He's a historian?"

"No. He's human, and the only one that cares enough about our past to come out of retirement to take on this challenge. He's old, cranky, and probably one of the most stubborn crew members you'll ever face. If anything, he's going to prepare you for a long career as a captain in the Concord."

"You think so?" she asked.

Tom nodded, his eyes crinkling at the sides as he smiled. "I know so."

"We'd better return." Treena started for the door, but Tom stopped her.

"He's here for a good reason. More than what Benitor

told me. He has to have some unfinished business internally. Otherwise, there's no way he'd have uprooted his old retired self from his cushy couch to do this mission. Find that reason, and he'll be yours," Tom told her.

Treena nodded, resolve firming internally. Tom was one hundred percent right. She was only going to need to discover Teller's motivation and utilize it to her advantage. "Thanks, Tom. Do you think I'm ready for this?"

His finger lingered over the entrance button. "I wouldn't trust anyone else with my ship." He pressed it, and she wasn't able to keep the grin from her face as they returned to their meeting.

---

*T*om spent all day on *Constantine* catching up with the executive crew. He toured the flagship with the team while Teller was introduced to the different departments. By the time he entered the hangar again, he was beat, physically and emotionally. He wasn't leaving with *Shu* until the next morning, and he had the option to return home for another night or head straight there.

Aimie said he didn't need to come tonight, but something told him there was unfinished business between them. He really did enjoy her company, but there were days he wasn't sold on the idea of being in a relationship. He saw the exact same thing in her eyes, in her actions, her words laced with little comments that implied they were together maybe too often.

"You seem distracted," Treena told him as she sat at the café table across from him in the courtyard.

"I didn't spend much time here when I was the captain," he said.

Treena turned and ordered a drink from the ServoBot and set her hands on the table. "Tom, you had other things to do."

"It's a special posting. You don't know what you have until it's gone." Tom hated the melancholic feelings resting in his gut.

"You can always change your mind," she told him, moving her arm out of the way so the ServoBot could place her steaming beverage on the table.

Tom laughed, fidgeting with his empty cup. "I can't do that. You've earned this, and besides… I'm about to see Aruto for the first time."

It was Treena's turn to laugh. "With Rene Bouchard."

Tom watched Treena silently for a moment and lowered his voice, making sure no one was close enough to overhear their conversation. "How are you really doing?"

She sat up straighter, her expression stony. "I'm… it's not simple, Tom. I've gone on for the last three years learning to deal with my situation, and just as I came to peace with it, I found out I was lied to and my body could be healed."

"I'm sorry," he whispered.

"It's not even the physical aspect. I don't mind putting the work in. When it hurts, it means I'm doing something. I'm gaining strength in my own body. It's the mental fortitude I need to see myself through my own eyes. I…"

"You're a unique woman, Starling. I can't tell you that I understand, because I can't know what it's like, but when I see you as yourself, I see the strongest person I've ever met. I see determination and beauty wrapped into one," Tom told her, knowing his words wouldn't be misconstrued as anything but platonic affection.

She grinned at him, holding the cup. He realized she never drank beverages, considering the fact that she was

Lineage

using a robotic body. "What's with the drink?"

She held it, staring at the hot liquid inside. "I have to get used to it, don't I?"

"So you *are* going to stop utilizing this android?" Tom hadn't been sure.

"I hope to," she admitted. "One day."

"Good. I'm glad to hear that," Tom said.

They chatted for another hour, Tom getting another Raca, and eventually, Treena shifted the topic of discussion to his nemesis.

"Where in the Vastness did Keen go?" she asked.

Tom tapped a finger on the table, shaking his head slowly. "It makes no sense. The Concord, despite my wishes, was reuniting him with his family. He could have been with Seda and Luci, but he escaped. There has to be an important reason for that."

"How are you attempting to track him?" Treena asked.

"We've set up feeds from any known Assembly bases, paid informants at each seedy space station within the Concord—and even a few outside our space—and now we wait," Tom said.

"And Seda?"

"She has no idea he was ever coming," Tom said.

Treena's eyes darted wide open, and her mouth squished into a pout. "I think you have your answer."

"What do you mean?" he asked.

"Seda. If she finds out that Keen was going to be brought to them, and that he chose to escape instead, she'll dish the dirt." Treena looked pleased with herself, and rightfully so. It was a good concept.

"Maybe I'll test your theory," he said.

Treena Starling rose from her chair, the courtyard café mostly empty at this late hour. Tom checked the time, seeing it was too late to return to Nolix and Aimie's penthouse. He'd send her a message instead. Tomorrow, he would venture out on a new mission, and he was anxious to be moving again.

Treena escorted him to the hangar and slowed as they neared the entrance. "Tom, I want to say thank you."

"For what?"

"For believing in me, and for guiding me. I'll take good care of her," she said.

"You might not want Constantine to hear you call the ship that," he joked. "You're going to do great things. Take care on your trip to Earth, and be careful with the Nek drive. The Concord hasn't mass-produced this technology yet on purpose. You're a test for it, so heed Reeve's advice and don't push it for expediency. Earth will still be there when you arrive."

Treena nodded, and Tom embraced her quickly, patting her on the back three times before letting go. "We'll be in touch."

She stayed in the hall as he entered the hangar, passing two guards. The door slid shut with a stinging finality.

"Constantine," Tom said as he strode over the metal floor toward his waiting shuttle.

"Yes, sir," Constantine said, appearing with a slight flicker.

Tom turned to face his grandfather's visage. This wasn't the real man, but he did hold his memories, making it eerily close to Constantine Baldwin. "Take care of them, would you?"

"I'll do my best." Con smiled. "It's been a pleasure working with you, Tommy." He let the nickname slip, clearly on purpose. Tom was going to miss him. In his youth, Constantine had been abrasive, challenging to live with, and opinionated. This version was softer, kinder, but with the intelligence and experience of the war hero.

Lineage

"I'll visit soon," Tom assured him.

"I'd like that." Constantine's AI lingered beside the shuttle as the vessel sealed up, and Tom departed, moving toward *Shu*.

Tomorrow, he'd be leaving for Aruto with Elder Fayle and Rene Bouchard's crew.

Lark Keen woke with a start, the banging on the metallic door resonating through the open room. "Will someone answer that?" he barked, but the others didn't move. He heard snoring throughout and wondered if he'd dreamt the noise. The knock returned, this time slightly softer, and he grabbed his PL-25, shoving it to his chest as he stumbled over the cots toward the door. One of his men was up, and Teeb placed a hand on Lark's chest, keeping him in place.

"Who is it?" Teeb barked. His long dreads hung low past his shoulders, and his thick Tekol frame covered most of the exit.

"It's me," a woman's muffled voice said.

"Open it," Lark told the man.

"We don't know for sure…"

Lark shoved the guy aside and lifted the squeaky metal level, tugging the door wide.

The Callalay woman grinned as she peered at Lark, then at the ragtag group behind him. "Isn't this just pathetic? The grandson of the great Admiral Keen, and self-proclaimed Prime Lark Keen, sleeping in a hovel like this with a bunch of wannabe thugs to protect him."

She was bald, her eyes light gray, her forehead ridges pronounced and symmetrical. She moved with liquid grace as she entered the room, walking past Teeb and stopping in front of Lark. "Are you sure you want to do this?"

Lark swallowed hard, nodding despite the trepidation burning in his gut. He should have stayed on that freighter. He could be with his wife and girl at this moment. Instead, he was about to start a war. "I'm committed."

"Good, then. I didn't think you'd have the stones, but I guess the rumors are true about you," she told him.

"Which rumors?"

"That you want power, and it takes priority over everything," the woman said.

"What's your name?" Lark asked her. He knew of her by reputation, but her name changed depending on who was speaking about her, or what kind of job they were running. She was a middleman, a hired hand that facilitated big jobs.

"You can call me… Prophet," she said with a smirk. "Grab your things. We're leaving."

The others were up, packing their meager possessions into duffel bags, and Lark went to gather his belongings, which amounted to a change of clothing, another gun, and a tablet. He had no personal effects, no pictures of Luci, nothing.

He was glad to be leaving this hole, and he followed Prophet from the rusty halls and up the short set of stairs into the cool night air above the surface. The world wasn't part of the Concord, residing only a system outside of the Border. It was dusty in this region, but swampy across the continent, making a sound hiding spot while they assembled the moving pieces into one place. This was phase two of the operation, and Lark was happy to be done with phase one.

"Where's the ship?" he asked, and the Callalay woman pointed into the distance.

"Wasn't going to bring it close in case I was being

tracked. We have to walk six kilometers." She stalked ahead like she was having the time of her life.

Teeb groaned behind Lark. "No one said we'd be walking. And in the middle of the night too. Who knows what's lingering in the dark?"

Prophet answered the hypothetical question. "There are no bipedal beings for about five hundred kilometers, but there are Stalkers, so you better keep your eyes open and your guns charged." She didn't slow as she told them this over her shoulder.

Lark mouthed the word—"Stalkers?"—and Teeb only shrugged. The other two hired hands trailed behind, chatting between themselves quietly. Coral and Slane. Lark didn't know them well, but they were apparently part of his Assembly. A couple of the lucky ones who'd been fortunate to not be uncovered by the Concord's elaborate digging after his capture.

Lark walked in silence, glancing at the cloudy sky. The ground was uneven and rocky, and twice he nearly rolled his ankles as they trudged toward their unknown destination. Only Prophet seemed to be enjoying the hike.

Two hours later, she slowed, and Lark realized how out of shape he truly was. A couple of months at Wavor Manor had done him no favors.

"Sir, what's that noise?" Teeb asked, stopping in his tracks.

Keen saw their spacecraft parked a good two hundred meters in front of them, and he tilted his head, trying to determine if Teeb was hearing things.

"What's the holdup?" Coral, a short Zilph'i man, asked. A second later, Lark heard the man grunt, falling to the dusty ground. Lark's gun pressed into his palm, and he spun around, searching for the attacker. Slane was backing up, and he tripped over a rock, landing hard on the ground.

A blast struck a stone beside the man, sending shards of rock into dust. The next blast hit Slane in the chest, and the hole steamed, his eyes wide and dead.

Teeb was panting, his gun tracking the shadows, but they couldn't see anyone.

"You can come out now!" Prophet shouted, and two masked soldiers emerged from the darkness beyond, pulling free their face coverings. "Keen, put the gun away. Those two fools were going to rat you out. We did some background checks, and they were working on delivering you to the Concord. Slane had communicated with Ridele twice before you met up with him, and the moment you were in Concord space again, you were returning to Wavor."

Lark's heart pounded in his chest. "And Coral?"

She shrugged. "They seemed tight. Thought they might be conspiring together."

Lark stared at the dead bodies and started forward. Teeb followed him, but the two female Callalay soldiers shook their heads, aiming their long weapons.

"What are you doing, Prophet?" Lark asked.

"We don't want loose ends." She lifted a finger, dropping it in a slicing motion, and Teeb was shot twice. He fell to the ground in a heap, and Lark could do nothing but watch.

"Was that necessary?" he asked, his mouth suddenly dry and sticky. Teeb was the one who'd enabled the rescue from the freighter.

"Your benefactor doesn't want any mistakes. Head to the ship," Prophet said, sauntering away. The two soldiers moved behind Lark, and even though this woman was supposed to facilitate his next moves, he couldn't help but feel like she'd just as soon shoot him and leave him for dead.

He was alone again.

Lineage

Lark entered the modified freighter, noticing the soldiers didn't let their fingers stray from their triggers.

FOUR

Reeve Daak grinned at Harry as the Bentom ball glowed in the center of the drive. "Today's the day, Harry."

"We're not using the Nek until we're outside of Concord space. You do realize that, right?" the engineer asked.

"Of course, but we're starting a trip with the very first modified drive in Concord history," she said.

"Don't you ever tire of making history? We've been at this for a year, and all we do is endanger ourselves each day," Harry said. "Wouldn't you like to have something a little less... explosive?"

Reeve's hair moved as she shook her head. "Nope. We're going to be legends. *Constantine* will go down as the most infamous ship ever, and our names will be etched right there with it."

"If you're into that kind of thing," Harry muttered. "We've done the tests, and we're confident this'll work, right?"

Harry was more hesitant about the technology than her. Reeve had been one of the engineers to create the shuttle used to race to Driun to warn the Ugna about the incoming Vusuls. With Hans' assistance, they'd applied the same concepts to modify the Bentom drive, but instead of manipulating the Nek to jump long distances, they'd harnessed the energy into millions of micro-hops. A craft this

Lineage

size might tear apart if they attempted to make a long-distance jump. But with the adjustments, they were able to increase velocity by more than they'd ever dreamed possible.

Reeve had spent every day and night over the last couple of months preparing for this, and she was convinced it would go off without a hitch. There might be a couple of hiccups, but she was prepared to deal with anything that arose.

"Bridge to Engineering." Lieutenant Darl's voice carried through the computer. "The captain has requested Executive Lieutenant Daak join us on the bridge for departure."

"I'll be right there," Reeve replied, patting Harry on the forearm. "Keep an eye on things. We don't want any of your dreaded explosions before we depart the Concord's capital."

Reeve wound her way toward the bridge, taking the elevator from the bowels. She loved her boiler room. Even though *Constantine* had been through some very tough paces, it was in prime shape and was a pleasure to work on. She preferred her office in Engineering, but as an executive officer, she was fully aware that her presence was expected for bridge duty. Her brother reveled in the role, and Reeve was impressed with how much Brax had grown in his short time as lieutenant commander.

Her daydreaming ceased as she passed through the bridge's entrance, and her gaze drifted to the seat beside Treena. The old man looked uncomfortable in his uniform, and she knew for a fact Teller hadn't worn that orange collar denoting the rank of commander in something like forty years. The choice didn't make sense to Reeve. Plenty of other people were qualified to assist Treena on this mission. There was usually more at play when it came to

Concord politics than met the eye, and Reeve was going to pay special attention to this man.

"Executive Lieutenant, please take your seat," Captain Startling said, and Reeve grinned at her as she passed across the bridge, moving to sit in Ven's empty helm position. The role of captain looked good on her friend, and Reeve couldn't have been prouder. She tried to think if she'd ever have the drive to seek a captaincy but couldn't imagine it happening.

Her brother, on the other hand, might be better suited than her. Brax winked at her as she peered over at his station along the edge of the bridge, and the captain stood behind them.

"Strange seeing you there," Darl told her. His dark hair was a little longer, his cheeks slightly thinner.

"I'm sure Ven's looking forward to returning," Reeve assured the man. She hadn't spent much time getting to know him, not after he'd permanently replaced Zare, and set it in her mind to make an effort integrating him into their group. He was always thrown into shifts with the executive crew, leaving him on the outside, and none of them seemed to even consider this.

"Incoming," Darl said, and the image on the viewscreen flashed from a view of Nolix and its heavy traffic to Prime Xune. His face was handsome, his expression stoic.

"Captain Starling, I wanted to wish you the best of luck in your mission. If Earth is what we've been told, this will be a monumental occasion for not only humans, but all of the Founders and partners alike. Seek out your ancestors, learn of your lineage, and return with a new ally.

"Commander Teller, on behalf of the Concord, we thank you for donning the uniform once again, and I hope you enjoy the task. Until we meet in the Vastness." The message ended before anyone could reply, making Reeve wonder if the feed was live or pre-recorded.

"Darl, detach from the dock," the captain ordered.

"Detaching."

"Executive Lieutenant Daak, bring us out," Treena said, and Reeve began guiding their giant vessel from the hectic space some distance from the capital, Nolix. She'd enjoyed time visiting her family below over the last two months, although it was much less than Brax, since she was in charge of the modifications to the drive, but it had been a welcome break. She noticed *Shu* out the right corner of the viewscreen, knowing they were leaving soon too. It was strange having Baldwin gone, but the crew seemed to be acclimating to the change. Treena was ready for this. They all were.

Ten minutes later, they were far enough from Nolix and the steady stream of incoming and departing spaceships for Reeve to have clearance for their exit.

"Set course for Driun F49," Treena said, and Reeve did. She wanted to test the Nek mods, but they'd promised to wait until Ven was aboard and they'd vacated Concord space, so she activated the star drive as normal, and soon they were racing toward their last stop before beginning their journey to Sol.

---

*T*om had sneaked onto *Shu* late at night, avoiding any familiar faces as he'd sought out his quarters. They'd given him a huge suite, one meant for dignitaries, and he realized his newly appointed rank of admiral came with additional perks.

He wore the uniform this morning and rubbed his smooth cheeks before moving for the door.

"Admiral. It is good to see you," Elder Fayle said, conveniently leaving her suite at the same moment as him. Tom wondered how long she'd been waiting behind her closed door for him to emerge.

"Likewise, Elder." He smiled, playing nice, but still had an odd feeling about the Concord's relationship with the Ugna. There were so many red flags popping up, but Benitor and the Prime were determined for him not to poke and prod over any of them. That alone set off more alarm bells in his mind.

"How are you enjoying the new role?" she asked as they walked through the corridor.

"About as well as can be expected."

"You're used to a little more freedom, I suspect. I always saw you as a 'wind through his hair' kind of person, not a man at a desk," she suggested, and he laughed.

"I thought you were part of the reason for my vocation change?"

"I was. Just because you thought you were better suited to careening through space doesn't mean that's the truth. I think you will learn more about yourself as an admiral than you ever could have as the captain of *Constantine*," Fayle told him, and when Tom was about to press her on it, the elevator doors opened, revealing Rene Bouchard.

"If it isn't my favorite admiral, Thomas Baldwin." Rene stepped to the side, allowing them space to enter.

"Rene," Tom said.

"Elder Fayle and I caught up yesterday. Were you aware the Ugna are already terraforming their planet?" Rene asked, and Tom shook his head.

"I didn't know that. Why terraform?" he asked.

Elder Fayle stared straight ahead as she replied, standing stiff as a board in the elevator. "We only want to make it as comfortable for our people as possible. Most of our training villages were on Leria, in the jungles, and we are seeking to duplicate that for the younger generations. It is really not that much of an endeavor."

Terraforming wasn't a new concept, but it was rarely done anymore. "I'll be pleased to visit one day and see," Rene told her, and Elder Fayle glanced at Tom, as if seeking his thoughts.

"I'm sure it will be up to the Ugna standards," was all he said.

The elevator stopped, bringing them to Deck Six near the bridge. "Do you mind if we do a quick overview with the crew?" Rene asked.

Tom noted how she asked Elder Fayle, not him. To be honest, Benitor hadn't explained the purpose for his trek to Aruto, and that was concerning. She'd told him she'd send the pertinent details, but they hadn't arrived yet.

"By all means, please," Fayle said, letting Rene take the lead onto the bridge.

Executive Lieutenant Conner Douglas was present, along with Commander Kan Shu. Hans, Rene's chief of engineering, stood behind a helm console, and Tom couldn't remember the name of her lieutenant commander. He stared at her, a young Callalay woman, and realized this wasn't the same officer.

Rene introduced them to Elder Fayle, and Tom greeted the familiar faces, stopping on the newest member of her team.

"Admiral Baldwin, it's a pleasure to meet you. I've been following your career since I was a little girl," she said, making Tom frown. He couldn't be *that* much older than her.

"Very good. What's your name?" Tom asked, and Rene seemed to realize she hadn't used her full name, only title.

"This is Lieutenant Commander Asha Bertol," Rene said with a glint of trouble in her eye.

And it clicked. "You're Cori Bertol's daughter!"

She nodded enthusiastically. "I sure am. He would be proud to see me on board *Shu*. We idolized Yin Shu."

As if the AI thought she was being beckoned, she appeared, smiling at the crew. "Hello, Thomas," Yin said in her patented stone-cold tone.

"Hi, Yin," he replied. It was odd calling his former captain by her first name, but no one expected an admiral to address an AI by anything but her name. She no longer held a title.

"This is going to be so much fun," Asha said, grinning widely.

Tom took in the crew. Things were changing. It was once mandatory that one of each Founder was present on the bridge, but now there were three humans, two Callalay, and no Tekol or Zilph'i. Tom had seen enough of those two races working on *Shu*. Cedric had been Tekol, but he'd died fighting the Statu.

"I can read your mind, Admiral," Rene said.

Tom raised an eyebrow. "Is that so?"

"It's exactly what I thought when I heard *Constantine* didn't have a Callalay executive officer. Precedents are shifting in this new era, and honestly, I kind of prefer it this way. I would rather build the best team I can, regardless of what race of Founders they belong to. How do you feel about it?" she asked, and Tom felt all eyes on him.

He really wished she hadn't put him on the spot. "You know I'm for traditions, but I have to agree with you on this one."

This seemed to break the tension, and Elder Fayle stepped from the edge of the room, reminding Tom she was there.

"Aruto. With so many Callalay"—Fayle motioned to Kan Shu and Asha Bertol, then to the AI of Kan's mother—"it's only fitting that we make this journey to your home together. I have been there. Once."

Tom frowned, wondering when that would have occurred. He wanted to ask the question but bit his cheek instead.

"The Ugna have a history with the Callalay, and I look forward to revisiting those bonds over the next few weeks," she said.

The trip to Aruto was a week, and Tom hadn't expected to be there more than a couple days at most. He really hated that he was in the dark on this, but couldn't say anything, or Rene would use it against him. Not that he needed her approval, but they were peers.

"Mother is going to love this," Asha told them.

Her father had been a remarkable man. He'd died twenty years ago, when Tom was first graduating from the Academy. Border attacks had been increasing at that time, and the Concord was working at recovering after the great War. They were stronger than any moment in the previous thirty years, and had sent out a few of their refurbished classic fleet ships.

Cori Bertol had been the captain of *Conquest* for ten years, and was the closest to react to an attack on Hunirom Perso, a newer Concord partner who specialized in viewscreen manufacturing. Unfortunately, *Conquest* vanished, never to be seen again, but there were signs of battle everywhere. Tom remembered hearing about it a lot during the year of his first posting, and the other crew members dreamt of being out there, fighting off the pirates that had apparently destroyed Bertol's ship, and recovering the Concord captain's body. That didn't happen, and eventually, Tom, along with everyone else, assumed the man was dead.

Tom almost forgot that Cori's wife had taken the

presidency in the next election, and since then, their borders had restricted visitation. Rumor was, she didn't trust anyone and blamed the Concord for failing to find her husband. But the mystery behind the Callalay's home ran far deeper than the last twenty years.

"If there's nothing else, then everyone take the rest of the day to settle, and meet me in the morning. That's when we depart," Rene said.

"I thought we were leaving today," Tom said.

"I found a couple of glitches in the systems, so my team is combing over them. We wouldn't want anything to go wrong," Hans told him, and Tom immediately thought of Aimie. Maybe he should give her a call, see if she wanted to meet up on the station.

Tom returned to his suite, noticing a file from Admiral Benitor, and decided to peruse it later. He called Aimie, seeing it was mid-afternoon on Ridele. She answered in her office at R-Emergence and smiled when she saw who it was. That wiped away any trepidation Tom felt about their relationship.

"Hey," he said.

"Hey."

"I'm sorry I didn't come home last night," he said.

"Home?"

"To your place, I mean," he said, catching her meaning.

"That's okay. I understand you're busy." Aimie was in a white lab coat, her office walls adorned with abstract Tekol art.

Tom had a sudden urge and couldn't stop his mouth before it said the words. He was feeling old, a little out of place in his life path, and with no real family left, he didn't want to wind up regretting his decisions. "What if we made it our home?" The second he said it, he cringed, not wanting to sound needy or desperate.

Lineage

"You want to move in with me?" she asked. Her expression spilled her true feelings. He'd made a mistake in bringing it up.

Was it too soon? Would she want to share her private home with a man, and one with commitment issues at that? "I mean, I *am* over there all the time, and this might be our solution to me always being late. But it was only an idea." He laughed, making light of it.

Aimie watched him through the screen impassively. "That seems impulsive. I know you gave up a lot to move to Nolix, but I can see the longing in your eyes every time someone mentions *Constantine*. If you're looking to plant roots, I don't think it's here. Take your trip, and we'll discuss it later."

Tom suddenly wished he hadn't said anything but could only shrug. "Sounds good to me." Maybe she was right about this. He wasn't ready to make a commitment like that.

"I might be visiting with some Ugna representatives about our robotics," she told him.

That was interesting. "Speaking of the Ugna, how's Brion doing?" He'd meant to ask after her brother the other day, but it had completely slipped his mind.

"He's doing well. He's working on the terraforming project on Driun. Says its coming along nicely," she said.

"Jeez, does everyone know about this but me?" he mumbled.

"Sorry, I didn't hear that."

"Don't worry about it," Tom said. "What else are you working on these days?" he asked, and Aimie started in, talking about their latest hardware that would revolutionize an issue with elderly Tekol. Tom listened, nodding and asking questions at the right time, but the unopened file from Benitor had him intrigued. It would have to wait, but only until the call was done.

Brandon checked the map again and determined this wasn't their supply transport coming for an early drop-off.

"We're going to need more than a few pulse cannons if we have to defend ourselves," Carl said, pacing the room.

They were in the Island, the fifth dome, the entire colony gathered into the mess hall. Brandon still smelled the steamed spinach and rice they'd eaten for dinner, and it was making him sick.

Carl was right. They were screwed.

Jun tapped the screen. "This could be random. Just because they're moving toward Mars doesn't mean that's their end goal."

"They sent a damned robot to issue a warning. They used his name. Said this place was unsanctioned by President Gordon Basher and Earth. They know we're here," Brandon said, running a hand through his shaggy hair.

"We were all aware that this was not only a possibility, but an eventuality," Kristen said. "We came to Mars, we repurposed the old domes, and it was only a matter of time before one of our supply runners caved."

The rest of the colonists muttered and groaned amongst themselves. "You knew the risks, right?" Brandon asked. "We didn't force anyone to come. We did it to start over. We left to escape his tyranny. All of us were aware of the possibility of being found out, and we made the choice to try despite the odds. Now we have to fight for what's ours."

Devon stood from near the rear of the room and raised a hand. He spoke with an old-world accent, from a small town. "What's the point in fighting a war we can't possibly win?"

Brandon was about to respond, when Theresa rose. "They'll kill us no matter what we choose."

"Damn right. We stay here, they'll come. We give up and travel to Earth, they mount our heads on Parliament's stone wall. Basher will make an example out of us," Devon said.

"What are you suggesting, Devon?" Brandon asked.

"We hop into our freighter, and we hightail it the hell out of here," he said loudly. A few others clapped and agreed with him.

"We don't have space for all of us, and how are we going to feed ourselves?" Brandon asked. "Not to mention, there's literally nowhere to go. You'll die just the same."

"But on our terms," Devon replied.

Brandon glanced at Kristen, who only shrugged at him. Jun and Carl were listening intently and waiting for Brandon to take the lead. "You'd rather run than stand up and fight? Would you rather waste away in the cold depths of space on an empty stomach than make our stand at the home we've been working on for a decade?" He hadn't intended to make a speech, but once he started, he couldn't stop. He jumped from the table, stalking down the center line between the mess hall's tables.

"We found each other—on Earth, in camps, in work details—and spread the word. We managed to escape, after years of planning. We did that. Us. Seventy-five humans, from different walks of life, with one similar goal. Leaving Earth and Basher behind. Every day I wake up, I feel nothing but gratitude for all of you and for what we've been able to accomplish. I will not leave on a freighter with nothing but a cooler full of vegetation and desperation.

"There's one ship coming. We can't tell how large it is based on our current information, but we can fight it off," Brandon said, his heart racing as he halted near the front of the kitchen.

"And then what? We stop this one, and they send more," Devon called from forty feet away.

"Then we do it again." Carl smiled as he spoke, patting a hand over his heart.

"How the hell are we going to achieve that?" Theresa asked, but Brandon saw the answer clearly.

"I have an idea," he told them, knowing it would be an uphill battle, but one he was willing to stake his life on.

FIVE

Ven waited near the outer edge of the city, anxious to leave. While he'd enjoyed most of his time among the Ugna, he didn't feel at home here, not like he did on *Constantine*. Ven had grown used to the camaraderie with Brax and the others, whereas the Ugna rarely spoke to one another unless it was necessary.

He glanced toward the city and spotted a few of the tall albino people moving through the streets, their pupils dilated, their feet hovering above the sidewalks. En'or was used frequently. He'd seen the injections when they'd fended off the Vusuls, and the destruction the drug could do. Or assistance, he corrected himself. The drug hadn't killed the invaders; it had merely aided the vessels, which were the Ugna.

Ven had refused to take an injection since then and longed to avoid En'or entirely.

"I was hoping to find you before you departed." Hanli's voice carried across the landing pad. She appeared from behind a shuttle and pointed at it. "Care for a lift?"

Ven walked toward her, pointing to the sky. "I was told the crew was sending a shuttle for me." *Constantine* should have been in position.

"I already contacted them and advised that you would be delivered," Hanli said.

"Why?"

"Do we need a reason to spend a few more minutes together?" she asked, but Ven felt the truth behind her words.

"It was High Elder Wylen's request, wasn't it?"

Hanli actually grinned in response. "You *are* intuitive, Ven Ittix. Come. I'll pilot it myself." She led him to one of the Ugna ships, an older model Concord shuttle, the First Ship logo whited out and painted over.

She powered the craft up, and he took the seat beside her, their elbows nearly bumping. Ven avoided contact, considering the rush of emotions evoked the last time she'd touched him. Hanli raised the vessel in the air, slowly guiding them from the city's edge. Ven peered at the forest beyond, the snaking river running alongside the valley's side, and felt a moment of clarity.

This would never be his home, no matter what Hanli or Elder Fayle suggested. It couldn't be. Not any longer.

"Will you consider my request?" she asked, failing to elaborate.

Ven sat still, hesitant to rouse her anger.

"Ven, will you not respond?"

"I have no place here," he said truthfully.

They moved through the clouds, the white mist blinding them through the viewscreen. "Is that so?"

"I fear I have changed."

"We have a fleet, Ven. They would give you a captaincy the moment you asked for it. Isn't that what you want? Perhaps we could command a ship together. *Gallant* or *Courage*."

He felt the longing behind Hanli's words and wondered at her motivation. Surely she wasn't only interested in him as a partner. There had to be political reasoning behind her advances. "Perhaps."

Lineage

"So you will consider it?" she asked.

He didn't have the heart to tell her straight away that it would never happen. He set a palm over her hand as they exited Driun F49, and he was glad her walls were up. She smiled at him, a glimpse of pure joy on her face. Maybe it wouldn't be so bad to be paired with her, scouring space in an Ugna vessel. He hated how his feelings shifted so much these days.

Constantine was massive, and his breath caught at the sight of her on the viewscreen. This was his calling, his true mission. Ven couldn't help but notice the three Ugna fleet ships nearby, as if they were standing guard against their own ally. He wondered if Brax was thinking the same thing on the bridge.

They entered the hangar, First Officer Hanli lowering to a gentle landing. She rose, hugging him briefly, and kissed his cheek. "Take care of yourself, Ven Ittix."

"Thank you. You as well." Ven left awkwardly, and the moment he was out of the shuttle, it lifted off, exiting the hangar in a hurry.

He was home.

"Push it," Constantine said, and Treena obliged, using her real arms to press the bar. This was the highest setting she'd tried yet, and everything ached. Sweat poured off her face, but she moved the weights. She slowly returned the bar to center and smiled at the AI.

"Thanks for helping me out," she told Con.

"It's my pleasure, Captain. You're doing very well," he said with a wink.

Treena hadn't spent that much time with Constantine

before this trip, but he was fun to be around. He carried so much wisdom and experience, she fully understood why the Concord had elected to create the AI projections based on the memories of real Concord heroes. Their expertise was invaluable.

She leaned into the bench and looked at her legs in the shorts. They were thin and pale, her knees too bulbous compared to the rest of her thighs and calves. She saw muscles and flexibility that weren't there before.

"Would you care for something to eat?" Con asked, and Treena considered it. Her body was fueled intravenously, like before, but she was slowly starting to eat solid food again. The first few times had been a challenge, but this was another area she saw improvement in each day.

"Why not?" She hadn't eaten real food for three years. The last time she'd had a true meal was dinner in the mess hall with Felix beside her, before they were attacked by the Assembly. Felix had devoured the noodle dish he always ordered, and she'd had rice and steamed vegetables. Life in space came with a lot of excitement, but until the fancy chefs of the flagships like *Constantine,* the food was bland, with few choices.

"How about Eganian noodles?" she asked, citing Felix's favorite bland dish.

"Are you sure you don't want something with a little more... flavor?" Constantine asked with a smirk.

"Nope. I'll take the noodles."

Constantine vanished, only to return five seconds later. "They'll be sent up right away."

"Thank you." She tried to stand, but her left leg buckled, sending her to the floor. Constantine reached out to stop her from falling, but she fell through his arm.

"Are you okay?" he asked.

Treena rolled over, using her arm strength to sit up.

"Bruised ego, maybe." She laughed and turned the leg braces on, setting them at eighty percent. She stood, brushing herself off. "I forget how weak I really am."

"And I forget that I'm not really here," Con told her.

"It must be strange. How are you dealing with it?" she asked, realizing the pair of them were quite the odd couple.

"It was normal at first, until I removed the blockade the engineers at R-Emergence created. Then I had this flurry of memories, feelings, and ideas flowing through my circuits again. I saw Thomas, a fully grown man, a forty-year-old version of the boy I'd raised. Or helped raise. Let's be honest, my wife did a lot of that before she passed, then the help cared for him more than I ever did.

"He was a good boy: smart, charismatic, strong-willed. Tom was me as a youth." Constantine smiled, his image wavering for a moment before solidifying again.

"You miss him, don't you?" she asked.

He stared at her, nodding slowly. "I didn't know if it was even possible, but the technicians embedded something special with these AI programs. I do miss him. We had started to grow close. Closer than we'd ever been in real life."

"This *is* real life. You're a fully aware entity, Con. Do you think I ever expected to be talking to you in my actual body? Technology has made some wonderful advancements, and I can't tell you how grateful I am to have you with me during this mission," Treena told him.

"I'm glad to be of assistance," Con said while the door buzzed.

"Enter," Treena said out loud, and the serving girl walked through the open suite door. She caught Treena's gaze and nearly dropped the food tray.

"I'm sorry, Captain. I…"

Treena hadn't even thought about it. None of the crew

had seen her like this. Most of them knew she was usually in an android body, but this was different. She looked like a husk of a person: a skinny, malnourished specimen, not the strong woman who stalked around the ship.

"There's nothing to be sorry about," Constantine said before Treena could reply. "Set it down, please."

The girl lowered the tray to the table with a shaky hand and turned, nearly running from the room.

"Is this what it's going to be like?" Treena asked the AI.

"For a while. You'll get used to it," he told her.

Treena wasn't sure if she wanted to. She was the captain of this glorious spacecraft, and with that came serious responsibility. Once word leaked that she was frail and scarred, the crew would lose focus and confidence in her leadership abilities. As much as she wanted to wallow in her own self-pity, she decided to focus harder. She would grow strong enough to stop using the android. But not today.

She walked over to the table, taking a seat. Her place had been modified to add the gym equipment, most of it donated from R-Emergence. There was a healing tank, a swimming simulator—which would strengthen her muscles—and the weight unit, which utilized bars and hand clips, mixed with gravity fields to optimize difficulty.

Treena sniffed, using her nose to smell the noodles. It brought her back to that last meal, Felix beside her, laughing about something that Max had told him earlier. They were dead, and here she was, the captain of a starship. "It's not fair."

Constantine stood at the opposite end of her table and smiled at her. "It rarely is. We have to take the punches and keep fighting on, because it's our only option, right?"

She felt a kinship to the man who'd been larger than

life before his death. If she couldn't have the guidance of her friend Thomas Baldwin, she was happy to have his grandfather by her side.

Treena lifted the fork with an unsteady arm and tasted the noodles.

They were terrible. Exactly what she needed.

---

*T*he file had been so limited, yet unsettling, Tom didn't know how to react to it. The Ugna had saved Aruto from destruction eighty years ago. He could only surmise the reason the Callalay hadn't wanted the Concord headquarters at their world was because of the seismic instability. According to the details Admiral Benitor had shared with him, Aruto had nearly been destroyed five thousand years ago. Volcanoes had erupted, covering a tenth of the planet in lava and half of it in ashes.

This was before the Concord was formed, but not by many years. The Callalay had grown desperate, seeking secondary homes, and when they'd managed to create interstellar traffic—more out of need than anything—they'd discovered other worlds.

Several details were still unaccounted for, ones that Tom would have to decipher himself while on Aruto, but from what he understood, the Ugna had been brought in to help save the planet thirty years before the Statu ever arrived. That time had been an era of peace in the Concord, and Tom was shocked to learn that the Callalay world had nearly met the Vastness.

Be steadfast, be vigilant, be strong. The Vastness welcomes all. Tom recited the Code, saying it to himself as he deactivated the projection and drummed his fingers over the desk.

If the Ugna had been recruited to stop the cataclysm of Aruto, it was no wonder their indiscretions were being overlooked. Tom recalled how quickly Benitor had agreed to the Ugna's terms when the Concord had needed their assistance in dealing with the Assembly, then the Statu. She'd approved their entrance into the Concord even before discussing it with the Prime, citing that it was better to ask for forgiveness than permission. Or something along those lines.

Tom had struggled to comprehend what power the Ugna had over the Concord, and now he saw it. Every time someone mentioned the fact that High Elder Wylen had been hiding one of the Pilia colony ships illegally outside of Concord space, the Prime or Benitor said it wasn't a concern to them. The sins of the Ugna had been forgiven before they occurred.

It made sense. "What other secrets are you hiding?" he asked. The Concord's Founders appeared to be comprised of secrets, their entire alliance built on mutual acceptance of some half-truth, rather than the full version. Humans were homeless, without origin, until they'd discovered Sol existed. How many of them knew about Earth?

Did the Ugna hold that secret close to their chests, or did the Callalay and Zilph'i, maybe even the Tekol, have knowledge of Earth and the human origin story? He longed to be on *Constantine* to learn the truth of what had happened to their people, but he also had a draw to learn about Aruto and the Callalay's deal with the Ugna.

Benitor had told him to stop digging into the Ugna, but why had she sent him on this mission with Fayle if he wasn't supposed to uncover any hidden conspiracies? Did Benitor only want him to build his relationship with the Ugna leader?

Tom stared at the screen built into his wall. It gave the

Lineage

impression of a window, and he watched the stars in the distance as *Shu* headed toward their destination. His stomach growled, and he decided it was as good a time as any to take Rene and Kan up on that dinner invitation. He sent a message, asking the captain if she and the commander were free.

The response came quickly. Dinner in an hour. Tom glanced at his ruffled uniform and decided to clean up and change.

A half hour later, he was pacing the halls, strolling to the fancy restaurant. Each flagship had one, and Rene thought it was a ridiculous feature, but since they constantly seemed to be caravanning some dignitary or another around, they'd become convenient, if not entirely necessary.

Tom arrived early, telling the hostess he was there to meet the captain. He was ushered to the back room, a private space with Tekol art displayed over the walls. He recognized one of the artists' works, since Aimie had the original at home.

Tom ordered a drink, a glass of his favorite Vina, and settled in. They'd been gone from Nolix for almost a week, and he hadn't made himself accessible to the captain yet. Not because he didn't want to. Their schedules just hadn't lined up until today.

He continued to work on tracking Keen, but none of his informants had found anything. He'd been in contact with someone named Slane. Tom was waiting for the guy to update him, but so far, nothing had come through. Tom feared the worst. But with one sighting, he expected others would follow. He needed to be patient.

"Hello, Admiral." Kan Shu stepped into the room. His eyes were kind, reminding Tom of his mother. He'd worked beside her for a few years and wouldn't forget the many lessons he'd received from the great Callalay woman.

"Kan. Good to see you," he told the commander. "Is the captain coming?"

"She'll be joining us shortly. A minor engineering hiccup to deal with," Kan said. "She asked me to keep you company until then."

Since he'd read the report from Benitor, Tom had hoped to have some alone time with Kan to pick his brain. "How are things going?" he asked the commander.

"Very well. Since we managed to help the Minon and Seeli, we've been staying pretty close to Nolix, with one border patrol near Greblok," Kan told him.

"Greblok. Did you visit their capital?" Thomas asked.

"Sure. We met with the new Regent and had a tour. It's really coming along. We also visited the remote Concord Academy." Kan ordered a water, and Tom swirled his glass.

"Did you meet a boy named Tarlen?" he asked.

Kan shook his head. "No, but there was a man named Penter that said he knew you."

Brax and Penter had stayed in touch, and suddenly, Tom felt bad for not reaching out to Tarlen for the last while. The boy would be older, a year into his studies, and Tom silently wished him the best. "I like the Bacal people," he said.

"Without their ore, the Statu would be alive," Kan said.

There was a lot more to them than the Greblokian ore, but Tom didn't say so. "Kan, I wanted to ask you something."

"Anything."

"Aruto. What was it like growing up there?" he asked.

"I didn't spend a lot of time on-planet, you know, because of my mother's schedule, but what I do recall, it is with fondness. My father and I lived two hours from Yunil;

our place had a lake, tall trees. It was nice," he said.

"Did you get bored, since you were an only child?" Yin Shu had been a very private person, as were most Callalay, but after a few years working with her, Tom had learned as much as anyone about the stoic woman. It had been difficult on her, being away from her husband and child so often.

"You know what it's like to have no siblings. We find ways to entertain ourselves. I took to my studies," Kan said.

"Which is how you're the youngest Callalay commander ever, isn't it?" Tom asked.

"I suppose so." Kan grinned at Tom. "My name doesn't hurt."

"Another thing we have in common." Tom sipped his drink and leaned over toward Kan, lowering his voice. "What can you tell me about the Ugna being on Aruto eighty years ago?"

Kan remained silent for a second, as if trying to recollect ever hearing something like that. "I don't know what you mean. The Ugna were nothing more than rumors and stories around the playground when I was a child."

That was what Tom had assumed. It had been the same for him. When he'd finally learned they were real, could read moods, and levitate things with their minds, Tom's mind had been blown. "Same here. So you never heard about them visiting your planet?"

"Should I have?" Kan asked, and Tom only raised his eyebrows in response.

"What'd I miss?" Rene asked, entering behind the hostess.

"We were just talking about what a smart and likeable boss you are," Tom told her, receiving a genuine smile. Rene's red hair had been braided at the center, falling long between her shoulder blades. She was in uniform, as was Kan, and Tom was glad he'd opted for the formality too.

"Admiral, I've been able to decipher your lies from truths for a long time." She took the seat to his left, her foot kicking him in the shin just enough to show it was on purpose. "Sorry, that was an accident."

"Sure it was. Tell me, Captain, how are things?" Tom asked. Being an admiral had changed things between him and the others, but he still felt like their peer rather than their superior.

"Smooth sailing," she replied, stopping when the server entered. She ordered a bottle to match Tom's glass. "I was hoping you could finally tell me what in the Vastness we're doing on this mission. *Shu*, one of our biggest and best ships, flying you and Fayle to Aruto? Something doesn't add up. There are far more pressing matters, not to mention the countless exploration targets we've yet to hit. We should be going with *Constantine* to Earth.

"Can you imagine? Finding our people's origin planet?" she asked him.

"If the rumors are true, Celevon—the Pilia home world—is technically our first planet, but humans as a race wouldn't have existed until they developed and adapted to Earth," Kan said, receiving a frown from his captain.

"Ever the stickler for accuracy, this one. I bet you have to deal with that a lot, having Reeve Daak," she said, and Tom noticed her catch the faux pas. "I'm sorry… I'm sure giving up *Constantine* was a difficult decision."

Tom didn't really want to discuss it right then, and his expression must have said as much. Rene changed topics. "What do you think they'll find?"

Tom did have a few speculations. "My guess is as good as anyone's. If we left Earth thousands of years ago as we predicted, it could be gone. Destroyed by nature, a supernova, an enemy. My best assumption? It's empty."

She shook her head before taking a long drink from her stemmed glassware. "I doubt it. I think we're going to meet more humans. And it's going to change everything."

"For the better?"

"That's to be determined," she replied.

"What about you, Kan? What do you think about Earth?" Tom asked him, curious what the obviously intelligent commander thought.

Their dinner arrived, and Kan poked at his food before answering. "I agree with the captain. It will be occupied. If it's a Class Zero-Nine world, I expect lifeforms, but they may be slightly different than you are today. Leaving a world has long-lasting effects on a race. We've seen it throughout history. We already have Callalay families living on Nolix for seven generations, and they're far different physiologically than the ones from Aruto."

Tom couldn't argue with that. "Treena will do the right thing. I can't wait to hear the briefing when they return."

"What about that Teller guy? Did you meet him?" Rene asked.

Tom nodded, chewing into his sautéed Tekol neerion. It was cooked to perfection. "I did."

"And?" Rene asked, leaning a little closer. "I heard he's a bit of an…"

Tom glanced at Kan and cut her off. "He's a little rusty. Has an assistant with him. I don't think being a commander is going to be simple for the old-timer."

"An assistant? We can do that?" Rene asked with a laugh.

"Apparently. But you might have to wait another forty years before the head office approves the request." Tom filled his glass again, and Kan received a chime on his wrist band.

"Captain, I'm needed on the bridge."

"Go ahead. Thanks for joining us, Commander," she told him, and Tom stood while the young man rushed off to some emergency or another.

When the door closed, Rene slid a little closer and set her hand on Tom's arm. "Seriously, Tom. What in the Vastness are you doing here?"

"I'm having dinner," he said flatly.

"Not this. I mean… you're wearing a gray collar. You always hated the admirals. You saw what they did after the War. Admiral Keen, then recently, Hudson. Damn it, Baldwin. What could possibly drive you to make this decision?" she asked.

"Maybe I wanted to make a difference from the inside," he told her, gauging her reaction.

"I don't think so. You loved your posting too much. The big hero, Thomas Baldwin, vanquishes the Assembly, stops the Statu, brings the Ugna to their new home." Rene clutched her glass as if she was scared to let go. "And after all that, you retire. It doesn't add up."

"Rene, as you can see, I'm not retired. And if I hadn't stepped down, would Treena have been promoted?" he asked.

"Yes, of course. She was primed for another vessel." Rene pushed her plate to the side and took another drink. "I don't think I'll ever understand you, Baldwin."

"That makes two of us," he said, raising his glass. She tapped it with hers, and they laughed.

"It's her, isn't it?" Rene asked, her tone low.

"Aimie?"

"Sure, the doctor. The one that works for the company that screwed over your good friend Starling," Rene said. The pair had been close too, even more so after working together against the Vusuls.

Lineage

"That might have played a part in it," Tom whispered.

"What is it? You feeling old? Did you see your lonely life flash before your eyes?" she asked, and Tom sensed there was more than her usual sass behind the comment. He looked into her green eyes and remembered their one passionate night together, long ago. Was she still holding on to that?

"Don't you ever think about it? We started at the Academy, and bam, we blink, and it's twenty-something years later. Did we not do enough in those years to earn some desk time?" he asked.

She smiled despite the mood she was emanating. "Be honest. You hate it, don't you?"

"It's only been a couple of months," he said, not quite answering the question.

"So you do hate it?"

He glanced around, unable to contain a smile. Rene had that effect on him. "I hate it. Oh, I hate it so much. What was I thinking?" It felt so good to let it out, and Rene laughed loudly as the server came in. She tried to hold back, but Tom cracked a laugh, and they went to it again as the dishes were cleared. Tom was blinking away tears by the time they were alone.

"That was good," he said.

"I haven't had a laugh like that in a long time. Thomas Baldwin behind a desk on Nolix. I never thought I'd see the day. If you hate it so much, what are you going to do? Ask for *Constantine* back?"

"I can't do that. It's Treena's. I'll figure it out. I always do," he told her.

Tom noted how close Rene's chair was to his, her cheeks flushed from the drink and laughter. "You know, if you'd been seeking company in the arms of a woman, you could have looked me up."

Tom nearly choked on his Vina and met her gaze. "Are you suggesting we should have made some sort of arrangement?"

"Something like that…"

"We're moving in together," he blurted out for some reason, and Rene went rigid.

"I see." She set her glass down and rose, moving toward the exit. "Tom, it was a pleasure catching up. Please don't take anything I said to heart. I was only kidding around."

Tom stood too. "Sure. And… I appreciate your company tonight. Maybe we can do it again soon."

She stopped at the door. "I'd like that."

Alarms sounded in the ceiling's speakers, and Tom followed Rene as she jogged through the restaurant. "What's going on?" he heard Rene ask through her communicator with the bridge.

"We're under attack."

SIX

*B*randon stared through the tinted glass dome, seeing the sunlight casting its glow over the vegetation. All this work, and for what? Moisture dripped from the ceiling, landing on the garden, a constant cycle of their greenhouse. His boots and socks were set by the airlock, and he walked through the rows of plants in the garden, feeling the dirt between his toes.

This might be the last time he'd ever come here, and it had been his favorite of the domes over the past decade. There had been repeated attempts to colonize Mars, but it had never worked out. By the time they'd understood enough of the technology to really make a go of it, the government had begun to change, shifting toward a single world order. At first, they'd all gone along with it. Brandon remembered gardening with his grandmother, and her recalling tales of that time.

They thought it was good, a united planet, but soon it was evident that democracy was no longer.

Brandon crouched by a tomato plant, brushing aside some of the leaves to see the basil plant underneath. He inhaled both, the scent titillating to his senses. One of the fruits was nearly ready to eat, and he plucked it off before finding another. Once he had enough for the giant sauce, he stopped. They were going to make a special meal tonight, maybe their last one before the incoming vessel arrived. Brandon was ready to give his life to keep this place and hoped that would be sufficient.

He foraged some basil and spent some time at the rows of onions. Soon he had a basket full of supplies, and he sealed it up, returning to his EVA. The others would be waiting.

Brandon took one last look into the greenhouse through the airlock hatch window and exited the dome, climbing into the rover. He moved toward the Island and slowed as he passed dome four. These had been created over two hundred years ago, about fifty years before the ultimate ban on colonization was issued.

Before that, corporations had attempted to set up stations on Mars, and on Jupiter's moons, using the bases for mining operations. Once the Visitors had arrived, everything changed.

Brandon continued on, stopping near the dome where almost all of their colonists were gathered. A few were still preparing for tomorrow's assault, including Jun and Carl, along with Devon. He grabbed the pack with food and entered the airlock. The moment he was through, his helmet came off, and he heard the shouting.

He dropped the bag, heading in the direction of the noise, and found two groups inside, facing off against one another.

"What the hell is going on?" he asked, and that was when he saw the gun in Sylvester's hand. He waved it around, pointing the barrel toward Brandon.

"You wanna know what I think? I think we're screwed. I'm taking the freighter, and you're gonna let us leave. All of these fine folks want to depart this colony," Sylvester said.

Brandon raised his hands. "Look, there's nowhere to

Lineage

go. You'll die."

"We're going to cut a deal. Basher isn't a monster," Paula said, her eyes wild.

There were about fifteen of them siding with the armed man, and Brandon hated to see the division.

"Paula, you of all people... you were torn from your family, sent to the mines. You really think that Basher will cut you any kind of deal?" Brandon asked, storming into the middle of the room to stand between the two opposing groups. He didn't stop there. "And you, Sylvester. Your own kid was killed by one of his militia. You want to trust the Visitors?"

The man smacked his lips, gaze darting across the room, but his gun stayed aimed at the others.

"We need to stick together. Work as a team and nab this ship. This will make the difference," Brandon said.

Sylvester was an older man, thin but wiry, and his neck tendons stuck out as he lowered the weapon. "Dammit, boss. I didn't... We're afraid. None of us wants to die."

Brandon took the gun from him, passing it to Kristen behind him. "I don't either, but the only way this works is if we take their ship. It was sent before the robot came with his ultimatum, so it may be a clean-up crew meant to escort us to Earth."

Paula nodded, draping a long arm over Sylvester's shoulder.

"I was about to start dinner. Does anyone object to that?" Brandon asked, and the tension eased as one of the younger kitchen workers grabbed his pack, carrying it through the mess to the swinging doors.

This was going to be their last meal on Mars, and Brandon intended to enjoy his fellow colonists' company. Time was running out.

"How long have you worked for our mutual friend?" Lark Keen asked Prophet in the cramped room on her modified freight hauler.

Her face was aglow with the light of her clear tablet, and she lowered the device, staring at him as if he'd interrupted something important. They'd been sitting silently for an hour or so, and Lark was exceedingly bored.

"Much like the Assembly, they've been operating from the shadows. Unlike the Assembly, they're still out there, and gaining power with each passing day." The jab was intended to sting, but Lark found he no longer cared about his failures with the Assembly. That was yesterday's news, and he was fighting for a way to improve his family's standing.

Sure, he could have continued on at the Concord's mercy and been with his family, a prisoner for life. Then what? What would have happened when Luci grew up? Or if they had another child while in custody? That wasn't freedom. Luci needed a future.

"It amazes me how they've managed to accomplish so much in such little time," Lark said, flipping a pillow in his hands.

Prophet laughed, a low, raspy sound. "Little time. They've been working on this for hundreds, maybe thousands of years. Cultivating their race, making allies with powerful people. They've done it all properly. Above ground, if you will."

"When do we arrive?" he asked.

"We'll be there in a few days," she told him.

He hated being in the dark like this. "Then what?"

"Then we hop into our Nek drive shuttle and head to

the final destination," she said. "Oh, if you haven't seen it, your uniform is in the closet." She pointed past him at the wall.

Lark rose, dropping the pillow to the bunk, and crossed the room, opening the sliding door. The uniform was familiar, the crest of the First Ship on the breast. He ran a hand over it. He'd never worn one, not for real. All those dreams of working side by side with his best friend in the universe, Thomas Baldwin, had gone to the Vastness when Lark had betrayed the Concord.

He would have finished the Academy, been picked up by a low-tier Border patrol ship, and risen through the ranks with his charm and work ethic, much like Baldwin had. Only that hadn't happened for Lark, because he'd met Seda, and her traitorous father had convinced him to travel another path. He'd been too young, too impressionable then, and much of what her father said of the Concord's faults were true.

Lark saw the folly in his methods. He hated that Baldwin had managed to unearth some of the truth of the admirals, including Lark's own grandfather, Admiral Keen. They'd gotten away with so much over the years, and Lark had been hoping to set it straight with the Assembly. He honestly felt like he could have accomplished so much without the meddling of his once-closest ally, Tom, but would that have been the best move?

He doubted it. Lark had no choice but to continue down a questionable path in order to secure a better future for his family. No matter where he stepped, trouble followed, but as he stared at the uniform, Lark told himself this was it. After this mission, he was done playing these games. He would take Seda and Luci and the riches promised him by his benefactor, and disappear for good.

"What do you think?" Prophet asked, startling him. He

realized he'd been standing there gawking at the Concord uniform for a good five minutes without moving.

"I think it'll do the job," he said, touching the gray collar denoting the rank of admiral. "Admiral Keen will rise again," he whispered, and closed the door.

Tom felt out of place on *Shu*'s bridge, with no real spot that was designated to him. He stood beside Commander Shu's seat, watching as the Veerilion cruisers attacked.

"What do we do, Captain?" Douglas asked.

Four enemy crafts were actively pursuing them, their pulse blasts striking the flagship's shields with little effect.

"Shields at ninety-one percent, Captain," Lieutenant Commander Asha Bertol said from her position at the side of the bridge. Tom almost expected Brax to be seated there, since the bridge was identical to *Constantine*'s.

Tom nearly answered the question from Conner before remembering he wasn't in charge.

"*To truly learn, one must be taught a lesson*," Captain Rene Bouchard said, quoting the Code. "Reach out to them one more time, and if they fail to respond, obliterate the lead ship."

Tom shook his head. It was probably better than they deserved, but there would be at least twenty lives aboard that ship. Unfortunately, they were attacking a Concord ship a hundred times their size, refusing communications.

Commander Shu tapped on his console, and an image wavered over the viewscreen. A Veerilion paced over their dim bridge, hands on hips. It was a thick creature, with a snout-like nose and deep-set black eyes. Tufts of hair stuck out from its head, and it said something in its native tongue before seeming to realize the mistake.

"How dare you come into our system unannounced," she said in Common. Tom now saw the subtle differences that told him this was a female of the race. The nose was shorter, flatter, the shoulders slightly narrower.

Rene rose, walking to the center of the bridge. "Excuse me? Are you not a Concord partner? Identify yourselves!"

"I am Omnik of the Veerilion, and we are defending our home," she told them, her anger as noticeable as Bouchard's.

"We have done nothing to warrant an attack. We are merely traveling through your…"

"One of you came and assaulted us two days ago. You knocked out half our satellites, damaged our docking station, and caused a tsunami that will take years to recover from," Omnik said.

Rene froze, turning to face the screen. "Excuse me? Who attacked you?"

"The Concord. The ship was clearly marked!"

Rene motioned to Kan to mute the call, and she turned to face Tom. "What is this about? Did Nolix give the order to raid the Veerilion?"

"Why in the Vastness would we do that? They're a peaceful people, with a great trade record. We've no reason to fight within our borders," Tom told her, frowning at the accusation.

"Kan, turn it on." Rene waited for the light to flash in the top right corner of the viewscreen, and she continued. "Omnik of the Veerilion, I'm sorry you were ambushed. I am Captain Rene Bouchard of *Shu*, and we're here to help. If someone stormed you under a Concord logo, I can assure you it was unsanctioned, and we will find out what happened and ensure someone pays for the assault."

The woman's snout sniffled, her eyes blinking three

times before she spoke. "How can I trust you won't attack us too?"

"We'll send our expedition vessel only. I would personally like to see any footage you have of the attack," Rene said, pointing to Tom. "As would Admiral Thomas Baldwin."

The woman blanched at the mention of Tom's name, and he nodded to her.

"If I would have known... I'm sorry. You can understand our concerns," Omnik said in a rush.

"Will you accompany us?" Rene asked.

"Yes."

"Good. We'll join you in a few minutes," Rene said, and the image of the Veerilion bridge vanished.

Yin Shu's AI walked over, arms crossed. "This is most intriguing, Captain. Do you mind if I join you?"

"Not at all. Who would attack the Veerilions pretending to be the Concord? It doesn't make sense," Rene said, exiting the bridge on the right. Tom followed and saw Conner Douglas chasing after them. Conner stopped at the edge of the hall leading toward their expedition ship, grabbing two PL-30s.

"You can never be too careful." Conner passed him one, and Tom grimaced as he strapped it to his hip.

"You want to know who would do this?" Tom asked, and Rene nodded as she climbed the few rungs leading into the smaller ship, nestled on top of *Shu*. "Someone that wants to create dissention within our ranks."

---

*T*reena was glad to be on their way. With Ven in his usual position on the bridge, everything felt a little more normal—except she was in the captain's chair, and an old man was seated to her left.

Commander Pol Teller snored loudly, a string of drool falling over his chin. Treena glanced at Missy, who seemed to finally notice the man was asleep. Missy grabbed a cloth and dabbed his glistening lips with it. Treena rolled her eyes and stared at the viewscreen.

"Captain, we're close to the Border. We'll exit Concord space in five minutes," Lieutenant Darl advised her.

"Good. Bridge to Engineering," Treena said.

"Engineering." Reeve Daak's voice was light and happy as usual.

"How is everything looking? Are we good to activate the modified star drive when we're past the Border?" Treena asked.

She heard some clicking and whining from the Bentom ball, and Reeve's voice returned. "We're all systems go, Captain. We're going to start by pushing it to twenty-five percent capacity, and continue from there until we're at full speed."

If everything went as planned, they expected the trip to take no longer than three months. Considering the vast distance, this would be a remarkable feat, setting a new precedent for interstellar space travel.

"What…" Teller's eyes snapped open as he gasped, and he glanced around. "Where are we?"

"Almost ready to start the new drive," Treena advised him quietly. She caught Brax grinning at her from across the bridge, and she tried not to smile back. What had they been thinking, sending this old man to do a young person's job? He couldn't last more than three hours without falling asleep.

"Are we sure this is such a great idea? I didn't live this long to be torn apart by some Nek and Bentom. In my day, we stayed where we belonged and didn't mess with distant rumors."

"Aren't you intrigued by the notion that we might find the birthplace of humanity?" Treena asked him.

"Sure, I suppose. Won't really change anything, though, will it?" he asked.

"How so?" Treena asked him.

Teller sat up, glancing at Missy, who brought him a bottle of water. He drank deeply and rolled up his sleeve as the assistant brought an injector. She pressed it to his forearm, and his eyes shot open as she inserted the medication. He grimaced and sank into his seat.

This was becoming a common occurrence on Treena's bridge. She'd asked Teller to do this in private the first time, but he'd said he needed the shot every couple of hours, so she'd relented.

"Even if we find some humans out there, what does it matter? Will it affect my children's lives? Will it change how the Concord deals with things? Not one bit. I understand why we're doing it, but why didn't we just send a scout in one of those Nek shuttles in the first place? See what's worth seeing." Teller's words actually made sense.

"We didn't want to risk the lives of the shuttle crew," Treena said. There had been numerous volunteers for the mission, including Brax and his sister. Even Treena had considered doing it, but Benitor had been adamant that *Constantine* make the trip. She wanted their representation of the Concord to be strong and admirable when they met with the leaders of Earth—if they existed.

"Sounds like a bunch of crap to me," Teller said, sitting up straighter.

Treena leaned toward him, lowering her voice. "If you don't mind, please leave the treasonous talk for the privacy of my office."

Lineage

He grunted, and Treena turned her attention to the viewscreen. Ven had been quiet since his return to *Constantine,* and she hadn't found the chance to have more than a passing conversation with the man after his brief stay on Driun F49 with the rest of the Ugna. She liked him, and his work was better than most, but the mere fact that he was Ugna still set off alarm bells on occasion. He'd done nothing but prove his loyalty to *Constantine* and the crew, but Tom had his reservations about Fayle and the others. After what Reeve and Ven had witnessed against the Vusuls, so did Treena.

"Captain, we are outside of Concord space," Ven advised her.

"Executive Lieutenant Daak, are we prepared?" Treena asked her chief of engineering.

"One moment, Captain. I'm getting a… never mind. It's all green lights from here," Reeve told her.

"Ven, let's see what this thing can do," Treena said, watching Ven initiate the customized star drive.

She clutched the arms of her captain's chair with a firm grip as *Constantine* shuddered, a long vibration carrying through the hull. The ship's AI flickered, disappearing for a few seconds before returning. They began to move, and she was amazed to see the stars streak over the viewscreen.

They were the fastest Concord vessel, larger than any of the Nek drive test models on Leria. It was unclear what they'd find on Earth, but Treena finally felt like they were on track to find out. She'd been anticipating this departure since she'd learned she was taking over *Constantine*.

Treena waited for another half hour before judging that to be enough time to test the new drive. She glanced at her commander, nudging him with an elbow. "I'm off to Engineering. You have the bridge."

He perked up, peering around. He'd been sleeping

again.

"You got it, Captain." Teller rose from the seat, his assistant Missy coming to help him to his feet.

"Ven, would you like to check out the modifications with me?" she asked her executive lieutenant. He turned, his red eyes startling against his pale skin.

"I would like that very much, Captain," he said, abandoning his position. Someone came to replace him as they exited the bridge.

Treena waited for a minute before speaking as they walked through the corridor and toward the elevator. "Ven, did you have a good time on Driun?"

"It was acceptable," he said.

"That's it?"

"Engineering," Ven advised the computer as the doors closed. "Captain, I am afraid I don't have much to tell you. I don't seem to fit in anywhere."

Treena saw the pain in his expression. "That's not true, and you know it."

"Will I ever be one of you? They seek to have me return to Driun when this mission is over. It is understood that I might...procreate with First Officer Hanli," he told her, and Treena broke into a smile.

"'Procreate'? Is that what goes for smooth-talking among Ugna?" She laughed, seeming to make him even more uncomfortable.

"Captain, I am sorry for mentioning any of this to you. It was out of line, and I apologize." Ven stepped off first as the elevator doors opened when they arrived on Deck One.

"There's more. What is it?" Treena walked out after him but grabbed his arm to stop him from passing her.

"I do not know what you are insinuating," he said plainly.

"Is it me? Are you upset about my promotion?"

"No, nothing like that."

"Do you miss Baldwin? We all do, Ven…"

"I don't trust them," Ven said after glancing around the elevator entrance, apparently making sure no one was nearby listening to their conversation.

"Who?" she asked, stepping closer.

"You heard about what happened. I close my eyes and I can see them all injecting the En'or. They hover there, eyes burning, and the power that emanated off them… it was too much. They killed the Vusuls, Captain. They did so without second thoughts or remorse. I was taught never to kill as a child. All life was precious. They lied to me then. What else have they been untruthful about?"

Treena peered toward Reeve's boiler room and set a hand on Ven's arm. He stared at the contact. "Your guess is as good as mine, but if your gut says something fishy is going on, then we have to trust that. You have an advantage." She wondered what Tom would make of this discussion.

"I hope I'm wrong, but I don't think I am. I was glad to have spent time there to see it with my own eyes, and feel the city and the people. Their spirits are high, but I sensed a lot of hidden thoughts, barriers erected to prevent me from understanding what was occurring. When I left, I also sensed an overwhelming relief from those around me. Even Hanli."

Treena assumed this must have been difficult for Ven. He was one of the Ugna, but his presence had disturbed them. Many would think of him as a traitor for joining *Constantine,* and those that didn't might see him as a tool to be used for their benefit. "And what of High Elder Wylen?" she asked curiously.

Ven locked his gaze to hers, a slight frown furrowing

his brow. "He is dangerous. I've been asked to spy on *Constantine* for him."

"Is that so?" Treena's hands flexed as she heard the news. "And what are you going to tell him?"

"Whatever we decide he should hear." Ven smiled deviously, making Treena smirk.

"I like this side of you, Ven. How about we continue this discussion later?" she told him, starting toward Engineering.

SEVEN

*V*eer wasn't a big world, mostly water, which was their main reason for being granted entrance into the Concord, according to the computer. They had riches beneath the glimmering surface of their giant seas, and Tom saw some of the finest beaches he'd ever witnessed as the expedition ship landed next to Omnik's shuttle.

The entire trip had taken four hours, and Tom's back protested as he stood. Yin Shu's AI projection wavered next to him, and Conner clipped her Link to his belt, allowing Tom's former captain to tag along for the ride.

"Whatever we see, we need to ensure they don't think we're the enemy," Rene suggested.

"Do you think they'd lure us here to harm us?" Conner asked.

Tom had been thinking the same thing, but it was Rene who responded first. "It's highly possible. What better negotiation bait than Captain Rene Bouchard and Admiral Thomas Baldwin, the most popular fleet captain in generations?" She smirked at Tom, and he returned a smile of his own.

"Let's hope that's not what this is about," Tom told her, and they exited the expedition vessel. Veer was a Class Zero-Nine planet, so they weren't in their standard EVAs, which was fine by Tom. The air was humid, the sun bright.

The sounds of lapping water carried across the landing pad, and Tom quickly saw the devastation from the tsunami Omnik had mentioned.

Buildings were crushed from the power of the ocean, and the repair was underway. Hundreds of the heavyset Veerilion people worked over a city block, while dozens of machines rolled alongside in a cleanup effort.

"As you can see, we've been hit hard. This city was our capital, and a quarter of it is destroyed. We lost over a thousand lives. Lucky for us, we realized the incoming attack and were able to vacate as much of the city as possible to our underground chambers," Omnik said, her voice choking with emotion.

Tom stepped toward her, watching the workers in the distance. "You did well to save as many as you could. We're going to figure this out and help in any way we can."

Omnik sniffed, and she stared at Tom with unrelenting black eyes. "I want them to pay."

"They will," Tom promised her.

An hour later, they were inside a Veerilion central command station on the outskirts of their capital city. Omnik remained behind her ground support team leader, who was booting up the footage. There were five feeds located around the city, and a few from satellites orbiting the planet. The Concord logo was unmistakable. It was a flagship identical to *Constantine* and *Shu*. Tom stiffened at the sight and glanced at Rene.

"No wonder they attacked us," Rene said quietly. "Tom, what in the Vastness is this?"

"We *are* building two more, but they aren't even near completion. Not to mention, they're waiting for *Constantine*'s feedback on the new Nek-modified star drive before deciding which unit to install. The Concord doesn't have a third vessel ready for space travel yet," Tom advised them.

Conner shook his head while they watched the giant spacecraft attack. Ten fighters, clearly Concord-issued, departed the hangar and began moving for Veer. The team leader switched to the localized feeds, and Tom grimaced as he saw the bomb being dropped far into the ocean to create a massive tsunami.

"Someone has one of our ships," Conner said. "How is this possible?"

"I don't know." Tom was angry. Clearly this was a Concord job, or someone had done one remarkable job of tricking the Veerilions. "I need to speak with the Prime."

They continued to witness the attack. The fighters fought from the sky all around the planet, and Tom was happy to see one of the enemy go down. "Where is that? Do you still have the pilot?"

Omnik swallowed and sniffled again. "The pilot is dead."

"Well, let's see the body," Rene said. "It might give us an idea who did this."

"I'm afraid that isn't possible," Omnik said.

"Why not?" Conner asked.

"Because they were liquefied."

Tom froze. "Did you say *liquefied*?"

"That's correct. Nothing was left of them but a pool."

"Where's the ship?" Tom asked, and Omnik's officer pointed to a distant spot on the screen.

"There," he said. "Would you like to see it?"

"Yes, please," Tom told him.

Omnik motioned for her officer to rise, and she introduced him as Erim. "If you'll follow me."

The big Veerilion led them from the room and into a sleek transport ship parked outside the facility. Omnik joined them inside, and soon they were lifting away from the capital, heading inland. The trip was short, and in ten minutes, they were landing again. Tom was anxious to see the fighter, but the fact that the pilot was nothing but a pool of liquefied matter set alarm bells ringing.

Conner leaned in, speaking quietly to Tom. "What if it's the same thing the Statu used?"

His question was obvious, but it still sent a wave of fear through Tom. "It can't be."

"What if it is?" Rene asked from his other side. "They were always clever, and they'd have a reason they chose Veer as their target."

Tom clenched his jaw in anger. "Stop it!" he shouted, far louder than intended. Erim and Omnik peered at him as they exited the transport. Tom lowered his voice. "It isn't the Statu, because we dealt with them. They're gone." He hoped this was true.

The landscape was much different this far inland. It was full of rolling hills and green grass. The nearby city stood tall, mostly undamaged from the attack, and the fighter lay where it had in the video, unmoved since the assault.

It was the same model as his old unit, and Tom stared at it as they crossed the field toward the crashed craft. Conner and Rene had flown them before, but only in training. Tom had logged a lot of hours inside those crafts, and this was definitely Concord-issued. The hull was intact, the bottom side burned, the nose slightly crumpled from the impact. Chunks of the ground encircled the front end, and Tom set a hand near the cockpit's rungs.

There were no markings on the side where the serial number and callsign should have been, and he inspected it more closely, seeing no evidence of tampering or paint removal.

"Should you be doing this?" Conner asked him.

"What, just because I'm an admiral, I shouldn't be

climbing around on a downed enemy vessel?" Tom asked with a light laugh, trying to break the tense mood surrounding them.

"Yeah, that's what I meant," Conner said.

Tom took the rungs, clambering to the cockpit entrance. He pried it wide, hinging the lid upward, and saw the sticky remains of the pilot.

"We scraped up what we could for testing in our laboratories. We can tell that the pilot was Callalay," Omnik advised him from the ground.

Tom leaned over the seat, searching for something else.

"The computer's fried," Erim said. "We tried everything but weren't able to retrieve anything useful."

This model was different than the newest iterations, and Tom pressed a lever, tilting the seat forward. The ship had a backup drive, one that only this generation used. He saw it plugged in along the floor, and he used his fingers to pry it free, pocketing the device. It might prove nothing, but it was worth a shot. Even if it was encrypted, he was confident Kan or someone else could assist in breaking the code.

Yin Shu's projection materialized beside him, hovering near the opposite end of the cockpit. "Thomas, there is no tag inside."

"You're right."

"This cannot be a Concord vessel," she suggested.

"It might be, but it hasn't finished production. See the seat?" He pointed at a spot near the front of the chair, trying to ignore the sticky substance on it. "The thread patterns are different than I remember."

"Are you certain?" Shu asked, and he nodded.

"Absolutely. This is a knock-off." Tom climbed down, happy to learn this was a replica. His boots landed on the ground with a thud, and he grinned at the others. "At least we know one thing. This wasn't us."

"Then who was it?" Rene asked.

He patted his pocket and shrugged. "We're going to find out."

---

*T*oday was the day.

Brandon powered the freighter up, glancing over his shoulder at Kristen. "You ready for this?" he asked her.

"It's going to work," she assured him for the fifth time since they'd woken up.

The suborbital defenses were in place, but Brandon hoped it wouldn't come to that. For this plan to work, they needed the incoming ship.

Carl entered the compact bridge, humming an old song. Brandon didn't know the words, but he'd heard Carl belting it out on occasion. He always sang when he was nervous.

"Where's Jun?" Brandon asked.

"She's… not coming," Carl said.

"Why not?" Brandon asked. "We had this planned out."

"I asked her to stay behind," Carl told him. "Devon can do her job just as well."

Brandon understood. Carl was trying to protect Jun, but he hated last-minute changes like this.

"Fine, but he'd better be on his game," Brandon said, hearing Devon's plodding footsteps from the cargo hold.

The seat vibrated as he flipped a switch, and he silently wished the colonists safety while they were gone. If the enemy made it to the domes, that meant Brandon had failed his task.

Kristen sat in the chair beside him, her blue jumpsuit a mirror of her eye color. "We're going to do this. I always knew there was a reason for holding on to this technology." She tapped the boxy unit connected to the weapons system. These old freighters were used for long hauling within the solar system, and their weaponry wasn't defensive. It was made to break apart rock or floating debris near the mining sites.

This craft, in particular, had logged over one hundred round trips from Jupiter to Earth over a span of fifty years. Brandon had been lucky to find it a decade ago, nabbing it for a bargain as it was being decommissioned.

The box Kristen indicated was another story. This device had the ability to disable drones and had been created to deal with haywiring units at the Callisto mining site over a hundred years ago. The incoming Invader vessel was going to learn about it first-hand today.

"You were right to bring it along. We hoped we wouldn't need to use it." Brandon averted his gaze, breaking eye contact with Kristen. "I'm sorry it didn't work out."

"We can do this," she said softly.

"No. It's too late. Sylvester was right. Even if this works, they'll come again, and again. We're going to die," Brandon told her, instantly regretting it. But Kristen didn't blanch at his comments; she only frowned.

"Then we take it to them. We steal this ship and head to Earth in it," she said, echoing his own thoughts. He hadn't wanted to share them with anyone, because the rest of the colonists would have said he was crazy for even thinking it.

"We still die, then," he said.

"For what we believe in. President Basher needs to pay, as do the Invaders. Let's do this. We've sat back and hidden for too long."

Kristen's eyes filled with tears, and Brandon nodded once. "I'm in."

"Are we ready to go?" Carl barked, causing Brandon to jump in his seat.

"We're good." Brandon fired up the propulsion lift, sending them off Mars' surface, kicking up a dust storm as they moved through the red planet's atmosphere.

"Computer, time to intercept?" Brandon asked as the shaking freighter moved into space, straight for the incoming enemy vessel.

"*Time to intercept is forty minutes, sir*," the female computer voice advised.

"Everyone know the plan?" Brandon climbed from the chair, letting the automatic controls take over as the thrusters sent them from Mars.

"We meet them, see what kind of bastards we're dealing with, and hit 'em where it hurts," Devon said, pumping a fist in the air.

"Something like that. Carl, you'll be in the engine room, making sure the shields stay charged. This bucket has a tendency to short out when it's being overworked. Devon, you're on the blasters. You're always talking the big talk, so let's see you prove it today, okay?"

Brandon waited for a quippy remark that didn't come. Devon looked terrified.

The trip to intercept went by quickly, with Brandon trying not to think about their next step. He told himself they needed to win this battle before anything, so he did his best to concentrate on the task at hand. Brandon certainly hadn't expected a Class Seven rover to show on screen as they zoomed on the approaching ship.

"Freighter, identify yourself," an even voice said through the speakers. Brandon hadn't even granted it access, and this concerned him. They must have had a way to hack into his old system.

"We're lost, and damaged from a chunk of rock bigger than a barn," Brandon said, using a fake accent.

"There are no asteroids in the vicinity, and reading your…" Brandon muted the call, and nodded to Kristen.

"It's time," he told her, flipping a switch to relay the message to Carl. "Be alert."

"On it," Carl's voice returned.

"Devon, ready to fire?" Brandon asked, and the man wiped an arm over his brow, his eyes brown and wide.

"Yep."

Brandon unmuted it and heard the tail end of the conversation. "…stand down, prepare for boarding."

The drones erupted from the rover: two of them, and both would be carrying a deadly robot. "Now!" he shouted, and Devon began pounding at the drones with the blasters. This particular model of freighter wasn't made for this kind of job, but Brandon had seen to the alterations himself. The drones' shields broke faster than could be expected, and they each exploded into debris. The rover was ten times their ship's size, with the Invaders' advanced technology. Still, it had one thing from the pre-invasion years, and that was the central processing chip Kristen targeted with.

The beam from the device flared, hitting the mark. Before the rover's crew had grasped what was transpiring, the bright lights along its outer hull dimmed. The thrusters cut out, going dark.

The rover was dead in space.

Carl's voice carried through the speaker. "Look, you didn't even need me."

It was true. The Invaders hadn't managed a single shot.

"We still might. We're going to have to clear it, so

everyone strap into your suits. Time to claim our prize," Brandon said as he urged the freighter forward, steadily closer to the very ship he was going to return to Earth in.

Lark didn't fully trust Prophet, but so far, she'd done nothing but stick to her word. She'd have no qualms about killing him if she felt he was going to betray her or their benefactor, but he was in this to win, not to return to prison. Once he did this job, he could be at the head of something like he'd always planned, with a strong ally.

He didn't fully comprehend how his mysterious collaborator had garnered any information about Sol and the inhabitants of Earth, but Keen was prepared to make the trek and play at being a Concord admiral.

Someone kicked his boots off the mess table, and he opened his eyes, seeing Prophet staring at him. The ridges on her forehead were prominent, the poor lighting casting silhouettes over her face. Lark guessed she'd spent most of her life in the shadows. "You almost done sleeping?"

Lark sat up, finishing his cold Raca. "Do you ever sleep, or are you a Begolyte night worm?"

A smile flickered across her face for a second. "You have a way with words, don't you? Let's hope they're nicer when you meet with the Earth president in a few days."

"What's the deal with these guys? Humans? Are you serious? I don't buy any of it." Lark rose, bringing his cup to the sanitizer.

"What's so difficult to understand?"

"Why have we never seen them before?"

"Your people left thousands of years ago, but clearly not everyone departed when your ancestors did," the

Lineage

Callalay woman said.

"I still don't see how they're going to help us gain control of the Concord," Lark told her.

"Neither do I, but I have some news. There have been three attacks by Concord ships on partner worlds over the last week. I think we have our opening. Chaos is within the system. People are finally beginning to hear about it, and protests are being planned for Nolix as soon as a few days from now," Prophet told him. She stepped close, her body blocking his exit from the room. "You'd better not screw this up."

"Why's this so important to you?" he asked her.

"Because I'm being paid a lot, and I never fail," she advised him.

Lark huffed, fighting to not roll his eyes. "Well, don't expect me to screw this up. My family is on the line."

"You've already failed them once. Why wouldn't you again?" she asked.

"Are we almost there?" he asked, not taking the bait.

"We're entering orbit as we speak," she said, moving aside so he could pass.

"Good. I'm ready to be done with this." He peered at his clothing, a real Concord-issued admiral's uniform. Part of him felt like a fool for donning the outfit. He was a traitor, though, and this was far from the worst he'd ever done. Impersonating one of the Concord leaders was nothing for Lark Keen, but Prophet's words cut deep. *I'm coming, Seda and Luci. Wait for me.* He pictured them, finding it harder to visualize his family. With each passing day, their memory faded slightly more.

The space station rotated around the planet below, a transport stop along a nothing system, where you could have your star drive tweaked, update your AI, or deal in illegal substances. It was within Concord space, and many places like this had been closed down over the years, but they always popped up again. This one was Concord sanctioned, and Prophet had said she'd chosen this one because of that fact. No one would search for them here.

Lark went to the bridge, watching over the pilot's shoulder while he brought them in to dock at the hideous space station. It was fairly big, with ten or so vessels berthed along its outer rim. He didn't want to be seen. Even if he'd never met anyone inside, there was an extremely high chance he'd be recognized. Prophet assured him his mug had been plastered over every newsfeed and transmission over the last few weeks since his escape. He was priority number one and the most wanted man in the Concord.

The reward was huge, and it made Lark wonder how much his ally was paying Prophet if she wasn't willing to turn him in to the Concord for the payout. The sum had to be astronomical.

"We're here." Prophet tossed him device, and he gawked at it, unsure what it was. "Clip it to your collar and put this on first. Do you really want to draw that much attention to yourself?" She passed him a brown cloak, and Lark covered the admiral's clothing with it. Once that was done, he placed the apparatus on the collar as she'd instructed, and his eyesight went blurry momentarily.

"What's this supposed to do?" he asked.

"Go look at your reflection," she told him.

Lark stepped away, heading to the restroom, and saw another man staring back at him. His hair was longer, dark, and he had the eyes of a Zilph'i. He moved a hand over his nose, and the image blurred. He'd have to be careful.

Prophet waved her arm, and he followed, entering the airlock. "Don't touch it, and you should be fine. We're going somewhere bleak, so don't worry about being spotted."

"And this contact will bring us to the Nek shuttle?" he asked.

"That's the plan," she answered.

Lark stepped onto the station, one step closer to completing his mission.

Only a few days had passed since Ven's return to *Constantine*, and he was already breathing easier. He was settling into his usual routine and finding it much better than biding time on Driun F49. This was the new version of himself, the role he'd accepted and thrived within. Being an executive lieutenant on Captain Treena Starling's *Constantine* was a dream come true.

He trusted the other crew members, unlike the Ugna he'd just spent two months with. The energy here was different, stronger, less contradictory. His quarters were as they always had been, neat and organized, and he exited them without a glance toward the drawer that held the vial of En'or. It had been some time since he'd used it, but he felt as strong as ever. It was something no one had explained to him, but Ven still saw the dancing lights behind his eyelids as he meditated. The Vastness called to him on occasion, not seeking his life as he'd once thought.

No. The Vastness wanted Ven to be aware of its power, to tap into the conscious stream of energy it held and pluck on the tendrils of the entire universe's existence. He didn't understand it, but he now comprehended the Vastness when he encountered it. It was the most beautiful yet frightening thing he'd ever witnessed.

"Ven, there you are," Brax said, running a hand over his bald head. "Have you been avoiding me?"

"No, Lieutenant Commander Daak," Ven said genuinely.

"Seriously? I thought we'd worked past the formal title. Did you forget everything in two months? It's Brax, and we're friends, right?" Brax patted him on the shoulder, and Ven nodded, happy to have run into the ship's chief of security.

"I am sorry. I've been distracted," Ven told him.

"What's new? Reeve and I are about to have our weekly, if you'd care to join." Brax pointed to the elevator.

"Why did you not request my presence?" Ven asked.

"We were giving you some time to acclimate to the new scenario," Brax told him. "Come on. We're already behind, and you know how my sister gets."

They made the trip quickly and ended up in their private meeting room, where Reeve sat working over a tablet. She kept her gaze on her screen when they entered, but she greeted Brax warmly. "Come on in, Brax, and we can start."

"Hello, Reeve," Ven said, and she glanced up, smiling at him.

"He managed to pull you from your quarters? Good." Reeve slid the tablet away, and the door opened behind Ven. He turned to see Commander Pol Teller standing there, his spine crooked and his eyes wide.

"Commander, what are you doing here?" Brax asked, and the old man smacked his lips together.

"If my crew are meeting in private, I thought it best to be included. I know how this usually shakes out," Teller said, walking proudly into the space. The meeting hall was basically an office, turned into somewhere the three of them could meet in comfort. There were only three chairs around a circular table, and Teller took one of them, leaving Brax and Ven standing.

Lineage

The commander's aide followed along behind him, and Ven sensed fear from her. She was young, and her hand shook as she passed the elderly commander his water.

"Well… what are you waiting for? Start your meeting," Teller barked.

Brax crossed his big arms over his broad chest and leaned against the white wall. "The commander doesn't sit in on our meetings, sir."

"He does now," Teller told him. "I've been out of the game for some time, and I want to catch up. And I've never been around one of…" He pointed at Ven, his long finger gnarled and bent. "*Them* before."

Reeve frowned at him, raising her voice. "This is Executive Lieutenant Ven Ittix, the only Ugna ever to be part of a Concord crew, and you should treat him with the respect he deserves."

Ven appreciated the support. Missy, the old man's assistant, let out a tiny yelp, and Ven looked at her as she receded from Teller, as if expecting his head to explode. Instead, the man laughed. Softly at first, then louder with each passing heartbeat.

"You have some gumption, Daak. God, I missed this banter. This camaraderie," Teller said, relaxing in his seat. "Do you know how good it feels to be in open space, doing something important?"

Ven felt his emotions escalating, pouring from his frail frame. The man was telling the truth. He was elated to no longer be relegated to his bed, going for short walks at home, being bored out of his mind. Ven had read up on the commander, and he hadn't been expecting this kind of reaction from Teller.

"What normally goes on in these meetings? Do you sit around and gripe about the commander and captain, or do you do some real work?" Teller asked, still seeming to be joking around.

"We discuss our teams and always seek procedural improvements," Brax said, and Teller grunted.

"You mean to say, you three think you can improve the processes that have been implemented for decades aboard these ships? I helped write the staffing guidebooks thirty years ago. Are you telling me they aren't good enough for you?" Teller asked, the mirth vacant from his gravelly voice.

"That's not…"

Teller broke into a grin and slapped his knee. "Well, you're probably right, because I had no idea what I was doing when I was first chief of crew. I hated that job." He glanced at Ven and gave an apologetic expression with his eyes. "It's like herding schoolchildren, that role."

Ven felt someone's alarm press into his mind, and he sought the source. Then another, and more… He turned toward Brax. "Something's wrong."

"What do you mean?" Brax asked, his arms unraveling from their resting position over his chest.

"I do not…" The alarms sounded, red lights flashing, and Teller's eyes grew wide.

"Missy, take me to the bridge," he ordered, and his assistant started helping him to his feet.

Reeve was at the wall, pressing the console screen. A picture of Harry appeared. "What in the Vastness is going on?" Ven saw people running around Reeve's boiler room.

"Daak, you better come quickly. The drive…" Harry swallowed, and Ven saw the worry etched on the man's brow.

"Spill it, Harry!" Reeve instructed him.

"It's the Nek drive modification. Something went haywire…"

Reeve paled, and Ven stepped behind her, listening

intently. Brax was already off, leading the new commander toward the bridge. "What is it?" Reeve pressed.

"The drive… it flashed… sent us off-course." Harry sounded nervous.

Ven finally asked the question over Reeve's shoulder. "Where are we?"

"I don't know," Harry replied.

EIGHT

*I*t had taken Kan Shu all of two hours to modify the Veerilion console to accept the device Tom had taken from the fighter. Yin Shu remained with them, her young AI projection acting as proud as a mother could be at her son's work. Tom was impressed as well.

"Easy as that, hey, Kan?" Tom asked, and the young commander only shrugged without bragging.

"It was only a matter of tying the receptors together and rewelding the casing..."

Conner shushed him as his fingers sped over the backlit keyboard. "This is interesting."

"What is it?" Rene asked, leaning over her executive lieutenant, trying to gain a better view of the screen.

"This has the ship's log, and it looks like the first tracking was done at... Aruto," Conner said.

"Aruto?" Kan asked, tapping his chin with a finger. "That's where we're headed. Why would the Callalay have created a series of fighters, then attacked one of our partners?"

"That's a damned good question, Kan. And it just so happens that we're traveling through only days after the assault. I believe in the Vastness, but not in coincidence," Tom observed.

Yin Shu came to the defense of her people, as Tom

expected. She was loyal to a fault: to her crew, to her Concord, but also to her race. "There's no proof that the Callalay manufactured them, or that they were even made there. They might have been built elsewhere and activated for the first time near Aruto to give the impression that the Callalay were behind it."

Rene nodded along. "That is a sound theory. It's what someone like Lark Keen would do."

"Lark Keen could have accomplished this," Tom said quickly.

"It's exactly what that bastard would do," Conner said. "I spoke with him once, and it instantly struck me how deviant he was. He's charming, charismatic, and while he's smiling at you, someone's sneaking up behind you with a PL-30."

"But he's been at Wavor Manor," Kan said.

"And then you guys freed him," Tom reminded them. "Do you assume he had no way of communicating with his people? He was broken out of his transport soon after, meaning he was indeed in touch with them. The Assembly might still be out there." Tom had done a lot of digging and hadn't found much proof of that, but they were good. He imagined some of Lark's old team remained in hiding.

"This is bigger than Keen," Yin Shu said.

"How?" Rene turned to face the AI. Omnik the Veerilion watched them with interest, staying quiet during their conversation. She stood near the far wall, as if trying to blend in with the desk.

"Vessels identical to our flagships and fighters? Tom, Rene, you've seen the numbers. The cost is extremely high to fund a project of this magnitude, not to mention the manpower and supplies needed. The Assembly wouldn't have stolen our retired fleet if they had those kinds of resources."

"Then who?" Tom asked.

"That's the key, isn't it?" Conner asked, spinning around in his chair.

"On to Aruto as planned." Rene tapped the console screen. "These fighters took off from nearby, but that doesn't implicate Callalay involvement. Either way, Aruto holds some answers. Tom, why are we going there in the first place?"

Tom had a distinct feeling that Admiral Benitor had sent him on this mission because of these impostors. She'd somehow known what was coming, or had learned of other attacks, and Aruto held some importance to the puzzle. But why send Fayle with him? "Headquarters wants the Callalay to be more involved in the program. They've been pulling apart for years, in little ways, and she seems to think the Ugna and the Callalay have a special relationship; hence the reason Elder Fayle is along for the ride."

"Interesting," Rene said. "Can we leave?" She glanced at Omnik, who was near the exit.

Tom rose, plucking the device from Kan's adapted console, and moved to the local woman. "We *will* track down who did this. I'm also going to request that aid be sent from Nolix to assist your rebuilding. It won't make up for the damages and lost lives, but it's a start."

"Thank you, Admiral Baldwin," Omnik said, stepping aside as Tom departed the room. A few minutes later, their two shuttles lifted from the landing pad, heading toward *Shu*. Tom was more anxious than ever to arrive at Aruto and find out what was really going on.

"How do we not know our coordinates?" Reeve asked

Harry, rushing into the boiler room. Harry turned to watch her enter, and he puffed out his cheeks as they filled with air.

"We're working on it, but the Concord holds no record of this region," he advised her.

Reeve's heart pounded. A new galaxy, somewhere far from their known universe, perhaps. She'd been on board with using the Nek-fueled advancements the entire time, but now she regretted their decision to rush the modifications to the star drive. None of them had seen this coming. Each of their test runs had been successful, and never, not once in their analysis, had the Nek drive sent them to another location.

"Check the stars for familiar constellations?" Reeve asked, but Harry would have done that already.

"Nothing on record. We're lost," Harry said, plopping to the seat at the desk.

"Will someone turn that alarm off?" she asked, her head pounding in unison with the bleeping effect. A second later, the lights kept flashing, but the noise was off.

Reeve stared at the images from the front of their vessel, noting they were in the center of a solar system, directly between the star and the last of twelve planets. "We have to fix the drive and find out our location."

"We've shut it down for the time being, containing the Bentom ball and Nek elements," Harry told her.

"Good. Constantine," Reeve said, seeing the AI appear to her right.

"Yes, ma'am," he said calmly.

"I need you to do me a favor. I have a load of old Concord partner details: ships' logs, trade routes, and exploration ventures," she said.

"I've already scanned the system network," Con informed her.

She shook her head. "These aren't in the Concord network. I've kept disk drives and hard copies of other cultures' space travel since I was a recent graduate. There's a whole storage bin full of the stuff." She waved him forward, making him follow her. "Kenneth!" she called to one of the system analysts.

He was a middle-aged man with a pot belly and a long beard. He cleared his throat, looking uncomfortable at the attention. "Yes, Chief?"

"I have a job for you." Reeve talked as she strode from the engineering room, entered the hall, and unlocked a door three rooms over. "You and Constantine are going to sift through this stuff, see if there's anything resembling details of this system. Any information that lines up with the constellations we're recording from the cameras." The door opened to reveal dozens of metallic crates, each labeled with a different Concord world's name. There was one for every partner.

"This is…" Kenneth blanched.

"Amazing," Constantine's AI said. "Good work, Executive Lieutenant."

The boxes were stacked and piled high, and Kenneth cleared a spot on a desk, powering up the sole console in the office. Reeve smiled at them. "Advise us when you find something." She closed the door and returned to Harry's side.

"Do you think they'll have any luck?" Harry asked her.

"I wouldn't have collected all that data if I didn't think it might come in handy one day. Today's that day," she said.

Reeve returned to the scans of the drive, trying to determine what had gone wrong and how she could ensure it didn't occur again.

Lineage

"While we're here, perhaps a little investigation is in order," Teller said.

He was more active than ever before, almost as if the detour had sparked some excitement in his life. He seemed younger, his eyes brighter, his snoring less frequent.

"What do you propose?" Treena asked the commander. His assistant wasn't on the bridge for the first time today, and she was glad the girl was getting a much-needed break from the old codger.

"There's a planet in this very system that's really close to a Class Zero-Nine world. Its parameters were only off by a few degrees on two of our checklists, but the air is fully breathable, the temperature near the equator balmy and hospitable," the commander informed her.

"And when did you find this out?" Treena hadn't been given the results of the probes yet.

"I looked it up." Teller pointed to the console embedded into the arm of his chair, folding it over his lap. "What do you say?"

Treena glanced to see Brax smiling at the edge of the bridge. She could see where his mind was. He wanted the adventure. "Lieutenant Commander Daak, what are your thoughts?"

"I agree with the commander on this one," he said, and Treena saw a connection between the two crewmates. Was old man Teller actually clicking with the others? She found it difficult to believe, and it was something she'd never have anticipated in a thousand years. "Reeve says it'll be a couple of days, maybe longer, before we have our location, let alone know if we can return. We may as well learn a little about this place while we're waiting."

Treena contemplated the situation and wondered what Tom would do. She dismissed the idea. She was the captain of *Constantine,* not Tom. He'd taken the promotion, and so had she. "Okay. Ven, set course for... what should we call it?"

"Planet X?" Brax asked with a laugh.

"Set course for Planet X," Treena said.

Ven's console lit up without the touch of any buttons, and the ship began moving toward the target, using the smaller thrusters. The star drive was out of commission for the time being. Treena hoped there was nothing on Planet X that would need running from.

"Course set. Arrival in three hours," Ven told the crew.

"Commander, how many missions were you part of during your tenure?" Treena asked Teller, and he turned to face her, his eyes glossy and full of memories.

"Too many to count. Over two hundred, if I were to guess," he said.

"Which type did you prefer?"

"My favorites were the explorations. I joined at the tail end of the War, when peace was on everyone's minds. Exploration grew, but funding wasn't available at first, not until the taxes increased among the partners." His gaze drifted past her, landing on the viewscreen. "But you know how it is. The Concord says it wants to seek new worlds, meet other beings, and bring expansion into the fold, but with each system we enter for the first time comes a lot of risks. They had all but cut those ventures by the time I was thirty. My favorite was a mission to explore a world we named Bessel Fourteen."

"Why did you name it that?" Treena asked, enjoying this strange new version of the commander.

"No clue. Think my captain's wife was named Bess or something." He frowned, as if trying to recall the details was causing him grief. "There it was, a world with very little greenery. The air was toxic to us, and I was one of the lucky ones sent to the surface in an EVA. You remember what those were like, right?" he asked, and Treena nodded.

They'd been forced to wear each of the last five iterations of EVAs at the Academy to understand the modifications each generation had to endure for the next. Treena distinctly recalled how heavy and bulky the energy packs were on that old model. They were designed to last ten times as long as the lighter versions, in case of emergencies, but the Concord had only kept them in production for two years before opting for the smaller style.

"They were terrible." Treena laughed, but Teller didn't.

"That's right. At the time, I thought I was being rewarded for my hard work," he said with a grimace.

"In reality, you were the low man on the pole, and no one else wanted to go," Treena said.

"You got it. I was sent with a damned rolling robot, to take samples, and the engineering assistant, who was young and foolish enough to join me."

"What happened?" Treena asked.

"The planet was teeming with life. We couldn't see it at first. I spent hours trudging along the rocky surface, with the slow-rolling bot checking samples of the dirt, the rock, the tiny fragments of moss somehow growing in dark crevasses. Galz noticed them at first. She was the engineering woman, a nice Callalay." Teller's mouth twisted momentarily. "You should have seen her face when she spotted the first one. I'd never seen such a thrill from anyone in my life."

"What was it? Did you find life forms?" The story genuinely had Treena interested and curious.

"They were made of gas. The captain had wanted to bottle one up and bring it home, but the science team advised against doing something so dangerous. They resembled clouds, hovering blobs of mist. I've seen a lot, but that was one of a kind."

The description sparked a memory from Treena's time at the Academy: a passing lecture about a gaseous being that had been discovered by the crew of *Longspar*. "You were with Captain Munter?"

Teller nodded, smiling again. "That's right. Munter took all the credit for the find, but it was really me and Galz."

"I have no recollection of Galz. Do you know what happened to her?" Treena asked.

"I pushed her after that. She went from being safely inside the engineering deck to joining a Border patrol vessel, trying to rise in the ranks. She died a year later," Teller said, his voice growing low.

"I'm sorry."

"It was a long time ago." He patted his knee and returned his gaze to her.

"Do you want to head to the surface on this one, Commander?" she asked the old man, and he hesitated before answering.

"I'd better leave that to the younger crew. Like that strapping Tekol over there." He pointed at Brax and leaned toward Treena. "But thank you."

"You're welcome." Treena had misjudged the man and was glad to see him opening up about his past. Perhaps he did have some wisdom and advice to share with a new captain after all.

She watched the world grow in the viewscreen as they headed for it, and hoped Reeve and her team could find out where in the universe the Nek-modified drive had sent them.

Lineage

Brandon clutched his weapon, hoping he didn't need it. They'd waited a full day after the life support cut out, as a precaution, but there was a possibility of live crew members inside. He didn't like the idea of suffocating them out, but they were the enemy, even if they didn't think so.

Most of the president's ships were manned by robotic crews after the Invaders had provided the technology to replace the erratic and untrustworthy humans. It was a huge part of the problem.

The corridors were dark, dim emergency strips glowing in unison along the floor. Carl and Devon were behind him, each armed as well, and Kristen walked at the rear, covering them.

His scanners were jamming, and it wasn't clear if there were life forms aboard or not. Brandon tapped the handheld device to his EVA's arm, and it blinked, the results unchanging. "Might only be us and the bots." His voice was loud in his own ear, and he glanced at Carl, who seemed ready for anything coming at them.

Carl had worked for these guys for twelve years before he understood the atrocities they'd done around the world. There were a lot of theories behind the president and just how the Invaders had affected his judgment, but no one knew the truth. Carl had begun seeking out others of a similar mindset, and that was when he and Brandon had teamed up.

They were about to acquire an Earth ship, and Brandon was more nervous than he'd been in years. As he walked through the corridors, trying to listen for sounds of movement, he wondered if he'd made the right choices throughout the course of his life. People on Earth could live out their lives in relative peace.

Brandon had been one of the lucky ones, only forced to work in the food supply chain. But he'd seen too many things during those ten years. All the deaths because the Invaders thought a region was over-populated. The meat factories had been something Brandon could never unsee. Even thinking about the writhing piles of flesh, he nearly gagged within his EVA, and he shoved the memories from his mind. *Focus*, he told himself, and stopped as the corridor turned at a forty-five degree angle. With his back to the bulkhead, he moved forward, gun raised, but the hall was empty.

He turned, seeing the others were copying his movements. He saw, too late, the silent robot entering the hall behind Kristen. The bot lifted an arm, the weaponry sparking as it shot bullets from short barrels. The first one bit Kristen in the leg, and she dropped to the ground, her helmet striking fiercely. Devon barreled over Carl, shoving him firmly, and took a series of bullets to the chest. Brandon couldn't move; he was frozen in place as Devon's arms fell to his sides. He groaned, letting loose a few swear words before charging at the robot.

"Devon, stop!" Brandon shouted, but the man was on a mission. His gun tracked forward, and he blasted at the robot while it fired more rounds of ammunition into his body. It passed through the fabric of the EVA with ease, but Devon managed to hit it, incapacitating the bot at the same time.

They tumbled together, Devon landing on top of the robot as they crashed to the floor. Brandon ran to his friend's side, but he was clearly dead. The robot's head was half melted, its eyes powered off.

"Brandon, over here!" Carl's voice was urgent, and he returned, helping seal Kristen's EVA with a sticky patch. It worked, but she was injured.

"Use the injectors, Kris." He held her helmet, and she nodded, pressing the controls on her arm. Her pupils dilated slightly as the painkillers entered her bloodstream. Brandon helped Kristen to her feet and asked if she was okay to continue.

"I'll be fine," she assured them.

An hour later, they'd managed to deactivate the whole robotic crew, and Brandon led their group to the bridge, ready to reboot the rover.

"I was wondering who it was," the voice said as Brandon entered.

He lowered his gun and saw the tall man's slim weapon pointed directly at Kristen.

"Who the hell are you?" Carl asked angrily.

"I work for the president," he said.

"Then you know we aren't turning ourselves in." Brandon took a step toward the guy, and as he neared, he saw the man was older than he'd assumed at first in the poor lighting.

"Stop where you are," he hissed. "Or she dies."

Brandon turned to face him. "What do you hope to accomplish?"

"You really don't get it, do you? The president is a reasonable man, but he can only be stretched so far. He's entrusted me to end this silently and swiftly, and that means you will lower your weapons and surrender."

Brandon smirked at the guy, and for the first time, it clicked that the man wasn't in an EVA. His hand trembled. It was an Invader. The man floated off the floor and started for Brandon, but Carl was faster. He pulled the device from his suit pocket, tossing it to the ground near the president's man. It vibrated and boomed, the concussion knocking Brandon off his feet.

When he rose, the man was struggling to his knees, but Brandon had his hands secured behind him. Kristen rushed over, limping on her bad leg, and pressed the injection into the Invader.

"You won't get away with this…" But they did. The Invader fell onto his front, his hands cuffed behind him.

"How the hell do they move things with their minds anyway?" Carl asked, but Brandon could only shrug.

"Maybe he'll tell us later." Brandon walked to the central computer, sitting in the chair. It squeaked under his weight, and he slapped the tool onto the screen. It pulsed, sending a surge through the electrical components, and the rover shook as it sprang to life. "Not to mention how they breathe without any damned air."

"It's not natural," Kristen said. Her pain was evident. They needed to find her some medical care, and soon.

The viewer started, and Brandon felt better as the lights flickered on throughout the bridge, everything regaining power.

He hated bringing one of the Invaders with him, but it was either that or kill him, and Brandon liked to think he had more of a moral compass than that. Plus, maybe the telekinetic alien could be of service to them.

NINE

"Why won't you tell me what happened on Veer, Admiral?" Elder Fayle asked Tom for the second time.

"Fayle, it's none of your concern. Do you understand that you're not in charge? That you're one of the leaders of a Concord partner, the Ugna, but not in a power position where you can boss me around and demand things of me? I don't know what you have on Benitor, but I'm not her!" Tom hated that she elicited such a reaction from him, but he couldn't help but retaliate when she pestered him.

She blinked slowly, and he wished that someone else was there to distract her. He hated being her link to Nolix and the Concord headquarters. Anyone else could have done the job, and Tom didn't believe Admiral Benitor's reasoning for a minute. Just because he'd been on Leria with her in the village didn't make Fayle his responsibility.

"I did not mean to offend you, Thomas. Are you always so quick to anger?" she asked. "I have a few meditation tips for you, if you would care to review…"

"That's fine," he said as calmly as he could. "We'll be at Aruto in a few days, and we can take our tour, meet President Bertol." It also wasn't a coincidence the newly appointed lieutenant commander was Asha Bertol, the Aruto leader's daughter.

For once, Tom wished someone had been clear on his

objectives before he'd been shuttled off on another diplomatic mission. With the attack on the Veerilions, and the well-manufactured fake Concord fleet, this had turned into something far different than what the objective had started out as.

"I look forward to it. Let me know if I can be of any assistance," Fayle told Tom, and left the courtyard.

Conner Douglas waved at him from the café bar, and Tom motioned to the chair across from him. "Have a seat, Douglas."

The other man did, setting his steaming cup on the table. "What was that about?"

"Nothing. She's… entitled." Tom didn't want to criticize Fayle in front of the crew, but Conner did have a level head on his shoulders.

"I can see that," he said. "Aruto is only a couple of days away."

"Yes, it is."

"Do you think we'll find out where these ships were built?" Conner asked.

Tom shook his head firmly. "Not at Aruto. I think this is a trick."

Kan Shu arrived, rushing to their table. "Admiral, we have word from Ridele. There have been two other attacks, each in this quadrant of Concord space. Denus was hit three days ago, and Thyle RP a day earlier."

"Why are we just learning of this?" Tom stood, following the commander from the courtyard. Conner was on his tail and nearly ran into him as Tom slowed at the elevator.

"Denus was struck hard. Blew out their communications. They said it was the Concord attacking. Some of the other partners are banding together, threatening a revolt." The doors closed, and they lifted toward the bridge.

"This is bad. We need to talk with the Prime as soon

as possible." Tom was the first to step off.

"He's already waiting, sir. In the captain's office," Kan informed him as they strode onto *Shu*'s bridge.

Tom walked across the rear of the bridge and into Rene's office, since the door was open in anticipation of his arrival. Rene looked up as he entered. "Bring the commander, please."

Tom brought Kan in with him, and they sat around Rene's desk, the image of the Prime emerging on the projection between the three of them.

"Prime Xune, it's nice to…" Rene started, but was cut off by Xune.

"Sorry to skip past the pleasantries, but we're in the middle of a crisis." He was scared: his usually coiffed hair was messy; his eyes had heavy bags under them.

"What's happening?" Tom asked, surprised no one had sent them notifications prior to this important communication.

"Admiral Benitor is missing," the Prime said.

"Missing? What do you mean, missing?" Tom asked.

"She's gone. Didn't show up at the office two days ago, and we've been searching for her since. It seems her place was visited by a shuttle three nights prior, according to the video feeds, but they were tampered with. We didn't see it leaving."

Tom's heart raced inside his ribcage. "And you think she's been abducted." The Prime remained stationary for a moment too long, and Tom put the pieces together. "That's not it. You think she's run off."

"We don't have enough information to formulate an exact comprehension of the events or reasoning, but Benitor is gone. Whether by choice or by abduction, it isn't clear."

"What about the attacks?" Rene asked. "We just came

from Veer, and we saw one of the fighters with our own eyes. Someone has been making Concord-issued vessels from our plans."

The Prime's eyes widened in surprise. "Why didn't you bring me this information? Of course I'd heard of the assault, but not of the ships."

"I sent the information to Benitor, but if she's not at the office, then…"

"She didn't receive it. Or she did, and that's part of the reason she's gone. What do we do, Baldwin? We have ten of our partner worlds threatening to attack Ridele. They're congregating as we speak. I expect a real opposing force knocking on our doors in less than a week."

Meaning they still had some time to figure this out. "The ships originated from Aruto," Kan told the Prime.

"We're being set up. Tom, is the door closed?" Xune asked.

Tom nodded after glancing to the office exit. "Go ahead."

"We suspect the Ugna and the Callalay have been conspiring behind our backs. The real reason we sent you there was because you seem to have a knack for discerning trouble and dealing with it. With the attacks and Benitor's disappearance, things have escalated too quickly. I need you to learn everything you can. Find out what Bertol knows, and for the sake of the Vastness, do not alert Fayle that we're suspicious," Xune ordered.

"Do you suspect she's involved?" Tom asked.

"I have to assume one of the Ugna leaders would be in the know. Keep her close, but not close enough to suspect what you're really digging for. When do you arrive at Aruto?" Xune appeared another five years older than he had at the start of their conversation.

"Two days, sir," Tom advised.

Lineage

"Good. Don't delay. They've been unreceptive to our communications, and that's not a good sign. I need to hear what the Ugna are up to, and if it *is* the two of them working against the Concord. This might be their game plan, to create dissention to attempt an implosion of the Concord. But not on my watch. We need to squash this threat!"

"We won't disappoint. Keep in touch, sir. Send a note if any news arrives about Benitor," Tom told him, and the Prime stared at him from the projection.

"Baldwin, I trust you. You've done more for the Concord than any one man in the last hundred years, including your grandfather. I need your help now. I'm in over my head. If Benitor was here… Just don't fail me. Too many lives depend on it." The Prime forced a grin, and the projected image snapped closed, leaving the three officers in the office, none of them wanting to speak first.

Planet X filled the shuttle's viewscreen, and Ven glanced at Brax Daak in the pilot's seat. The lieutenant commander was more at ease this trip, as if his experience over the past year had aided some of his hang-ups about space travel.

"Why are you watching me like that, Ven?" Brax asked with a smirk.

"I am only ensuring you are stable," Ven told him truthfully. He wasn't trying, but he felt Brax's emotions break through his barrier. He was confident, and contrary to their dilemma of being stuck in an unknown system, far from home and their destination, he seemed happy.

"And what did you find?" Brax asked him. He always was perceptive.

"Why are you happy?" Ven couldn't understand the

emotion at a time like this.

"You and I are heading to the surface of a world that no one from the Concord has seen before. They might name it after us." Brax entered through the atmosphere, the shuttle shaking slightly at the transition. He stayed elevated for longer than normal. "Where to?"

Ven used his mind, playing with the controls, and the tiny probes dispatched from their compartment in the underbelly of the shuttle. "We will have that answer soon."

"We already did scans," Brax told him.

"The captain asked that we be thorough. I'm going the next step." Ven watched as the probes returned countless streams of data into the shuttle's system.

"While you're waiting, I'll enjoy the sights."

Planet X's surface was snow-covered below them, the entire landscape a frozen tundra, and Ven peered at the screen as they neared what he assumed must be an expansive ocean. Giant cracks formed in humongous icecaps, each of the sections dozens of kilometers wide. It was exhilarating, yet terrifying.

"You wouldn't want to be stranded at this place," Brax whispered. "Anything good on the sensors?"

Ven assumed he knew what Brax constituted as *good*, and searched for signs of life. He didn't expect to find any and was shocked as the image of a jungle-like terrain, four thousand kilometers from their position, appeared to have man-made structures jutting from the overgrowth. "I found something."

Brax peered over, bumping into Ven's shoulder. "What is it?"

"Head to these coordinates." Ven passed them into the computer, and Brax accepted the location, setting course on his map.

"Someone lives on Planet X," Brax said, smiling again.

Lineage

"More likely, someone *lived* here," Ven replied. "I have sent the data to *Constantine*. Let us investigate."

Usually, they'd bring along more than two crew members on a mission like this, but Teller had suggested only they make the journey. The captain had wanted Brax to bring Nee instead, but Teller had been adamant that Ven go, for some reason. Captain Starling had accepted the proposal without preamble, but Ven had seen an odd twinkle in the old man's eye when he'd peered over at him.

"I've never seen a world so close to being a Zero-Nine," Brax said. They were above a temperate desert, the ground nothing but rocks and dusty sand for hundreds of kilometers. "If someone tweaked it a bit, even with minor terraforming, this would be a great world for the Concord."

It made Ven think about the terraforming the Ugna were doing on Driun F49. "That is a valid point. When the Nek drives become commonplace, we could have access to distant planets like this with greater ease."

"Ven, we might be looking at the newest Concord colony." Brax guided the shuttle lower as they crossed a long, narrow body of water that separated the desert from the warmer and more humid jungle beyond. Twenty minutes later, they flew a hundred yards above the stone structures they'd seen from the probe's feed, and Ven felt a slight tremble in his hand as he spotted the city below. It was much more evident from this position, and Brax remained quiet as he found a clearing to land their shuttle within.

"We need to be cautious," Ven said as the doors opened. They were in uniform only, but Brax grabbed two armored vests from the storage compartment, tossing one at Ven. He clasped it over his torso while Brax did the same, and Ven clipped a PL-30 to it near his chest. Brax opted for the larger XR-14 and jumped onto the damp grass.

"You don't really think anyone's living in there?" Brax asked, and Ven shook his head.

"Not any longer. But someone used to, and what did we learn at the Academy about ancient races?" Ven asked his Tekol friend.

"They liked to leave surprises behind for future visitors. And they were rarely pleasant ones." Brax started forward, taking the lead as he headed toward the structures a half-kilometer away. The trees were tall: thick veiny green leaves clung in bunches to long, thin branches, reaching for the bright star. The sky was cloudless, adding to the heat of the midday, and Ven was already sweating.

A swarm of minuscule insects roamed the jungle nearby and instinctively swooped at Brax. He spat a few out and waved his arms in defense. Ven lifted a hand and used his mind to disperse the cloud of bugs.

"Thanks," Brax said, continuing on.

Ven had a strange feeling of trepidation at this adventure, and nearly stopped Brax twice before they'd gone three hundred meters into the dense forest. Vines draped over high branches, and something about it reminded him of the forest on Driun. He glanced to the treetops, expecting creatures to drop from above and attack, but none did.

The ground was soft, everything humid and sticky. Bright flowers grew anywhere the sunlight broke from the canopy above, sending a sweet smell across the entire region. Brax sneezed three times and sniffled as they walked past the blooms. Ven stepped over a moss-covered log, almost slipping as his boot hit the wet vegetation beyond it. His hand touched the fallen tree and left an imprint in the soggy growth.

There was something familiar about this region, and he realized it reminded him of his village on Leria. Nestled far within a jungle, with deadly animals and insects surrounding it, they hadn't been permitted to leave the grounds very often—not unless they were accompanied by an Elder.

Ven recalled the time Fayle had brought him alone into the jungle, leading him through an intricate path system toward a waterfall. A year later, when he was older and feeling more rebellious, he'd attempted to duplicate the steps they'd taken that day but had failed miserably. He couldn't locate any of the landmarks Fayle had guided him past. After hours of wandering the jungle, scared and alone, Elder Fayle had found him.

His skin had angry red welts from bug bites, torn from barbed branches, but Fayle hadn't shouted or reprimanded him. She'd hugged him close and whispered something memorable in his ear.

"If you ever are lost, I will find you, Ven Ittix. Lose your path, and I will guide you home."

Brax had stopped, turning to face him. "Ven, you okay?"

"Yes. I was just..." Ven thought about his resentment toward Fayle recently, with her odd actions, and again pictured the Ugna as they'd destroyed the Vusuls in unison. Did he even know Elder Fayle at all? It seemed like she was trying to protect him from High Elder Wylen at times, but why?

"We're almost there," Brax told him, pointing through the thick brush. He separated a cluster of vines with his sizable weapon's barrel and let Ven through first. The city was beyond.

To call it that was a little bit of an exaggeration. It was a village at most, with square stone structures, each covered in mossy drapes, some dripping with liquid.

"It must have rained earlier." Brax touched a damp stone and flicked water from his gloved finger.

The ground changed, the wet grass giving way to a rocky path. Ven took the stone sidewalk, using it to carry him through the village. There were half-crumbled buildings on either side, and at the endpoint, a round structure centered the space. And it hit him.

"This can't be," Ven said, spinning around. It was so obvious.

"Ven, what is it?" Brax asked, grabbing him by the shoulders. He felt the fear from the Tekol officer, his own worries oozing out alongside Brax's.

"This is impossible." Ven sank to the ground, his knees pulling tight to his chest as he rocked slowly. The building walls appeared to be closing in, as if seeking to squash him, trap him for eternity. How old were these ruins? At least a thousand years. It didn't make sense.

Brax hauled him from the ground, grabbing Ven by the collar. He shook him lightly, and Ven felt the impact as the big man slapped him across the cheek, bringing him out of the trance. Ven's eyes widened, and he locked gazes with Brax.

"If you don't tell me what's going on…"

"I know who built this," Ven said.

"How? Who did it?" Brax asked, gazing over his shoulder at the stone remnants.

"The Ugna. This is an Ugna village."

Lark was glad to be exiting the space station. A Concord cruiser had come in the middle of the night, docking right next to Prophet's ship. As if that hadn't been bad enough, he was sure he'd gone to the Academy with one of the crew he spotted walking through the corridors of the station.

Lineage

He was in disguise, but if the device failed for a split second, he'd be found out. Prophet had assured him it was infallible, but from his experience, nothing ever was.

They'd waited for two days here, and finally, her contact had arrived. "Late is better than never," she told Lark for the second time, and again, he had no choice but to agree.

"Thank the Vastness the blasted Concord vessel departed," Lark said from the dark corner of the food court. A dozen vendors from around the Concord were located there, sending far too many different smells through the recycled air, making Lark sick to his stomach. He couldn't wait to leave.

The man arrived, and Prophet pointed at him from under the table. "That's him."

He was Zilph'i, which wasn't unusual at a Concord-approved station like this, but he went to the Eganian food vendor, ordering something very much alive, the worms slithering over his plate. This was the sign. It was their contact.

Prophet stood, Lark joining her as they walked past the contact, making sure he noticed. He set his food onto a table and followed them. Prophet didn't slow until they were well past the storefronts and storage containers, where she stopped and leaned against the wall. Lark saw that her fingers didn't stray far from the gun at her hip, and he suddenly wished he were armed too.

"Greetings," the man said, coming to a halt twenty yards away.

"Kell?" Prophet asked.

"That's me." The man shifted from foot to foot, clearly nervous.

"Where is it?"

"Close. We'll need to fly."

Lark had been hoping the damned thing was docked at the station but assumed that wasn't a possibility. The sooner he made the trip, the sooner he returned to his family.

"Then what are we waiting for?" Prophet asked.

"There's a small matter of payment," Kell said, his voice cracking slightly.

"You'll be paid when we have the shuttle." She was a cool customer. Keen could have used someone like Prophet at his side during his tenure as the Assembly's leader.

"That wasn't the deal."

"You want to leave? Go ahead. We have the credits and will pay you when we're happy with the shuttle," she told the man.

"Do you have any idea how difficult it was to procure a Nek shuttle?" Kell asked too loudly, and someone from farther down the hallway started toward them.

"We're leaving. Lead us to your transport," Prophet said. "And stay quiet."

He nodded, and Lark walked past the prying station guard, who carried a flashlight like a weapon. He let them pass without issue, and Lark breathed a sigh of relief. Ten minutes later, they were entering the airlock of a corporate freighter, meant to haul goods within the Concord, and once the doors shut, Prophet motioned for Lark to cut the device.

He did so, and the Zilph'i man stepped away in shock. "You... it's you. Keen. The entire Concord is searching for you."

"And you're growing a conscience suddenly?" Prophet's hand hovered beside her gun.

"No. Nothing like that..."

"This changes nothing. Bring us to the Nek shuttle,

and do it expeditiously," Prophet said.

The man tapped a communicator along the bay's wall and advised the pilot to depart. Keen looked around the ship, finding it devoid of any goods: no crates and no load of ice were attached to the freighter's towing hasps at the rear of the craft.

"I take it you're new to the business?" Lark asked the man.

Kell nodded. "Why do you say that?"

Lark pointed at the empty shelving, the bare floor. "What in the Vastness is an ice hauler doing out here with no payload, and nothing inside the holding bay? If you were flagged and boarded, what would you tell them?"

"Uh… I would have said I needed passage…"

"Who? You? Some nobody Zilph'i with enough money to hire a hauler? Why would you come this far? This station is a dump. Next time… because there *will* be a next time… you buy some goods to move around. Sell them, even. Find a contact at the world you're traveling to, make a deal to bring supplies, and earn some side credits while appearing legitimate."

Keen saw something spark in the man's eyes. "That makes a lot of sense," Kell said. "I'm only doing this…"

Keen raised a hand, stopping the man from going on. "Quiet. I don't want your story. How long until we're at the shuttle?"

The man's expression grew sheepish. "We're already there."

"What do you mean?" Prophet walked up to him, pressing a finger into his chest.

"I mean that the shuttle is here. In the next bay." Kell motioned to the doorway ten steps from their position.

"You brought it with you? That wasn't part of the deal. What if we were followed, or if you were caught before you arrived?" the tough Callalay woman asked, clearly angry. Keen was beginning to like her more and more.

"But we weren't…"

"Show us." Keen walked to the doorway, and the Zilph'i man came seconds later, using a retinal scanner to gain access to the freighter's secondary bay. Usually, it was the one that was climate-controlled, for the transport of frozen goods or animals used to a certain environment. When the doors opened, Lark smiled at the sight of the Nek shuttle. It was brand new, the First Ship logo on the doors. The Nek drive took up a quarter of the rear section of the hold, and he strode to it, silently admiring the construction.

"How did you acquire it?" Prophet asked, but the man shook his head.

"I can't tell you that."

"Fine." Prophet glanced at the exit. "Does it work?"

Their contact entered the shuttle first, and Lark saw something in Prophet change. He didn't like the vibe she was giving off. The engines powered on, the drive humming loudly before cooling and calming.

"Are there any tricks to it?" Prophet asked.

"Nothing that isn't in the system's…" The woman punched Kell hard in the gut, and he keeled over, gasping for breath.

"What are you doing?" Keen asked.

She didn't reply, only dragged the tall, skinny man from the shuttle, tossing him to the ground. Her gun was in her hand. "How many are on this ship?"

"Just the two of us," the man said through grinding teeth.

She fired, the weapon's blast striking him in the chest. His eyes were still open when he hit the floor.

"Prophet… you…"

Lineage

She threw the gun to Lark. "You deal with the pilot. I'll figure out how to operate this thing," she said.

Lark held the gun, staring at Prophet while she casually entered the shuttle. What had he agreed to? He'd done a lot of things in his life, but he always kept his end of a bargain when buying supplies and gear. She'd killed this man without a second thought.

He closed his eyes, and when he opened them, he stared at the dead body, wondering if there was another path he could take. Anything, other than doing as their benefactor said, led him back to Wavor Manor, where he would rot, never being reunited with his Seda and Luci.

He took the gun and strode through the freighter's corridor, heading for the bridge.

TEN

The space around Aruto was as peaceful and quiet as Leria. Earon, the human home world, and Nolix, the Tekol planet, were such opposites of the Callalay and Zilph'i's. The Founders had different ideas of how to live. Tom appreciated the simpler places like this, happier for no traffic and smaller, more spread out cities.

The density of Ridele wasn't something he'd expected to grow used to. Imagining his new home made him think about Aimie. He'd basically offered to move in with her. As much as he cared for the woman, was that in his best interest, or even more importantly, her best interest? She'd been about to retire, and with Tom an admiral, they could have traveled together, him bringing her along on diplomatic missions—at least, the ones that didn't involve war-starting chaos, like this trip.

Now that she'd decided to continue working, which was completely her right, their situation had changed slightly. Not to mention, Tom wasn't positive he was cut out for this role. The Prime's reaction to everything had been a bit of a revelation, though. He'd asked Tom for advice, sought important decision-making from the newest admiral, which meant their leader had faith in him. So did Tom, but this was where he belonged: out in the Concord, trying to make things better. Perhaps doing so as an admiral while using someone else's ship, like *Shu,* wasn't the worst idea either. He could avoid the long shifts on the bridge but stay part of the adventure.

"Bringing us in, Captain," Douglas said from the helm position, and Tom snapped out of his daydreaming.

Lieutenant Commander Asha Bertol was practically bouncing in her seat. She'd mentioned that she hadn't been home for three years, and she'd just finished her duty as executive officer aboard *Xinape*. This after spending the previous five years since the Academy in a junior rank on a Border cruiser.

"Captain, we're being denied clearance to the station's docking bays," Conner said.

Rene rose from her seat and strode toward Douglas. "What are you saying? Did you tell them who we were?"

"Sure did. They just replied saying our access was denied," he said.

"Find someone on the communicator. I want answers!" Rene barked, and a minute later a Callalay man's dark ridged head surfaced on the viewscreen.

"Greetings, and welcome to Aruto. We hate to inform you, Aruto is not taking visitors at this time…"

"And why not?" Rene asked.

He even managed to smile. "That information is out of my jurisdiction. I apologize for the…"

"They were expecting us. I am Captain Rene Bouchard of the flagship *Shu*, and this is Admiral Thomas Baldwin from Ridele, here at the bequest of Prime Xune. You may have heard of him… leader of the Concord." Rene was fuming, but the man's expression didn't shift.

"I'm sorry…"

"We know, 'Aruto is not taking visitors at this time'," Rene finished for him. She reached over Conner and killed the feed. "What's happening? We're being railroaded, and

Aruto is involved. They have to be."

Tom moved beside her. "Lieutenant Commander Asha Bertol, why did your mother close access?"

She stared at him with big brown eyes, her cheeks reddening. "I don't know, Admiral."

"You're the daughter of the most important person on this Founder's world. We just learned that our top Callalay leader, Admiral Jalin Benitor, is missing, taken from her home in Ridele. Someone is trying to start a war within the Concord, using ships that are exact replicas of our fleet, and now your mother is telling us we're not welcome on Aruto? This isn't adding up, not unless she's involved," Tom said, and the girl relented.

"She's scared," Bertol said.

Tom saw the fear in the crew's eyes: Kan Shu, Douglas, and the few non-executive members. "Bertol, in the captain's office, now." He turned, walking toward the room off the rear of the bridge, and he heard Bouchard, then the young Callalay officer, follow.

When the door closed, Tom stepped closer to Asha. "What has she done?"

"Who?"

"Your mother, Lieutenant Commander." Tom's hands found his hips, and he was feeling particularly annoyed at this delay.

"She hasn't done anything. She's terrified. The Callalay have had a long-running relationship within the Concord. We were an integral part of the Concord's beginning. Things have been changing, and with Prime Pha'n being removed from power, it's started something of a revolution within our ranks," Asha said.

"What does this have to do with anything?" Rene asked her officer.

"Everything. Mother has seen the shift when no one

Lineage

else has. She refuses to let you bring the Ugna to Aruto."

And there it was. Tom moved away, leaning against the desk. "Why? I thought the Ugna and the Callalay had a bond."

Asha shook her head. "This is not true. Yes, there was a time they helped save our planet. Without their assistance eighty years ago, our race might have been somewhere other than Aruto, but the price was high."

Tom was starting to understand. "What did they want in exchange for their help?"

"According to my mother, whose father's father was our leader at the time, they demanded a favor. That's it. But now that we understand the cost, Mother says we shouldn't have made the barter. We should have sought help from our Founder friends, not the Ugna," Asha told them with a trembling lip.

"What was the favor?"

"They would one day seek entrance into the Concord, as a race. When that day happened, they wanted to be accepted without issue," Asha said.

Tom glanced at Rene, who wore a deep frown as she digested the news. "You were there, Tom. What happened?"

"Fayle offered to help our diminished fleet with the Ugna vessels. She only asked that they be given a planet and entrance into the Concord. It didn't seem like a big deal," Tom told her.

"But it was… and who was the Prime at the time?" Rene asked.

Tom was fully aware she knew, but he was following her logic. "There was no Prime. There was Prime-in-Waiting Harris, but Admiral Benitor was really in charge." The betrayal hit him in the chest.

"And she agreed to their terms?" Rene asked.

"Instantly. I recall her saying something about being able to convince the others and mentioning that it was easier to ask forgiveness than permission." Tom slapped a palm to his forehead. "We've been played. Benitor brought them in, and now she's missing."

"Are you saying the Ugna have been planning their entrance into the Concord for eighty *years*?" Rene asked.

"Something tells me it's been a lot longer than that," Tom whispered. "Asha, can you reach out to your mother? Tell her you're coming with Rene and me to the surface. I need to speak with her."

Lieutenant Commander Asha Bertol nodded and exited the room, leaving them alone.

"If we're shooting straight here, Tom, what does this lead up to?" Rene asked.

Tom considered the question. "The Ugna want to control us. They might be the ones attacking our partners under the guise of the Concord. We have to stop them."

He thought about Treena and the crew of *Constantine*, and wished they were with *Shu* at Aruto to help him solve this riddle.

---

*T*reena walked through the village, struggling to imagine it before the centuries of growth and vegetation had torn the foundations; had cracked and broken through the pathways. This had been an ancient Ugna village, according to Ven's theory.

"Could they not have copied the style?" Treena asked her executive lieutenant as they stood atop the highest ground in the town, staring over the entire layout. Drones had spent last night and this morning mapping it out, and

Lineage

Ven was confident the exact same footprint was used on Leria, and a version was being duplicated on Driun F49.

"This is Ugna."

Brax climbed the last few steps, sweat beading over his brow, and he sat, gawking at the jungle village. "There have been multiple cases of different villages creating the exact same artwork, or similar buildings and carvings. To be fair, there are more than six cases I've read about where different races, from different eras, had etchings almost identical to one another, even though they were thousands of light years apart."

Treena smiled at Brax. "I had no idea you were such a xenobiologist and anthropologist."

"Just a little light reading. I have to keep up with Reeve's conversations somehow," Brax said.

"You could be right, but Ven is positive this was created by his ancestors." The man was even quieter than usual. She was anxious to know if Reeve had learned anything more about their location, but so far, the chief engineer hadn't contacted them on the ground. In this case, no news *wasn't* good news.

"What I want to know is how we ended up in this system. Of all the places for our star drive to malfunction and send us, we stopped near Planet X and found an ancient Ugna village? The odds are low." Brax looked Treena in the eyes, and she didn't have an answer for him.

Ven did. "I do not think it is an accident we found this."

"Then what? Someone sent us?" Treena asked.

"It is possible." Ven finally broke his stare at the ruins and met her gaze with red eyes.

"How? You'd need some serious clearance and technical abilities to force the Nek to activate and drop us this far from anything. Reeve would never allow such tampering," Brax said.

"Not deliberately, but I think Ven is right. This can't be a coincidence. Someone wanted us to find this." Treena tried to think of who, and even more so, why.

"To what end?" Brax asked.

Ven started descending the ruins. "To show us that the Ugna are a far older race than we imagined. They are not just of the Concord. Driun F49 has over a million Ugna. We're aware that High Elder Wylen had one of the Pilia colony vessels, and that most of their population came from outside Concord space."

"And Benitor and the Prime told Baldwin not to press the matter. I know for a fact he was doing some searching on his own accord before they asked him to cease and desist. They aligned him with Elder Fayle on a mission too, so they're all-in with their partnership of the Ugna. Is that how you see it, Ven?" Treena asked.

"That is what I think as well. There are so many secrets surrounding the Ugna, far too many for me to accept. Perhaps they refuse to share them with me because of my connection to the Concord or because they keep it to the top-level Elders alone. I get the sense that none of the other Ugna, the regular people trained and raised like myself, have any idea what is truly going on." Ven led them over the decline, and a minute later, they were lined along the overgrown walkway.

"Where were these people when you were on Driun F49? The ones born and raised outside of the Border." Brax wiped his brow again, and this was one of those cases when Treena was thankful to be in an android's body. Perhaps she wouldn't always be, if that was her end goal, but right now, with the sweltering heat and the swarms of bugs annoying Brax, she counted it a blessing.

"I did not meet any. I was told they were going through

Lineage

a transitional phase," Ven advised.

"Which means?" Treena heard some commotion from across the village, and they started walking faster toward the few engineering crew members sifting through the drone data.

Ven slowed, appearing to gather his thoughts. "The Ugna have different phases during training. As you know, we are fed En'or, injected with the drug to assist our growth and strength. I believe they are dosing the newcomers, which they suggest helps acclimate them to a new environment. They will each be isolated, fed the drug, and instructed to spend days, weeks, even months, to meditate and improve their mental capacity while on a new planet."

"This doesn't sound right," Brax said. "They brought nearly a million people from around the Concord, and over half of them from hiding beyond the Border. They drug them and instill powerful telekinetic abilities. If the Ugna turn out to be a foe, not a friend, we're going to be in for a real fight."

Treena tried to gauge Ven's reaction to this comment. She'd been thinking the same thing but didn't want to express her concerns with her executive lieutenant present. It was too late now.

Ven's expression didn't alter. "I believe you are accurate in your assumption. Fighting the Ugna would prove deadly."

Treena imagined facing off against a ship full of beings that could kill your entire crew with their minds, and cringed. They had to be wrong about this. If the Prime trusted them, and Tom almost did too, Treena had to follow their lead. "It can't be. The Ugna were scared. They hid for fear of persecution. You saw how bad it was when word leaked over Driun F49. The opposition to their entrance into the Concord was unprecedented."

"But we stopped that," Brax said. "Tom managed to convince their ringleader. Of course, he *is* dating her."

"We don't have enough information. Let's see what they found and return to *Constantine*." Treena avoided a particularly uneven section of the path and walked up to one of Reeve's crew, spotting a strange device uncovered from the brush. "What's this?"

The woman pulled a long vine away from the object, which was placed on a stone pedestal. It was about waist-high on the dais and clearly of a different time than the ruins. Treena thought the shape and design was a little familiar, but she couldn't put her finger on it.

"That's used in terraforming," Ven said.

"Terraforming?" Brax asked, setting a hand on the unit. "This thing looks old, but I see what you're saying. It's similar in style."

The engineering woman nodded along. "That's exactly what it is."

"Why is it here?" Treena asked her. "Were they trying to make this a Class Zero-Nine world?"

"On the contrary," the woman said, flipping her ponytail over her shoulder. "I believe that Planet X was a Zero-Nine planet, but they adjusted to change the parameters."

"Why would they do that?" Brax asked.

Ven answered. "To keep people from seeking to colonize. They didn't want anyone to find it. Or they planned on returning one year and wanted it to be clear of settlers."

"It appears like they set the device to run for a century, but that time was up long ago," the engineer said.

"Can you find a time stamp from it?" Treena asked, her mind racing with questions.

"We'll do our best." The woman waved the other crew members in, and they began to work on moving the tool onto a hovercart so they could bring it aboard *Constantine*.

"The mystery continues." Treena started for *Cleo* when the transmission came in.

"*Reeve to the captain.*"

"Go ahead, Daak," Treena replied.

"*I think we might have our answer.*"

"You've tracked our location?"

There was a slight pause before Reeve spoke. "*Almost. Anything we need to know?*"

"We think this is an Ugna village," Treena told her.

"*The Ugna? That doesn't make sense.*"

"No, it doesn't. Keep working on it. I'll be there soon." Treena ended the communication and watched as the engineers hauled the terraforming device toward *Cleo*. She was anxious to be moving, to find Earth and learn more about human history.

"We can't keep him sedated forever," Kristen said. Her skin was pale, and there was a constant sheen of perspiration over her forehead as they sat on the bridge of their recently-acquired vessel.

"Do you really want to trifle with an Invader?" Brandon asked her, and she shook her head.

He'd invited their colony doctor, Val, in for this discussion, and he turned to her. "What do you think, Val? Do we have enough supplies to dampen his abilities?"

She pursed her lips, the wrinkles accentuated at the pose. She was older, with long gray hair, but her nimble hands and mind had saved many of their lives during the difficult decade in the old abandoned colony on Mars. "I think we should be able to bring him out for a while. I'll have another dose prepared, should he prove an issue. But from everything I've heard, the drug should counter their telekinesis, at least temporarily."

Carl was the only one refusing to sit, and he stalked back and forth across the bridge, his bootsteps loud against the composite floor. "You can't seriously be considering this, Bran. We have the rover. Let's kill the Invader and be done with it. They're bad news."

Brandon was fully aware of this. They were the reason Earth had gone from being great to being oppressed. *If only the Invaders had never found it.* Brandon watched his people and struggled with the decision he needed to make. The Invaders were the key to this. If there was a way to get rid of them, maybe they could reclaim the planet.

"I know what you're thinking," Kristen said. She had this remarkable ability to read his mind at times, almost like one of the Invaders they hated so much. "We can't win. We've been through this. It's why we left in the first place."

Brandon gripped the arm of the chair, his fingernails digging in. "That's not what happened, and you know it!" He was getting angry, and he rose, moving behind his chair to rest his forearms on the headrest. "We escaped because we wanted to fight them. We came to Mars to regroup, and when we found the colony, we decided to rebuild a dome so we didn't need to crowd in the freighter forever. But somewhere along the way, we lost sight of our initial plan. We turned to cowering and hiding, rather than regrouping and forming a plan.

"There are others like us, people that want to rebel against the Invaders, and I know how to reach them," Brandon assured them.

"If they still exist," Kristen whispered.

"Where there's oppression, there will be seeds of resistance. This is a universal truth. I will find help, but we have to go to the moon first," he said, not wanting to plead with them.

Carl was already behind him one hundred percent. It was the rest of the colony he was concerned about. Once someone had mentioned using their two vessels and heading away from the planet, moving deeper into the solar system, the others had taken hold, happier to starve out there than die by a blaster on Earth.

"And then what? We find another ragtag group of hungry people, and we sacrifice ourselves against President Basher and his allies?" Kristen asked.

She was usually behind Brandon, so seeing her turn on him was a big surprise. He stared at her leg, the bandages covering her wounds, and he tried to give her some empathy. She wasn't thinking straight.

"They won't go for it," Val advised him. "There are over thirty colonists who want to retaliate."

Carl fumed, his face contorting in anger. "Then we'll stop them!"

"No." Brandon raised a hand, sighing deeply. "We won't. Val, tell them they can have the freighter. Anyone that wants to stay can. I'm taking this rover and going home. Ten years is too long to continue hiding."

"They'll come to Mars again, and this time, they won't stop until the colony is destroyed," Val said.

"Then our friends better join me or head out in the freighter. Those are their choices." Brandon was at peace with his decision, even if he didn't love it. It was better than getting into a fight with his own allies. They'd been through too much together to end it like this. "And, Val, it's time to awaken the Invader. We need to find out some information."

Brandon glanced at Carl, who looked prepared to interrogate the captive with impunity, and then at Kristen, who appeared his polar opposite.

"I'm in, Bran, you know that. You're a good leader," Kristen finally said, and he smiled at her, walking over to set a hand on her shoulder.

"I'm glad you're with me. Let's go ask our friend some questions."

ELEVEN

*T*he capital city of Aruto was in an odd location. Thomas was used to Founder capitals being adjacent to a giant body of water. It was common because the worlds had set up trading within their own continents thousands of years earlier, with boat docks and harbors to move goods around the planet. Once the race developed air travel, followed by space transports, boats were rarely used.

Tom had spent a few dinners on boats over the years and always enjoyed the open sea air. The first time, he'd felt sick from the constant bobbing over the turbulent waves, but eventually, he'd grown used to the movement and even began to appreciate it.

Beacon, the largest city on Aruto, was nestled high in the Boshua Mountains. Tom peered at the snow-capped peaks as they exited the expedition vessel, finding the sight awe-inspiring.

"This is beautiful," he whispered, and Elder Fayle stopped at his side.

"I never forgot this majestic view from my first visit. One's faith in the Vastness rings true when you see something like this, right, Admiral?" she asked, no condescension in her voice.

"I agree with you there. Kan, thank you for showing the Elder around today," Tom said, nodding at the Callalay commander. He was home, though he hadn't grown up in the city, and Tom needed to distract Fayle while she was on Aruto. Asha Bertol's mother, the Callalay president, had been adamant that the Ugna woman should step nowhere near her head office during her stay on Aruto. She'd also ordered a full-time Callalay escort to oversee the woman's whereabouts. Kan Shu was the perfect candidate.

"I still do not understand why I am being traipsed around with Commander Shu," Elder Fayle mumbled under her breath.

She hadn't taken kindly to the news. Tom felt like she was aware something was wrong, but she wasn't speaking up, so he didn't try too hard to convince her of anything.

"We have a meeting with the local Concord Academy, and then we'll try to reconvene at the embassy later tonight, okay?" Tom smiled at the Elder, hoping she bit. She was an expert at reading emotions, and Tom tried to keep his energy positive, knowing it probably did nothing to hide his trepidation.

"Okay. I'll see you then. Come on, young man. Show me the sights," she said to Kan, and the commander helped her into a waiting transport shuttle, telling her about the city.

"Kan's good," Tom told Rene, and she nodded once.

"The best."

Asha Bertol was already walking down the path, and when the doors to a cruiser opened wide, the girl started running for the ramp.

"Asha, on the other hand…" Tom didn't finish. The girl had earned her position, he was told, yet she seemed too young, too naïve for the role of lieutenant commander. But it wasn't his place to say so.

"She's a great asset. Without her, we'd be in orbit, twiddling our thumbs." Rene nudged him in the arm, and he smirked as they walked toward the president's unmarked cruiser.

This was a big moment. Tom peered past the shipyard to the hundreds of homes lining the side of the mountain, most of them below the freezing line. There was a cluster of buildings near the center of the city, but none of them were over ten stories. He appreciated that they kept their skyline low, so everyone could benefit from the glorious views. Tom thought how much more he'd enjoy living somewhere like Beacon over Ridele, and wondered if they'd take outsiders.

He laughed, thinking of that conversation with Aimie Gaad. He doubted there was any way the woman would ever move to Aruto, even if they were able.

"What's so funny?" Rene asked.

Tom glanced at *Shu*'s captain, noticing her green eyes sparkle as she looked at him. Her lips curled into a grin, and dimples formed on her cheeks. He averted his gaze, suddenly feeling self-conscious. He'd been spending too much time with her lately. They'd never been a real couple, but he was remembering why they'd sought comfort in each other's arms years ago. She was full of life, and not to mention beautiful.

"Nothing. I was only thinking about retirement," he said, half lying.

"Do Baldwins ever retire? I seem to recall Constantine working until he died, and now he's stuck on a ship named after him." Her face held that mischievous expression he'd seen so many times.

"This Baldwin will retire one year," he said firmly. They were nearly at the ship, but Rene slowed, taking hold of his arm.

"And then what? Are you going to have a family?" The question caught him off guard, and he stammered a reply.

"Wha… I don't know. Why are you asking that?"

Rene laughed, shrugging. "It's as good a time as any. Are you?"

"I don't know," he answered. "We haven't discussed it."

"Meaning you and the doctor?"

"Yes. Aimie Gaad," he said.

"Just don't settle, okay, Tom?" Rene said, walking away.

Settle? "She's a doctor and an executive with R-Emergence. I don't think I'd call that settling," he told her.

She glanced at him from ahead. "I didn't say anything about her wealth or career choices."

They arrived at the cruiser, and Tom was left flustered, unsure what in the Vastness Rene was implying.

"Admiral Thomas Baldwin, this is my mother, President Kalio Bertol," Asha said. "And this is Captain Rene Bouchard of *Shu*."

The woman stood tall, her shoulders covered with a black cloak. The Callalay woman's ridged forehead was glistening in the sun, and when he locked gazes with her, he nearly gasped. "Jalin?"

She shook her head, smiling at him, the spitting image of the recently missing admiral. "I'm afraid not, Admiral. But Jalin Benitor is my sister."

That explained even more. Tom wondered why he'd never been told this, and why it wasn't listed on any of their records. "Very interesting. Asha, why didn't you say anything?"

The president answered for her daughter. "It's not something we wanted to advertise. You know the Concord hierarchy was under scrutiny in the Statu aftermath. Jalin thought it best to keep our relationship under wraps. But you've seen the resemblance, and I suppose the Booli is

Lineage

out of the sack. Come, we have much to discuss."

Tom let Rene go first, his mind still reeling from their conversation and the news that Jalin, the missing admiral, was a sister to the Aruto president. How did this connect with her distrust of the Ugna? He was determined to find out.

The trip was quick, Tom remaining standing while the cruiser lifted, taking them to the city headquarters. They exited a few minutes later, Rene staying on the other side of the president and her daughter. Tom hadn't expected something flashy, but this was a far cry from a palace. The building was peaked, in deference to the mountain crests around them. It was five stories high, with a few Callalay people walking to and from separate structures across the street. Everyone acted pleased, their chatter carrying through the peaceful morning air.

"This is my office," the president said. "It's not anything compared to the building you work in, Admiral, and it's nothing like *Shu*'s bridge, Captain, but it's important to us. It was one of the first structures we built in this valley, over five thousand years ago. My ancestors settled this spot, and only in the last few centuries did we really expand the small village into the capital city you see today."

Her voice was so much like Jalin's, but her enunciation was different. She was more poetic, where her sister was pragmatic.

"I like it," Rene said plainly.

The president laughed, and Asha smiled beside her mother. "Good. Come, I'm sure you'd enjoy some refreshments."

"I'd rather cut to the chase, President Bertol," Tom said, following her into the entrance of her headquarters.

"In good time. My husband, Cori, always used to tell me I rushed things. He told me that some quiet contemplation was the key to any solution."

Tom spotted the guards around them: from the ship's pilot that had trailed them, to the armed workers trying to act casual this entire time. "Your husband was a well-respected man, and apparently a wise one as well."

They entered the foyer, the ceilings squat and low. It was obvious they'd put a lot of refurbishing into the ancient structure over the centuries. Tall windows were cut into the stone exterior, allowing for natural light in what would otherwise have been a dark space.

Asha spoke in hushed tones with her mother in front of them, and Rene glanced at Tom while they followed the pair into a circular room. The floor was a step-down, with a flat surface beside the drop. It was stone, and the round bench had lush seat cushions. It made Tom think about his school growing up. They would use a room like this to show the students a projection play, one you could watch from any angle of the amphitheatre. This place could likely house a couple of hundred people, but for now, it was secure for the four of them.

"Please, help yourselves." The president motioned to a cart with refreshments near the right side of the circle. Tom did that and poured them each a clay cup of the green liquid.

"Are these original?" he asked, indicating the glasses.

"They are. Our ancestors used this building, drank from these cups, and had their most important meetings in the Round Room. This is our custom." The president accepted the beverage graciously and took a seat on a purple cushion; long gold tassels were sewn into the corners of the pillow. "Tell me why you used my daughter to gain access to Aruto."

The room was extremely wide, and Tom sat on the far edge so they could face one another, Rene taking the seat

Lineage

beside him.

"We were sent by the Prime. Surely he made you aware of our visit?" Tom asked.

"Not that I was informed of. I did know my daughter had recently been placed upon the great *Shu,* and we are very grateful for the opportunity, aren't we, Asha?" The president regarded her daughter, who sipped from the red clay cup at her left.

"That's right. We *are* grateful." The young woman seemed genuine, her smile wide.

Tom tried to delay the flurry of questions he had for the president, but found that after a couple of minutes of small talk, he couldn't. "Why are you afraid of the Ugna?" He'd been told some information by Asha, but wanted to hear it from President Bertol's lips.

"You should all fear them. What they can accomplish is beyond what any Founder has been able to achieve. They went from being a mystery, with a meager population, to having a force of over a million. And we let them into our fold, invited them in." She slammed her cup down and placed her hands on her thighs. "Do you have any idea how tough it is to extinguish pests once they're inside your walls?"

"Are you saying the Ugna are pests?" Rene asked.

The president leaned forward, her spine straight. "They're not pests, because those are controlled by nature, by needs and actions based on survival. The Ugna have done this before, I can assure you, and they're not planning to hide within the walls for long. They will spread out and take over before you're able to stop them."

"Why didn't you tell us?" Tom asked, not liking where this conversation was heading.

"I told Jalin my theories, but she didn't buy them."

Rene tapped Tom on the shoulder, drawing his

attention. "I'm beginning to understand why Benitor sent you here. She knew you'd uncover the truth of the matter, and it seems like you are." She shifted her stare to the president. "Are they behind the incidents?"

"It's unclear. One can only assume so, given the timing," Bertol said.

"And are you sending a force against the Concord?" Tom asked.

"I would never do that. I was about to transmit my opinions to Nolix, Leria, and Ridele, advising them of my concerns with the Ugna. If they buy in, we may be able to thwart the coming attacks from within," she said.

Tom pictured their own partners banding together to fight Ridele, thinking the Concord had anything to do with the recent assaults within Concord space. It was unsettling, to say the least. "We need evidence."

President Bertol stood, waving them to follow her. "I may have what we need. I have record of them working with the Assembly, using wormholes to leave outside the Border, and recently discovered a manufacturing station that might be where they're creating this mimic fleet."

Tom passed through the exit, his heart racing. "How did you find this?"

She glanced at him as they strode through the domed corridor, and she smiled despite the dark news. "I followed the credit trail."

"And you think this lines up?" the captain asked Reeve, standing behind her seat in her Engineering office. Doctor Nee bumped into her chair, leaning in close.

Reeve pointed to the screen, where the old star-map

Lineage

image sat behind the current one. "This is old data, but if we adjust the angles slightly…" She ran a finger across the screen, tilting the modern constellation layout, and they clicked together. "There we are."

"Where are we?" her brother asked.

Reeve switched the program, bringing up the details of a long-gone race, the Ziota. "The Ziota lived thousands of years ago, and one of our ancient explorers, *Exex VI*, found their world, gathering their books and anything remaining within a computer system. This map was part of it. It appears that this system, the one with Planet X as the sole Class Zero-Nine world, was known as Dagrilo.

"We're farther from Concord space than any of our present vessels have ever been." Reeve glanced behind her to the gathered crew.

"Can we make it home?" Captain Starling asked.

Reeve was nervous but confident the drives still worked. There was something else she needed to share with them, and she cleared her throat. "Okay, this is going to sound a little strange, but here's what I found. The Nek mods are fully operational. We can set course for Nolix, but it will take eighteen months to arrive."

"Eighteen months!" Brax shouted. "That's like forever with a normal star drive."

Reeve smiled at him. "Like I said, we're far from home."

"If this Planet X in the Dagrilo system had Ugna living on it, how did they fly from this position to the Concord with their rudimentary engines all those years ago?" Doctor Nee asked.

"That's the question we don't have the answer for. They had one of the Pilia colony ships; that's the most likely answer," Reeve said.

"The same ship that originally brought Eve's people to

Earth?" Brax scratched the top of his head, as if it might help him think through the problem easier.

Treena crossed her arms and dropped her chin. "Let Reeve finish. We can use the new star drive to jump to Nolix. You sounded like you had another option for us."

"A few, honestly. We can also use the Nek jump." Reeve paused, gauging their reactions.

Ven Ittix had remained silent this whole time, and he finally spoke. "Is it safe?" he asked.

"We made it here with a jump. I'd say it's safe. But there's an issue," Reeve told them.

Brax frowned at her. "What is it?"

"It looks like someone programmed this jump into my system. Someone breached *Constantine*'s firewall and directed us here," Reeve said.

"Sent us to Planet X? This has to be a mistake!" Brax stood taller, his gaze drifting across the boiler room. Reeve guessed he was searching for an assailant that wasn't there.

"It's not." Constantine's AI surfaced. "I've run the reports you wanted, Executive Lieutenant Daak. There was a breach, as you suggested—one that was hidden very well."

"Who would send us to this system?" Treena asked.

"I've been thinking about that. There are two options." Reeve spun around in her chair, facing the entire executive team and Harry. Doctor Nee tapped his fingers on his hips impatiently. "One. They wanted us out of the way."

"Of what?" Brax asked. "We're going to visit a long-dead world."

"We don't know that." Treena stepped forward. "Earth may be thriving. Reeve, what's your other thought on it?"

"They sent us to find Planet X. To see proof that the Ugna were around this long ago."

"Why?" Brax asked.

"They wanted us to see how ancient the Ugna are, and how influential. Ven, did you hear anything about this colony?" Nee followed up.

All eyes went to the tall Ugna officer, and he slowly shook his head. "It appears as though I have been kept in the dark about many things related to my people. It does not surprise me one bit, and the fact that we brought so many from outside Concord space was always a concern of mine, and of Thomas Baldwin as well."

"But the question becomes, who breached the firewall?" Treena asked.

Constantine's AI shrugged. "Currently, I have no manner of determining that. Whoever did this had access to advanced technology."

"We need to make a decision: do we stay, head home, or continue toward Sol? And do we use the Nek jump or star drive?" Reeve asked, making an internal bet with herself on what the captain would answer.

"We go to Earth. And we jump there," Starling ordered, and Reeve glanced to her brother, whose face had slightly paled at the response. He'd jumped before, and so had she, along with Ven. It was engrained in them to be dangerous, but they'd survived before. "Don't bring us too close to Earth. Bring us deep in Sol so we can survey what we're dealing with. I have a feeling something might be waiting for us, something big and dangerous. There's a conspiracy going on, and *Constantine* has been thrust in the middle of it."

Treena exited the boiler room, the others trailing after her until only Harry lingered at Reeve's side. "Well, Harry. Time to lock in our destination." She was nervous about what would transpire over the next couple of days, but she was also ready to test the new drive's capability.

TWELVE

"Today's the day, Keen. Are you ready for this?" Prophet asked him from the shuttle's cargo hold. Beside them sat twenty empty containers, and he'd spent the last hour removing the contents, storing the Nek inside the shuttle. He'd asked her why they needed so much of the ore, but she'd sidestepped the question with a grunt.

He was back in his admiral's uniform, feeling out of place in the garb. He glanced toward the airlock, where they'd ejected the two bodies yesterday. It was nothing compared to what he'd done in the past, but he'd clung to his ideals then. He'd had goals and was trying to better the Concord, which meant he could be unscrupulous if necessary. "The results justify the actions," he muttered to himself before realizing he hadn't answered her. "I'm ready."

The shuttle was underwhelming. It was an earlier iteration of the Nek-powered ships from Leria, and half of the vessel was taken up by the modified engines. The shuttle had no ID tags within, but it did have the First Ship logo on the side. He couldn't go in there with an unmarked craft, pretending to speak for the Concord, if he didn't look the part.

"Why didn't they send someone? If their own people are there, why send me?" Lark asked the question that had been lingering in his mind all week.

Lineage

"Because you're human. They tell me it's been centuries since they've spoken to their people in Sol. They didn't have things like jumpships to go back and forth, and the trip takes too long to send regular convoys." Prophet always had answers, and for a hired hand, she seemed to know an awful lot about their benefactors. Lark wanted to have faith in her but had seen her kill in cold blood a few times in their short acquaintance. He'd built a fence around their relationship and didn't want to get too close to the Callalay woman.

"Inside." She pointed to the door, which was winged up and open. He obeyed, heading for the passenger seat, and a minute later, Prophet was beside him, manning the controls. The shuttle vibrated as she powered it up, his seat cushion absorbing most of the tremors. The viewscreen flicked to life, and the ship's dash hummed as the lights flashed on.

The idea of hopping from here to Earth was suddenly terrifying. Lark was so sure they'd be torn apart, ripped to shreds and dead in the middle of nowhere. It wouldn't matter. At least then it would be over. Seda and Luci could live out their days never knowing what happened to him, but they'd be safe and alive.

He hated the idea of them thinking he'd taken off, abandoned them forever. "You're sure this will work?"

Prophet shrugged unapologetically.

"And if they gave us a faulty ship?" he asked.

"Then we die, Keen. Are you afraid?" she asked, her dark eyes boring into his. For the first time, he noticed she wore contacts.

"I'm... let's get this over with." He turned his attention to the controls and used them to open the cargo exit before Prophet guided the shuttle from the freighter's hold. Once they passed the energy field, the doors shut again, sealing in the empty ship. He wondered who would eventually discover the empty vessel.

Prophet flew the shuttle from the vacant craft and headed in-system, using the dash console to choose a destination for the Nek jump.

"Can I see?" Lark asked, peering over her arm at the screen. It showed a series of mathematical equations he didn't comprehend, and a 3D image of a galaxy. Prophet zoomed in, matching some equations with a blinking location, and five minutes later, she glanced at him with a grin on her face. Beads of sweat dripped from her ridged forehead as she broke the silence.

"It's ready. Time for our mission," she told him.

It felt like he'd been on this quest for ages already, but this was only the beginning. He had an objective. At this moment, chaos was beginning to ensue within the Concord, and it was his job to meet with Earth and promise them an astonishing future.

Lark closed his eyes as Prophet started the jump clock. The computer spoke the numbers in a male voice, counting down from ten, and when it hit one, he opened them in time to see his life flash before his eyes.

The man blinked groggily, his mouth open halfway as Val stepped to the side.

"You're sure he can't use his abilities?" Brandon asked her, and she nodded.

"Cut off for at least an hour." Val had been keeping him drugged, but they'd finally brought him out of his sleep state to question him.

"You'll pay for this," the Invader warned, his voice

Lineage

drowsy. The tall pale man was strapped to a chair, and Brandon stepped a few feet in front of him.

"That's fine. I never expected to. I have a few questions, and you're going to answer them," he told the man.

"I will do no such…"

"How were we discovered?" Brandon asked.

"You fools think you could hide on Mars from us? That we didn't know about your little group?" The man spat on the floor of the room. It was empty, with the exception of a robot charging port.

Brandon wasn't going to let this man get under his skin. "Then why did it take ten years to make a move against us?" he asked.

"Your president decided you were too inconsequential."

"And what changed?" Brandon asked.

The Invader's eyes narrowed, his pink irises sending shivers through Brandon's spine. "Something's about to happen."

"What?" Val blurted out. Brandon had asked her to stay silent, and she gave him a remorseful look.

"That's none of your business."

"Tell us, and we might not kill you." Brandon let his hand rest on the gun's hilt as he took one step closer.

The man laughed a mirthless cackle. "You really have no idea about anything, do you, human? We're so far ahead of you, it's a wonder we've let you survive this long."

"The president wouldn't let that happen," Val said, and Brandon silently chastised her. Not to mention, he hated President Basher.

The man laughed again. "Basher… you still believe he's human. You're more gullible than even I suspected."

Brandon's blood ran cold, and he tore the gun from its holster, aiming it at the Invader. "What are you talking about?"

"It doesn't matter any longer. They'll be gone soon. I can feel it."

Brandon darted forward, using his free hand to strike the Invader across the cheek. Their eyes locked, and the man only smiled, blood dripping from his lip. "Basher is one of us. Have you even wondered why he caters to us so?"

This was too much. Brandon backed up, glancing at Val, who was frozen in place. "You're lying."

"I don't think so," the man said, a glint of hatred in his eyes. He sat up straighter, and Brandon felt the pressure building up in his skull. Val staggered toward him, obviously feeling the same thing. The Invader had broken the drug barrier and was trying to kill them.

The pain grew, and Brandon barely felt the gun drop from his grip. His knees hit the metal floor, and Val used his shoulder to prop herself up as she lunged for the bound Invader. Brandon heard her grunt as she jammed the device into his neck, and his head hung limply, Brandon's pain instantly subsiding.

Brandon rolled onto his back, hands on his temples, and groaned. "He was trying to kill us."

Val helped him to his feet, her own legs wobbly. "And he almost managed it."

Carl banged on the door, and Brandon opened it. His friend peered over his shoulder to stare at the unconscious Invader. "What the hell just happened? My brain almost exploded!"

Val hiked a thumb toward the center of the room. "It was him."

"Better to kill him and leave him in space. The freighter is off, traveling for Alpha Centauri. There's only the twenty of us left behind," Carl advised them.

Brandon decided they would need to dispose of the Invader, but he wished there were a way to learn more from the man before doing so. "Carl, find someone to help. Toss this bastard out the airlock. We're heading for the moon."

The lights danced across her dreams, morphing into shapes: familiar faces from her past, planets she'd visited, ending with the shadowy figure of High Elder Wylen.

Elder Fayle gasped, sitting up in bed. It was too hot and she tossed the blankets aside, feeling the cool air against her skin. She was burning up, and she longed for a shot of En'or to calm her, but that wasn't going to help. Not anymore.

She'd spent the day with Kan Shu, being shown around Beacon, the capital of Aruto, nestled snugly within the Boshua mountain range. It was peaceful, idyllic... deadly. The moment she'd set foot on the world, she felt the president's disdain for her and her people, and she understood why.

Regardless of her awareness of Kan's motives, she had enjoyed the day in his presence. He reminded her of the good people within the Concord, the kind of soldiers and fleet crew that would be killed in the coming incursion. She needed to make a decision, and soon.

Fayle planted her feet on the cold floor, letting them sit on it bare while she cradled her forehead in her hands. She'd been a part of it all. They would indict her, but perhaps she could save lives before it was too late. People like Baldwin, whom she'd grown to respect. Ven Ittix would be devastated by the news, but he was strong, resourceful. He'd never forgive her, but her deception would strengthen him. Maybe he could lead their people if they stopped this early.

Another attack would be happening in two days. Here, on Aruto. That would be unprecedented, a strike against a Founder, but Wylen wasn't aware of President Berton's suspicions.

She climbed from the bed, catching a glimpse of herself in the mirror across the room. The lighting was dim, the gentle glow of orange lights from outside lamp posts carrying past the bottoms of the drapery. She was old, and tired of living a lie.

Fayle dressed, splashed water over her face, and exited her room. It was late, somewhere around halfway between sleep and rise, and she found the room at the embassy where Baldwin was staying. She knocked on the door softly at first, then harder, until the disheveled admiral answered. He wasn't wearing a shirt, and when he saw who it was, he nodded once, as if understanding why she was there.

"Come in."

Tom knew why Fayle was here. It was obvious from the first moment he locked eyes with her. Elder Fayle looked weary, exhausted from a long day, and he suspected he did as well.

She stepped into his quarters without a word, walking past him. She sat at the cushioned couch, tapping a light on.

"Thomas, we have something to discuss," she said with authority.

He threw on a robe and took the seat opposite her. Tom rubbed sleep from his eyes, wishing he were clearer-headed for the coming discussion. "I'm all ears," he urged her.

"Please listen to what I have to say, and try not to react too harshly until I am finished," she told him, and Tom's pulse quickened.

"I'll do my best," he promised her.

"I know you've been doing some digging on the Ugna," she said, her tone not accusing, only matter-of-fact.

He shrugged. "I'm sure you would do the same if our roles were reversed."

"True. I think we're more alike than you'd ever assume, Baldwin. Starting with my people. I've always looked out for them, cared for them, even if it took some drastic measures, much as your Concord has done for centuries. You have all done horrible injustices for the sake of the partners, especially the Founders.

"Did the president speak to you about our involvement here eighty years ago?"

Tom remained silent for a few moments before shaking his head. "No, she didn't. But I know about the bargain."

"Aruto was experiencing tectonic shifts unlike any the planet had ever seen. They tried everything, but they were at their wits' end. We offered our assistance," she said.

"In exchange for a future favor," he finished for her.

"That's correct. A favor Admiral Benitor obliged us with," Fayle said.

"I heard. I have to admit, when the Prime find out about this, I expect they'll rescind your entrance into the Concord and remove you from Driun F49." Tom gauged her reaction, but she was stone-faced in the dim room. She could have been a statue.

"You think you understand what's happening, but you don't."

"So you aren't behind these attacks within the Concord?" he asked, trying to keep his tone even. Fayle flinched, just a slight twinge of her cheek, but he saw he'd struck a blow.

"May I continue my story?" she asked, and he let it go for the time being. He motioned for her to continue, and she did. "What I'm about to tell you will end my time under High Elder Wylen's custody. I will be stripped of any title and will be alone, no longer a member of the same race I've devoted my entire life to protecting."

"Tell me what it is. What do they want?"

"High Elder Wylen is bringing reinforcements. I know you've been searching for Lark Keen as well, correct?"

Tom nodded once.

"He's involved. One of our ships freed him. He's on his way to Earth as we speak, if he isn't already there."

"Earth?" Tom shot out of his chair, all signs of sleepiness gone. "Why?"

"Because the Ugna own the planet. We've resided there for over a hundred years, amassing a fleet," Fayle told him, and Tom thought she seemed relieved to spill her secrets, as if the burden of holding them inside was threatening to ruin her.

"They have a fleet on Earth?"

"Yes. With humans on their side," she admitted.

"What's their motivation, Fayle?" Tom wanted to rush and warn the others, but something was missing from her story.

"They're going to attack Aruto in two days, with another Concord flagship like the ones you've been hearing about. They'll destroy a Founder's home world, then sit back while the entire Concord burns," she told him, and he felt the color drain from his face.

"Why would they do that?"

Lineage

"To get what you have. The Ugna want to rule over the Concord."

THIRTEEN

*H*er muscles ached, her feet burned, and her eyes stung from the sweat dripping over her brow, but she pushed on. "One more lap?" Constantine asked Treena, and she blurted out an unintelligible response and kept moving.

The gym was empty with the exception of her and the AI until the door opened, revealing Dr. Nee. He was the only other person on *Constantine* she'd given the access code to. Treena didn't want any others stopping by while she was in her real body. Not yet.

Inspired by the doctor's arrival, she drove herself even harder and finished the lap in record time, nearly falling over as she passed the green beam of light that marked the oval track. She stayed on her feet and reached for a water bottle, using her own muscles to lift it. Her hand gripped the bottle, and she sucked through the straw, the water cool as it passed through her throat. Treena hadn't realized how much she loved water until she'd begun to drink it again. She smiled as Nee came over, his lab coat as clean and pressed as his white gloves.

"Take it easy, Treena. You don't want to overexert yourself," he said, scanning her from a meter away.

"If I don't push it, I'll never be the woman I was," Treena told him, and waited for a reply, telling her she couldn't be that version of Treena Starling.

Lineage

"I have no doubt you'll be even more formidable than you were," Nee said, grinning like a proud parent, even though they were close in age.

"That's hard to believe, but if you say so." The water bottle slipped from her grip and landed with a thud on the floor.

"Let me." Nee grabbed it, setting it on the table beside them. He took her hand in his gloved palm and bent her fingers up and down. "The mobility is improving, but it will take a while for you to have full control."

Treena picked up the water again, as if to prove to herself she could do it, and took another drink. "Like I said, practice makes perfect. Thanks for the help today, Con." She glanced at the AI, who was standing a few feet from her, unmoving.

"You're welcome, Captain. Is there anything else you need?" he asked.

"Not today. See you in the morning," she told him, and with a smile, he vanished from the gym.

"How are you feeling?" Nee asked, his voice lower now that they were alone.

"Pretty good. I only have the leg braces at ten percent today, and…"

"Not about that." Nee touched her elbow, helping her to the bench near the change room. "About the mission."

She let out a warm breath and sat. Her backside was too skinny, the flesh taking its time at filling out, but it felt incredible to feel pressure against her skin. She might be in a weaker body, but she was alive. "I can't say. We're risking our crew by using the Nek drive, but what choice do we have? We were sent to investigate Earth, and that's what we're going to do. This whole Ugna mystery has me a little uncomfortable too."

Nee squatted, taking a seat to her right. "Same with me.

I only wish Ven knew more, but he's as upset about the revelation as anyone."

"I was hoping we'd have some idea of what we were getting into," Treena said. "Do you think Tom would have made the same decision?"

Nee patted her knee gently and nodded. "I think you two are cut from the same cloth. His choices would be similar, and if it helps, I think the entire crew agrees with your decision."

"And you?"

He looked surprised she'd asked him that, but he recovered quickly. "One hundred percent."

This pacified Treena, and the tension she'd been carrying since they'd arrived near Planet X started to wash away with her sweat. "Thank you, Nee."

The handsome Kwant waggled his eyebrows. "You know, we do take a few psychology classes during our lengthy educational process. If you ever need to talk about anything, I can be the ear to listen."

Treena let him help her to her feet, and she clicked the braces up to forty percent, aware her fatigued muscles wouldn't carry her to the room without the assistance.

Nee stayed with her, using a private lift from the end of the corridor to the officers' quarters, and when they arrived at her suite, she turned and thanked him. "See you on the bridge nice and early? I'm assuming you'd like to be present while we become the first Concord fleet ship to intentionally use a Nek jump."

"I'd like that very much. Have a good night, Captain." Nee gave her a slight bow of his head before walking toward his own suite a few doors down.

Treena entered her room, barely recognizing it anymore. Most of the training machines had been moved to the private gym, but there was the healing tank and a few exercise units in case she felt the urge to train between quick shifts.

Treena's clothing was drenched in sweat, and she removed her sports bra, letting it drop to the floor. She caught her reflection in the bathroom, and she walked over, her skinny legs limping slightly. The face that stared back looked happier than it had in some time: the cheeks fuller, the hair thicker. Her eyes shone, a glossy expression that replaced the sad look lingering within deep sockets few months ago.

Could she do this? For real? She glanced behind her, at the closet, and walked over to it, tugging the door open. Inside sat the android she'd been using since destroying the first one inside of the Statu wormhole during *Constantine*'s maiden voyage. This was a perfect specimen. She ran a finger over her avatar's nose and shut the door.

For some reason, Felix's face entered her thoughts: his goofy smile, his callused hands, his natural scent. She'd loved him so much. Treena sank to her bed, and the image changed into a different man. She pictured Conner Douglas instead.

"What would you do, Felix?" she asked out loud.

When no one answered, Treena went to the steam shower and let the warmth soak into her aching muscles. Tomorrow, she'd return to the android, but tonight, she was the real Treena Starling. She resolved to begin working even harder to ensure her return to form.

After a light dinner and plenty of fluids, Treena's head hit the pillow. Despite the monumental morning ahead of her, she fell asleep faster than she had in weeks.

One second, Lark was one place; the next, their shuttle was near an unfamiliar space station. Dozens of large vessels lingered near a moon. He balked in surprise, and Prophet cheered beside him, the noisy reaction catching him off-guard.

"You want to warn me when you're going to yell in my ear?" he asked, but she only wagged a finger at him.

"We did it. Can you believe it? We made it," Prophet said, a laugh attached to her words.

"Did you not expect to?" He suddenly felt sick to his stomach as he realized they'd just traveled an astronomical distance in mere moments.

"Sure. I trusted the Zilph'i technology. Come on, we have some work to do," she said, unzipping her jumpsuit. Beneath it was a different uniform, one he'd seen before.

"Isn't that an Ugna symbol?" he asked, pointing to a crest on the arm of the gray garb.

"It is." She opened a communication, and Keen tried to assess what he was seeing. The ships were almost familiar, and his eyes widened when it clicked.

"These are similar to the Ugna vessels that assisted Baldwin when they came after the Assembly," he said as a statement, not a question.

"That's right. They're remarkably close," Prophet said.

"But how? The Ugna are here?"

"Very good, though they aren't known by that moniker in these parts. They're the Invaders," Prophet told him, and the hair on his arms rose at the title.

"Doesn't that sound a little... ominous?" For some reason, he wasn't overly surprised that the Ugna were present. Their benefactor was one of them, but he hadn't been very forthcoming with details.

"They did invade." She shrugged, as if that was enough

Lineage

of an explanation.

"So we have to convince these people to tweak their drives and return with us to the Concord?" Lark asked.

"That's right," Prophet said. "Should be simple."

Lark pointed at the console, seeing the incoming transmission arrive. He tapped it and listened.

"Unidentified vessel, remain where you are. Power off any weapons systems." The voice was female, and it spoke perfect Standard. He raised an eyebrow as he peered at the Callalay woman beside him. She flicked the shuttle's engines off, and Lark pressed the blinking icon.

The group of single-manned fighter crafts arrived, encircling their shuttle, and he cleared his throat, ready to play his role.

The image of a woman in an office appeared, and he smiled at her. "Greetings. I am Admiral Lark Keen of the Concord, and I'd like to meet with your leaders."

The woman seemed confused, and her jaw dropped. "Where are you from? I don't recognize your design."

"As I said, I come from the Concord. We have much to discuss with your leaders. Please guide me to them," he said with as much confidence and authority as he could muster.

The image stayed on, but he noticed the woman's mouth move without hearing anything. She'd muted herself. A moment later, the reply came. "The Keepers will escort you to Earth."

The screen flashed, and he was once again looking at the space station through the viewscreen. The fighters, which were clearly called Keepers, began flying forward, and Prophet powered up the shuttle, following them. They were shorter than the Concord versions, each with stubby wings that would allow them to shift quickly within a planet's atmosphere. The Keepers were dark gray, with yellow lines along the sides leading to two bright orange thrusters.

"Good work, Keen," Prophet told him. "We're almost there."

"I wasn't expecting this," he admitted.

"What did you think? Our friends went to all this effort to break you out and send you to Earth for fun?"

Lark stared at the space structures as they headed toward Earth. There were huge floating pods in orbit, making a structure that would almost compete with Earon Station in size. Humans. How was it possible the Concord hadn't been aware of them?

Space vessels came and went from what had to be docking zones as their Nek-modified shuttle flew after the Keepers. It all appeared very organized and well-created. "They seem to be more advanced than we are."

Prophet chuckled. "The Concord always does think it's the epitome of advancement. They're too close-minded to believe for a moment there might be other races that could rival them for power. That time has come."

This was really happening. Within a few months, the Concord would be no more.

Three of the Keepers broke formation, their orange thrusters burning brightly as they arced away. A communication poured through the speakers. "Follow us. Do not activate any weapons or you will be destroyed immediately."

The Keeper pilot's deep voice issued the warning, and Prophet didn't flinch as they advanced to the human planet. Keen was amazed by what he saw. White cloud cover was thin, overhanging part of a large continent, but it was the ocean that drew his attention. It was so beautiful, and something urged him to walk the beach, a primal instinct like he was returning home. He shook his head,

Lineage

trying to clear the cobwebs.

"You holding it together, Admiral?" Prophet asked.

Hearing the fake title returned Lark's focus. He had a job to do, and he was going to do it to the best of his ability.

The remaining three Keepers descended, the shuttle following behind, and ten minutes later, they were en route to an island country, with another piece of land to the left of it. It was daytime, but they passed through some thicker clouds as they neared the shore, and everything turned gloomy. Rain poured over the shuttle, the dark sky casting a murky net over the entire region.

The Keepers led them toward ground, and soon they were flying over farms, and Keen noted there were huge robotic machines working the land instead of people. The crops ended quickly, and everything turned as they moved for a cityscape. The homes grew closer together; the buildings became taller, until they were in the epicenter of a metropolis.

"You will land there. Arms up when you exit the shuttle," the same male voice said before the last of their escorts raced off, leaving them no choice but to rest on the tallest skyscraper in the city. The closer the shuttle came to the landing pad on top, the bigger Keen realized the place was.

Prophet kept silent while she flew and only spoke when the ship was settled on the rooftop and powered off. Rain still fell in fat drops over the viewscreen, and Lark wiped nervous hands over his dark pants. It was showtime.

He followed Prophet to the exit, and she opened the door. Ten armed human guards waited for them, and Keen's eyes were drawn to the bald albino woman behind them. She smiled, her red eyes almost glowing in the cloudy afternoon.

Keen cleared his throat and stepped off, using his most

charismatic voice. "I'm Admiral Lark Keen with the Concord, and we're here to ask for your help."

The woman motioned for the guards to lower their weapons, and they obeyed.

"We've been expecting you." The woman turned, walking away, and Lark followed.

"They're going to attack us?" President Bertol paced the room, her hands behind her back.

"That's right," Fayle said.

"This is ludicrous. The Ugna dare fight us, when we were the ones to help them in their time of need," Bertol said, and Fayle lifted a hand.

"You misunderstand. The Ugna were always going to force their will. By entering the Concord, they could invade from the inside, taking over when the time was right," Fayle said.

Tom could see how much it pained Fayle to be offering this information. He struggled to decide if she should be detained or rewarded for the news. It was too late, but as his grandfather used to say, it's better late than never.

"Their motivations are irrelevant at this point. We need to mount a defense," Tom said, standing. He pointed to the president's seat, and she huffed, taking his suggestion. Once she was seated, he continued, pressing a button on his tablet. A 3D image appeared in the center of the table, and Rene leaned on her elbows, staring through the diagram to lock gazes with him. "This is Aruto. From what the Elder is suggesting, they'll arrive in thirty hours, using the same replica of *Shu* that assaulted Veer. They're not expecting any kind of retaliation. They'll come in, send the

Lineage

fighters to the surface, hit Beacon, and retreat, claiming the Concord sent a hit out on one of the Founders.

"The partners are already up in arms with the rumors surfacing. They think the Founders are taking over, that they're sending our fleet against vulnerable planets in an effort to strengthen their own grip."

"What's the Prime saying about this?" the president asked.

"We're about to find out," Tom said. "But first, here's what we're going to do." He pointed to the diagram, icons scattered around the planet of Aruto.

Twenty minutes later, their first plan was in place, and Tom glanced around the room. Kan Shu was present with Rene Bouchard and President Bertol, and a man named Representative Tajo Harrn, Bertol's head of defense. He was a short, round man, with a stuffy black uniform on that he looked entirely too uncomfortable in. His ridged forehead was deep-set, his eyes deep in the sockets.

"I'd prefer if we continued the discussion without the Ugna in the room," Tajo said.

"She's the one who told us what's moving for us," Tom reminded the man, but he shook his head.

"This could be a trap. For the sake of our people, President, I advise we do this behind closed doors. She could be feeding them details." Tajo's gaze could have melted ice.

Tom motioned to Fayle, asking her to rise. "Thank you for bringing this to our attention, but I have to agree with the representative. You're to be reprimanded and placed in a cell on *Shu*."

He expected a retaliation from Fayle, but none came. "Very well. I understand."

Rene ordered a shuttle to Beacon, and two of the representative's men entered, ushering Fayle from the meeting room.

President Bertol waited until the door was closed to speak up. "And you trust *her*?"

Tom nodded. "I don't see that we have a choice. If we ignore the information, then we're vulnerable. Do you want to find your world under attack?"

Tajo slammed a palm onto the table. "We are not some trivial planet to be trifled with. We are a founding race of the Concord. *Freedom is not to be taken for granted. Sometimes one must fight to have peace.*"

His Code quote struck Tom in the chest, and he nodded. "Then tell me what we can work with outside this plan I drafted."

They discussed it, Tom learning how powerful the Callalay really were. Tajo spoke of their intense suborbital defense system, and the drone army waiting at the space station near their largest moon. "Anyone who comes here will be given a fight they didn't anticipate."

"Good." Tom glanced at the man, seeing a smile peel across his face. He was beginning to like the guy and guessed Brax would too. "There's just one stipulation."

"What's that?" the Callalay president asked.

"The flagship. The one the Ugna somehow built to trick our people." Tom watched as the woman nodded, following along. "We can't destroy it. I want it."

Tajo grinned, his rugged brow twisting into a frown. "I may be able to assist you with that."

"Admiral, a message is coming from Ridele," Kan Shu said, and Tom waited as the projection of the Prime appeared.

"Prime Xune, we…" Tom started.

"Admiral. Tell me you have good news. Tensions are high at Ridele. There are over fifty offensive vessels nearing Nolix, and I don't expect they're coming for peace talks," Xune said. He looked terrible. He was always so put

Lineage

together, straight-backed and perfectly styled. It was obvious he was tired, his hair disheveled.

"Is someone with you?" the president asked, and Xune leaned over, giving Tom a view of his office nemesis, Admiral Anthony West.

"I've placed Admiral West in charge during Benitor's absence," Prime Xune said.

"What are you doing to find my sister?" President Bertol asked, and Tom noticed West's shocked expression. At least Tom hadn't been the only one left in the dark about the relationship between the Callalay leader and Admiral Benitor.

"I think we have a lead. She was sighted at Earon," Prime Xune said.

"Earon? What in the Vastness is she doing there?" Rene asked.

"We don't know, but our contacts are following up with it. Tell us what you can, Admiral."

Tom did, explaining everything about the Ugna's plan and Fayle's involvement.

"This is bad, Baldwin. They've created a disaster. I need you to prevent this assault at Aruto. I'm sorry there's no time to send reinforcements." Xune stared at him from the projection, and Tom could only nod in understanding.

"We'll stop them, and I have a plan to hijack their flagship. The Ugna are powerful, sir, but we're the Concord. We've been around for a long time, and nothing will destroy us," Tom assured him, his words carrying more confidence than his heart.

"We should have seen this coming. Damn it, we were too blind to them. The moment we learned about their numbers, we should have acted," Xune said.

West leaned on the Prime's shoulder and rubbed a hand through his gray beard. "We're ready to make a move against Driun F49, sir."

Xune glanced over his shoulder at the man behind him. "Nolix needs all the protection at this point. We need to send a statement to the people that the Ugna are behind this, and that we're united together to stop them at any cost."

Tom glanced at Rene, who was tapping a finger on the table. "Captain Bouchard, do you have a suggestion?"

"I don't think you should implicate the Ugna quite yet. They won't be aware they've been named. There's no way they would ever suspect that Elder Fayle, one of their leaders, would have betrayed them. I'd suggest making the statement to all Concord partners, but saying there's an external threat posing as the Concord, and that everyone must remain vigilant and on guard during this trying time.

"Assure them that the Founders are united, and that Admiral Thomas Baldwin is in charge of the investigation. That way, their faith will be restored, and maybe the incoming contingency of partner vessels will talk rather than fire." Rene seemed to realize she was fidgeting with her hands and placed them under the table.

Tom glanced at the Prime's image, and he pursed his lips while thinking. "Great idea, Captain. West, see to it."

"But, sir, I've already drawn up the statement..."

"Then change it! Make sure Baldwin's name is there. Bouchard is right. His name is the beacon that will keep this from spilling over. He's the hero we need. Do you hear that, Tom? Don't fail this. Stop them. Get that ship and bring the attackers to justice." The Prime ended the call, but not before Tom heard Admiral West complaining from the other end.

"We have our work cut out for us." Tom remembered Reeve's dire warning about the Ugna, and how they'd floated in rows on the colony ship's bridge, each injecting themselves with En'or before killing the Vusuls.

The meeting room door opened, and a guard poked their head in. "Sorry for the interruption, but there's been an incident."

"As if we need more to go wrong," the president said. "What is it?"

"The shuttle with your guest…"

"Out with it!" Bertol said impatiently.

"It's gone." The guard blanched. "The shuttle didn't make it to *Shu*."

Tom raced for the exit.

Elder Fayle had escaped.

FOURTEEN

Ven was ready for the jump to Sol. Judging by the urgency of emotions from the other members of the bridge crew, so were they. He couldn't read Captain Starling, but that was because her real body was in her quarters. So far, he'd heard she was recovering well, but he hadn't yet seen her physical form since the revival.

"We're about to embark on something unexpected, everyone." The captain walked to the center of the bridge, standing between Ven and the viewscreen. "We weren't planning on using the Nek jump drive function for this mission, but due to the unnatural manner in which we were sent to Planet X, and the speculation of foul play, I'm anxious to return to Concord space as soon as possible. The mission comes first, though. We'll make the leap to Sol, investigate Earth, and when we're able, using Executive Lieutenant Daak's expertise, we'll go home. Does everyone understand?"

No one objected, and Ven caught Brax's gaze. His brow was furrowed, his mouth tightly closed.

Reeve arrived on the bridge, walking through the entrance quickly, finding a seat beside Ven. Darl stood at the rear of the bridge, going over system checks, and Reeve flashed a grin at Ven as she sat beside him.

"Everything is running at optimum, Captain.

Lineage

Constantine is ready for the trip," Reeve assured the bridge.

"Very well. Ven, please move into position. Reeve, count it down." The captain went to her chair.

Ven felt unease emanating from Commander Teller. He peered behind him at the older man, and his rheumy eyes were wide, fearful.

Ven guided their immense starship deeper in-system, using the localized thrusters only, diverting most of the energy from the Bentom ball into the Nek field.

Reeve's fingers darted over the console, and she pressed an icon, the digital numbers blinking on the viewscreen's top right corner. It started at twenty, and Ven glanced to see the engine's processor bar at full. They were really going to intentionally do this.

During the few seconds before launch, Ven wondered how they'd ended up here. Who had programmed the location into their system? Had it been an enemy or an ally? Sometimes the difference between the two was negligible. He didn't know if the Ugna were his friends or foes. He almost felt Elder Fayle's fingerprints all over it, and when he closed his eyes, he could nearly hear a warning from his old mentor.

"Three, two…" Reeve counted out the last few numbers aloud, and Ven tried to keep his eyes open while the jump transpired. He felt like he was floating momentarily, and the colorful lights of the Vastness emerged, dancing across his line of sight. It was the same feeling he'd had when he'd died saving Lieutenant Commander Brax Daak's life in the Nek shuttle. Just when he thought he might be dead, he gasped, coming to.

His vision focused, and he found that he was hovering above his console as *Constantine* arrived in a completely different solar system. The crew around him was clapping, cheering their survival.

"Report," Starling said as Ven lowered to his seat. It didn't even seem like anyone had witnessed his odd behavior—or they were growing used to his differences.

"Captain, we're in Sol, all right. I recognize the patterns from the resources we'd found. There should be a planet…" Brax paused, using his controls to zoom and locate a ringed planet. "There she is. Saturn."

"How long until we reach it?" Captain Starling asked, and Ven ran the calculations.

"Twenty minutes, Captain," he said. Ven lowered his voice, turning to Reeve. She was red-cheeked and smiling. "Good job, Reeve."

"Thanks. I'm glad it worked out," she replied.

He didn't remind her that if it hadn't, they'd all be dead, the ship broken into a million pieces, scattered around space somewhere between Planet X and Saturn.

"I've sent the jump probes," Brax advised them. "We should have details soon."

Within five minutes, the feed for the local drones had flashed into the system, and he accessed them, bringing the footage onto the viewscreen. He was shocked to see the complex structures near the planet's many moons.

"What is this?" the captain asked. "Mining operation?"

"Captain, judging by the readouts from the probes, I'd say it's a weapons manufacturing plant, as well as a mining operation." Brax zoomed again, pausing the image on the surface of one of the moons. There were high structures, dozens of giant machines rolling along. He canceled the image, switching to another. This one depicted a floating station, and Ven saw the dozens of fleet ships under construction, many large and docked within metallic-framed bays.

"I'd say you're correct in your analysis," Commander Teller said. His assistant was present, holding out a bottle of water for her boss, and Ven returned his attention to the images. Who was running the operation? He closed his eyes, extending his senses toward the manufacturing station. He felt only a single entity.

"Captain, I think we should investigate. Sensors indicate one being inside the station," Ven said.

"Shouldn't we leave it and continue on to Earth?" Teller asked.

"No, I agree with Ven. We should make contact. Get some intel before rushing and showing our cards. Darl, can you communicate with them?" Treena asked.

Lieutenant Darl attempted to broadcast a greeting, but their communication went unanswered. "Nothing, Captain."

The captain motioned to Brax, and then pointed at Ven. "I'd like you two to take *Cleo*. Make contact with whoever's on that station. Be careful."

Ven exited his post, keeping calm about the entire scenario. They'd made the jump a few minutes ago, and they were already rushing off in the expedition ship. As he reached the edge of the bridge, Reeve was already running diagnostics on the drive, saying they were in the clear.

"Looks like we have all the fun, hey, Ven?" Brax clapped him on the back as he jogged into the elevator. They rose a deck and darted up the rungs leading to their craft.

"I do not think this is fun, Brax," Ven admitted.

"Then tell me what you consider a good time, Ven." Brax entered the ship, powering it up from its perch on top of *Constantine*. Ven already felt a difference in the man. Not so long ago, he was fearful of space, scared to pilot a craft like this between points A and B, but Brax had changed a lot in the past year or so. He was more confident, a better officer. Ven hoped he'd grown as much.

"I meditate for my enjoyment," Ven told him.

"I'll never understand you." Brax undocked *Cleo* and drifted toward their destination, the thrusters propelling them forward. Upon closer examination, the station was long; interconnected with outstretched metallic tubes. The vessels under construction were lined up beneath the structure, and that was where Brax guided them.

Ven searched again, sending tendrils of energy from within. He pointed to the right. "The human is in there. In the main building, near that largest bay."

Brax pressed the comms to life, using the automated message. A second later, the dash comm beeped, and Ven tapped it, accepting the incoming communication. It had no video accompaniment, only verbal, but the message was clear, the female voice crisp.

"*I don't know what the Concord is, but if you're here in peace, come on in,*" the woman said.

Brax grinned. "They speak Standard. How very interesting."

Ven's eyebrows lifted. The chances of them using Standard were very low, making it quite the coincidence… or not.

"Thank you. Can we enter the main bay safely? I assume our door docks aren't compatible," Brax replied.

"*Use the bay. That's fine.*" The woman sounded excited, and Ven wasn't sensing any ill will.

Brax did just that, and Ven stared at the construction zone. The vessels were mostly skeletal frames at this point, but the general shape was recognizable. He tried to picture them with a hull but couldn't place the familiarity.

Cleo was tiny compared to the enormity of this operation, and Saturn sat in the distance, the perfect backdrop for the station. It was impressive, and Ven's attention shifted to the station itself as they entered through the

Lineage

immense bay door's energy barrier. The room was full of raw materials, different types of robotic arms, rovers, and shuttles. At one point, this had likely been a giant operation, but now, there was only a sole occupant on the entire station.

Brax settled the expedition vessel in an open space in the center of the processing floor and grabbed his PL-30 from behind his seat. "Better bring yours too, Ven. We're supposed to greet her, but we have to be cautious. It wouldn't be the first time someone played friendly to trick a newcomer into relaxing."

Ven fully agreed and grabbed the weapon and holster, strapping it around his chest. He ran a scan from the exterior hull to ensure air quality. "It's safe," he told Brax before they opened the doors to their craft.

Brax went first, climbing down the decline onto the space station, and Ven heard the sound of footsteps coming at them. The woman stopped about twenty meters from their position, her jumpsuit greasy, her long dark hair pulled into a ponytail. She removed her gloves and dropped them on the floor.

"Sorry, sir. I didn't recognize the ship. To what do I owe this honor?" she asked.

"You wouldn't..." Brax started, but Ven saw she was looking at him, staring in deference.

Ven stepped in front of her. "Do you know who I am?" His voice was quiet.

She shook her head. "No, sir. Only that you're one of the Invaders. I hope I didn't do anything to upset you. The funding has been cut, and I'm trying my best. I know you found ways to automate the processes, but we need more bodies to keep the machines running at optimum capabilities. I would be farther along in the..."

"The Invaders? I do not follow," he said.

"I'm sorry. Is that offensive? I know that's not what you're really called. That's the human-created name that stuck. I thought you were okay with it…" She stared at the floor, and Ven didn't need to be clairvoyant to sense her nervousness.

"I am not an Invader. I am Executive Lieutenant Ven Ittix of *Constantine*. This is Lieutenant Commander Brax Daak, and we hail from the Concord," he said, and she met his gaze again.

"You're not from here?" she asked.

"No. We've come to investigate Earth," Brax said, and Ven saw her finally realize that Brax wasn't human. He was a foot taller than her, twice as broad at the shoulders. While his face was similar, it was rounder, his eyes different.

"You're not a human…" She walked closer.

"I'm Tekol. I come from Nolix, the Concord's home planet."

Ven thought she might freak out, but she surprised him by smiling. "I knew it. Someone's come to save us."

"Save you?" Ven asked.

"You're not one of the Invaders? You look just like them. The skin, the eyes." She touched his cheek, her fingers warm.

"I am Ugna, but more importantly, a member of the Concord fleet."

"Then you will help?" she asked.

"Tell us what happened," Brax said. "Better yet, come with us onto *Constantine*."

She glanced between them, but she nodded eventually.

---

*F*ayle released the two guards wearing their EVAs,

leaving them to float in space with a distress signal on a loop. She told herself they'd be fine. They were only an hour from Aruto, and she needed to make better time. She was risking a lot by leaving like this, but considering the looming attack, Tom and the president couldn't waste resources on searching for her.

She found the waiting ship where she'd instructed it to be: on the far side of the seventh planet's mid-sized moon. Fayle hated having to do this to Baldwin, but she'd gone too far to stop now. Years of working with Wylen, in preparation for the Ugna's internal attack. She'd deceived so many people, including most of the Ugna she'd ever been in contact with. Wylen expected her to guide the other Elders through the coming months, but she had other ideas.

As she flew the shuttle toward the moon, Fayle recalled the first meeting she'd ever had with High Elder Wylen. It had been fifty-seven years ago, when she'd been nothing more than an up-and-coming acolyte. She'd been stripped from her family, much as the others had, and four years later, the mysterious stranger had stopped in their village on Leria.

Even at that time, while she was a mere slip of a girl, Fayle hadn't been able to remember her parents. In the early years, she'd wake in the middle of the night, sheets drenched with sweat from nightmares of the faceless family she'd been stolen from. The Elders would see her pain and feed her a shot of En'or, and somehow that helped. She now understood why. The drug was terrible, a powerful enhancer, but also as addictive as anything sold in any dark alley in Ridele.

She glanced at her trembling hand, knowing it wasn't fear that caused it. She hadn't used En'or in a few hours. Wylen and his predecessors had been fully aware of what they were doing. He'd created an army of dependant soldiers. They would do what he wanted, even if she fought against him, but Fayle did think they could win the upcoming internal struggle.

She landed the shuttle, the vessel latching to the rocky surface, and she waited for the cruiser's hatch-field to seal around her exit before she opened the doors.

It was Concord-owned, the First Ship painted along the side, and Fayle thought about the history behind the symbol. The Ugna were older than the Concord, which was a difficult concept to imagine. Wylen claimed there might be millions more of them, including the ones at Sol.

Fayle should have come clean sooner, but she hadn't decided which side of the fight she would stand on. After witnessing the passion Thomas Baldwin held for his position and for the partner planets' safety and well-being, she'd changed her mind. If that man could give away his ship and move to Nolix for what he thought was the good of their people, then she could do the same for the Ugna.

"Are you well?" First Officer Hanli asked as Fayle entered the cruiser. The woman was wearing a plain brown jumpsuit, her hair long and loose. She looked like a stranger.

"Yes." Fayle ran a hand over her pants, nervously fighting a crease. "Thank you for coming. Is she here?"

Hanli was one of the few she felt she could trust. They'd discussed this eventuality years ago, when the woman was a mere child—recruited from a young age, just as Fayle had been. It was surprising how cyclical deception was.

"She's here and waiting for you in your cabin," Hanli said. "Have they heard from *Constantine*?"

Fayle had expected that would be the woman's first query. "No, but I'm sure your friend Ven Ittix is fine. Show me to the cabin." Her steps were shaky, and she fought the urge to reach in her pocket for the shot of En'or.

Ven was no longer taking it, and it scared her. An Ugna without En'or was rare… and he was already powerful. As she walked the long corridor behind Hanli, Fayle thought about the Temple of Sol and Father Hamesly. He'd told Ven the truth, that Ugna didn't need the drug. And that name. What did Hamesly know of Sol and the Ugna? Maybe it was time to discuss it with the man.

Hanli stopped at the door, turning toward Fayle. She took the Elder's hands, and Fayle found the girl's were cool to the touch. Her eyes were wide, but her words were strong. "We are doing the right thing, Elder. Our people deserve a choice."

"Thank you, child. I will meet with you later. Please proceed."

Hanli departed, leaving Fayle alone in the corridor, near the door. It opened with the press of a latch, and she smiled at the face greeting her from a comfortable seated position on a couch. The woman set her tablet on the tabletop.

"Hello, Admiral," Fayle said.

Jalin Benitor smiled in return. "Elder Fayle. It's time to get to work."

FIFTEEN

Almost all of the people Lark encountered were Ugna, and this disturbed him greatly. The gangly pale folks wandered the halls with grace, rarely saying a word. They'd been sent to quarters for the first night, with the promise of speaking to the Earth president the morning after. It was now midday, and Lark was growing tired of waiting.

"I expected them to be a little more enthusiastic about meeting a representative from millions of light years away," he muttered to Prophet. She sat quietly at the two-person table in the elaborate courtyard. The ceilings were glass, but all they did was showcase the miserable rainy day outside. The dark clouds matched his mood, as if he was being personified by the inclement weather.

"It's a tactic," she replied, setting her fork to her plate. "The food is good, though."

Another tactic. Lark knew them like the back of his hand. He considered himself an expert negotiator, but sometimes there was no mutually beneficial outcome. It was how he'd ended up at Wavor Manor. "Whatever it is, I'm…"

The Ugna woman from yesterday appeared, striding toward them. Her dark red pantsuit accented the color of her eyes, and she motioned for them to follow. "President Basher will see you."

Lineage

"About time," Lark mumbled, but spoke louder, in his diplomatic tone: "That's wonderful. I look forward to it."

She didn't respond. The walk was somewhat quick, five minutes through a maze of halls and doors. Lark noticed more humans, but they were all head-down, set to their tasks. They walked as if they had the weight of the galaxy on their shoulders. He almost noted how most of them were in matching blue uniforms, whereas the Ugna were expressing free will.

Prophet strolled beside him, matching his stride easily, and their guide stopped at a set of ten-foot-tall double doors made of a rich wood. The flooring was pure white, so clean Lark imagined you could eat off it. Whoever this Basher was, he ran a tight ship.

Two men opened the doors from the inside, and Lark entered the large oval room. The flooring was covered with a dark purple carpet; tapestries hung on the walls, depicting scenes of what could only be human history. His gaze settled on one in particular. Enormous ships descended from the skies as thousands of people stared toward the incoming vessels.

"I have always appreciated that one too," a voice said, and Lark noticed the man moving from a desk near the far end of the room. This had to be Basher. He was middle-aged, maybe a little older than Lark, six feet tall, and fit. His clothing was similar to a style used within the Concord, but it was different enough to feel alien. The man stopped when they were ten feet apart and grinned at them. "When I was told someone from this mysterious Concord had arrived, I didn't believe my people. Then I was told one of them was human, and I knew for sure someone was pulling my leg. But her…" Basher stared at Prophet. "She's unlike anything we've ever seen."

"Her name is Prophet," Lark said, not liking the way

this president was assessing his escort.

"Beware of false prophets who come to you in sheep's clothing but inwardly are ravenous wolves." Basher smiled again. Lark didn't like the man's choice of words. He didn't quite follow them, but there was a veiled threat interlaced with the man's constant grin. He hoped his benefactor knew what he was getting into.

"I think you know my race, President Basher." Prophet lifted an arm, and an empty vase lifted from an end table, floating in the air toward her.

"You're one of them?" Basher asked, and Lark's heart skipped a beat. This whole time he'd been flying with an Ugna, and she'd never told him. She'd been able to read his emotions, and only the Vastness knew what else. Betrayal burned deeply within him, but he tried to act like he'd been aware all along.

"I am one of the Ugna," she said.

"But you look…"

"You are as well, aren't you, President Basher?" she asked, the vase falling from the air and shattering on the floor. A human guard opened the door, asking if everything was okay, and the president dismissed him.

Lark shook his head, confident this man wasn't one of the Ugna, but he shocked Lark by smiling in response. A second later, the broken bits of the vase rose from the ground, returning to their shape. He closed his eyes, humming something, and the pieces glowed hotly. A moment later, the vase hovered to the table and lowered. It had been repaired.

"Impressive," Prophet said.

"What is it you want?" the president asked.

Lark thought it was time for him. "I'm Admiral Lark Keen of the Concord, and we need…"

Prophet raised a finger, silencing him. "Now that we've

confirmed he's Ugna, we don't need that any longer." She turned her attention to Basher. "The Ugna have joined a multi-world conglomerate and own a home world within the Concord. There are riches unlike anything you've ever seen. My boss, High Elder Wylen, has sent me to come for you, to promise you a seat at the head of this Concord if you bring your people and help him secure victory."

"Surely you have enough strength to do this on your own," Basher offered.

Lark watched the conversation with a detached sense of foreboding. The Ugna were really making their move. One race trying to take over the entire Concord. He thought about the humans in the halls, heads low, their expressions sad and depressed. Was that what he was playing with? Was he going to assist the Ugna in enslaving the entire Concord?

"We can, but our foothold is tenuous. We need allies. We want your fleet," Prophet said.

The president ran a hand through his medium-length brown hair and peered at Lark. "How do we progress?"

Prophet grinned. Slipping a tablet from her pocket, she passed it to him. "This. We have the means to modify star drives, and enough Nek to fuel jumps to Concord space. The job will take a few weeks, if you have a facility and the workers. It's all there."

The president peered at the clear tablet, rotating it in his hands. "How many worlds are we talking about?"

"Over forty. Each with resources to spare," she said. "You will have a seat at the head of the newly formed leadership."

President Basher glanced at Lark again, as if the human's presence was making him uncomfortable. "I will think about it."

"Don't think too long. The offer expires at dusk."

The president left them alone, and Prophet went first. Lark was frozen in place, staring at the tapestry, feeling like he was watching the aliens invade. Life in the Concord was about to change forever. He'd been promised a good life, one with power and riches for himself, but most importantly, a life with Seda and Luci.

Could he trade his own happiness for the lives of everyone else? A year ago, he would have said yes, but now he wasn't so sure.

Cassandra's eyes darted nervously, and Treena gave her a slight smile, hoping to ease her mind. "Thank you for coming to speak with us."

The woman suddenly looked ten years younger, like a kid in trouble. She had to be at least twenty-five or thirty, but Treena guessed life hadn't been easy alone at this empty workplace. The manufacturing station didn't seem to have the most comfortable living arrangements. "Who are you?" Cassandra's voice was small.

"I'm Captain Treena Starling, and this is Commander Pol Teller," she said. "You already met Executive Lieutenant Ven Ittix, and Lieutenant Commander Brax Daak." Reeve wasn't present. She'd opted to head to the station to see what kind of operation the humans had going on near Saturn.

"Where are the buggers?" Teller asked abruptly. His aide Missy passed him a glass of water, and he muttered something about wanting a stiffer drink.

"Excuse me?" Cassandra asked.

Treena took over. "Ven said you recognized him. Called him an Invader. Are there Ugna around? Or on

Lineage

Earth?"

The woman nodded. "They've been here for a long time. I hear rumors of life before them, but it was long before my time, or my parents and grandparents."

Treena was shocked. They'd expected something on Earth—maybe an abandoned world with secrets of humanity's past—but not this. Not humans still living under the rule of Ugna. Someone had known they were coming and had sent them to Planet X to see proof of the ancient Ugna village. It was to warn them and perhaps prepare them for what they were about to find.

Treena wanted to know everything, but she decided to tell the woman about them first, to gain her confidence. "We're from the Concord. Far away."

"But you're human. At least you two are, right?" Cassandra asked.

"That's right, Cassandra. Humans live on a planet named Earon, and are one of the four Founders of the Concord. We have over forty partners within the group."

"What are the Founders?" she asked. "And you can call me Cass."

"Four races joined to start the Concord. Callalay, Humans, Zilph'i, and the Tekol. Ven is technically Zilph'i, so I assume the Invaders are descendants of them as well. Brax is Tekol. Together, they formed a government and invited partners to trade goods. We have a fleet created to defend our worlds and Border, as well as to explore new opportunities outside of Concord space. We recently heard of Sol and Earth, and were sent to investigate."

Cass took a drink of water. "This is astonishing. The Invaders told us we were alone. That they've explored the known universe, and Earth was it. That's why they came. To help advance us. To partner with us. But since they've arrived, they've slowly taken over. My grandfather once told me it wasn't always this way. That at one time, we were free.

"There are a few lucky ones like me. Most are working the fields at home, sweating in the plants, slaving on their stations at the moon. I have an aptitude for robotics, and when my teacher died out here a year ago, I didn't tell them."

"They don't know you're alone?" Brax asked her.

Cass shook her head. "They don't care. This place practically runs itself. It's mostly automated. I only ensure the bots are up to code, but they do the rest."

"Do you have access to the buggers' network?" Teller asked, and Treena really wished he'd stop calling them that.

"Some. I don't have entry to everything, but if you'd like to learn about Earth, you'd be able to find a lot of information, if that's what you're after," Cass said.

"Good." Treena noticed a red light blinking on her tablet, and she slid it over, checking the message. It was Reeve. She tapped it, the projection of the chief engineer shooting from the tablet's center.

"Captain, something's happening," Reeve told them.

"What is it?" Treena asked.

"I don't know." Reeve glanced around. "The machines started moving, and a notification keeps chiming."

Treena turned her attention to Cass. "Tell us."

"Looks like new orders came in. Can you patch the details in?" Cass went on to explain to Reeve how to access them, and a few minutes later, Cass was reading the newly-sent instruction out loud to their group. "I don't understand. They're bringing twenty more ships. Protectors."

"What are Protectors?" Brax frowned while he asked.

"They're the Invaders' main vessels. They can each house over five hundred crew and have enough armaments to destroy a moon within minutes. The instructions are strange, though," Cass said.

Treena scooted her chair closer to the woman. "What makes them odd?"

"The engines. There are some modifications I'm to prepare for. Something about Nek mods."

Brax stood, bumping into the table; he knocked over a water glass. "Nek? How in the Vastness did they gain access to that?"

Treena thought about it, and the answer was clear. "Someone stole a Nek shuttle and brought the plans. And if I have to guess, it was the Ugna."

Brax cracked his knuckles. "We have to stop this."

Treena smiled. "We will. With Cass's assistance."

Brax crossed his arms. "I say we destroy the facility."

Teller chuckled. "You have a lot to learn, son. Warfare is more than just blowing things up. You need to be cunning, prepared, and always a step ahead."

"What do you propose?" Treena asked the old man. He was proving to be useful, despite her earlier reservations.

"We let them arrive, dock, and begin the manufacturing. But we tweak things a little bit. If they're heading for the Concord, wouldn't it be helpful if they were short twenty of these Protectors?" Teller's eyes shone.

"Who said anything about them coming for the Concord?" Brax asked.

Treena had been thinking the same thing, but it was Ven who answered. "I fear he is correct. I have watched my people, felt their moods, and have seen the actions of the High Elder. He wished to befriend me, but I could never betray my people, and I don't mean the Ugna. I think the Ugna are making their move, and we need to stop them before it's too late."

His words solidified Treena's decision. "Cass, how

long before the fleet arrives?"

"Less than a day," Cass replied.

"Can you make the changes to the programming without anyone noticing?" Treena was anxious to start their plan.

"I can, but…"

"But what?" Brax asked, perhaps a little too forcefully.

"If I do this, I want help."

"We'll take you with us," Treena promised her.

Cass shook her head. "My family. They're on the moon. We have to rescue them."

Treena glanced at Brax, and the Tekol puffed his cheeks out. "If we time this right, we may be able to do that."

He had a big heart and a soft spot for saving people. Treena went to the exit, stopping to face the room's occupants. "Then it's settled. We'll set the trap, rescue your family, and return to the Concord to warn them of what's happening. Everyone get to work; we have a long day ahead of us."

The moon was different than Brandon remembered it. The nearby space station was twice the size it had been, and the gray surface of the moon held a real city, not just a ragtag spattering of structures. There were buildings over ten stories in height, and he noticed a huge greenspace within the giant crater centering the cityscape.

"Brandon, it looks like there's even an artificial atmosphere. They've stepped up their game," Carl said with awe in his voice.

"Any issues on clearance?" he asked Kristen.

Lineage

"None at all. This rover is one of their vessels. The Invaders don't expect a group of Mars runaways to be returning on it. They haven't even reached out." Kristen stayed in her seat, slowing their craft.

"Are you sure we need to stop here first? Why not go straight to Earth?" Jun asked.

"We've been through this. I'm not going anywhere without my brother. Plus, he's the only one that can lead us into the president's palace," Brandon said, hoping Clark was still alive. They'd had a lengthy fight the day before Brandon had departed for Mars. The moment Clark had told him he wouldn't be joining their group was the hardest day of Brandon's life. He'd met someone on the moon, and she wasn't willing to risk it. Most humans weren't. They were subservient to the Invaders and powers that be, most losing any hope of ever breaking the shackles that bound them to the aliens.

"If he wouldn't help us a decade ago, why would he now?" Carl spat.

"Because he's my brother, and he'll do the right thing." Brandon's words were sharp as a knife, and Carl backed away, hopefully sensing that was the end of it.

Brandon returned his attention to the city and directed Kristen to dock at the station, as they'd previously decided. The radar blinked, and Brandon ran to the pilot's side, checking what could have set off the ship's sensors like that.

"I don't like this," Kristen said softly.

Brandon didn't either. A giant envoy of Protectors moved away from Earth, heading past the moon and beyond. "There have to be twenty of them."

"Do you think they're going to Mars? Is this about us?" Carl asked, but Brandon didn't have a good answer.

"How could they know? That's far too much artillery

for a small group of dissenters. Twenty Protectors! That's almost their entire fleet," Jun exclaimed.

That wasn't true. Brandon knew for a fact that they had at least twice that number of Invader vessels. They were huge, each capable of carrying hundreds of the Invaders. The assumption was that they were manned by humans these days, the ones who'd bent knees and proclaimed their services to the alien beings. From what Brandon had seen before they'd escaped, most people were happier working for them than against them. It wasn't something he could live with.

"What do we do? Should we run?" Kristen asked.

"Stay here." They were almost docked, and their ship slowed, coming to a stop near the station. He peered out the viewscreen, and one of the immense vessels thrust past them, close enough to see through the screen. "Something big is happening. They've never had so many together. Not since the day of the invasion."

Brandon had seen the old footage, the recorded newsfeeds that had survived the invasion in subsequent years. The original leaders had fought them off without success. Years later, President Gordon Basher was all in with the enemy, and Brandon had to wonder how they'd brainwashed him. The president was charming and loved by many. The people of Earth seemed to think he was their savior, solely responsible for keeping them alive when the Invaders could have ended their lives at any time. Basher was another in a long line of presidents since the Invasion, but to Brandon, they were all the same. Cowards.

Carl shook his head slowly. "I don't like it."

"You don't have to. With everyone's eyes on the Protectors, this is the perfect time," Brandon said. "Kristen, dock the craft. Carl, you're coming with me. Grab the gun and wear the mask."

Brandon slipped into a uniform, the same brown jumpsuit the other human workers would be donning. He placed a black filtered mask over his face and wore a skull cap that kept dust from covering his hair on the moon's surface. Carl did the same, and they moved for the exit.

"Wait!" Kristen shouted, jogging to meet Brandon. She pulled his mask aside and kissed him firmly before placing something in his hand. "Don't forget these."

He glanced down, seeing the stolen ID tags they'd stowed before leaving to Mars. He'd almost walked onto the moon without identification. That was a quick way to wind up dead. "Thanks."

Brandon tossed one to Carl, and they clipped the tags to their chests, exiting the ship. It was time to find his brother and take this on the offensive.

SIXTEEN

Tom checked the time. They had an hour before the attack. He sat in his quarters on *Shu*, anticipating the pending battle. He used to hate waiting, but the older he became, the more he appreciated it. So many things could go wrong during times of war, and decisions were often made in the heat of the moment. The time before could be used for contemplation, planning, and recharging.

He was only too aware of how little time there was for any of those things during the altercations. Tom was oddly calm about the entire thing. Elder Fayle had escaped, and they'd found the two shuttle guards within Aruto's system, bringing them home unscathed. Fayle had gone out of her way to keep them unharmed, and despite President Bertol's assumptions, Tom did guess Fayle might be on their side.

He'd sent the message to Aimie Gaad nearly a day prior, and finally, an hour ago, a reply had arrived. He sat at his desk, awaiting her call, and it came right on time. She was always punctual, if anything.

Tom smiled as her face projected over his desk, but she didn't return it. "Aimie, what's wrong?"

"Ridele's going crazy. People are starting to protest, and it's getting dangerous. Are the rumors true?" she asked.

"Which ones?"

"That the Concord is attacking its own?" Her voice

Lineage

was quiet, her face nervous.

"No." He straightened, intertwining his fingers on his lap. "Aimie, everything will be okay. I can't tell you much, but it's not us. We're being attacked from the inside, and they're trying to pin it on our government."

"But it's not? Are you certain?"

"One hundred percent," he assured her. "I wanted to talk to you…" He didn't know if this was the last time he'd speak to her, considering the battle he was charging into. The president had suggested he hide in a bunker far below Aruto's surface, with her and the other representatives, but he'd refused. Bouchard had seemed thrilled about having him aboard.

"I need to speak with you too," Aimie said, her face long.

"You first," he urged, his stomach tying in knots in preparation. This wasn't the first time he'd had this conversation, but he'd hoped that part of his life was over. That he might be able to finally settle down, but from the look on her face, that wasn't his path.

"I can't keep doing this. R-Emergence has been vandalized again, and there are over a hundred incoming ships heading for Nolix as we speak," Aimie said.

"The Prime is working on explaining the situation, but it's a delicate matter," Tom said, wishing he could tell her the truth.

"Tom, I'm leaving." The words came out quickly, and Aimie averted her gaze, staring at her hands.

"Good. Go somewhere safe and ride it out. I'm hoping to be home within a week," he said.

"No. That's not what I mean. I'm going to retire, like I'd suggested before. I might start my own small business, maybe do research on a planet far from the Founders' reach." She met his stare again. "I hate what the Concord has become."

It hurt: not just because he was the poster boy for the damned Concord, but because he actually believed in what it stood for and wanted it to thrive like he'd dreamed it could. "Aimie, you're not seeing the entire picture…"

"I've seen enough of it. I feel terrible about the bad things R-Emergence has done in an effort to gain a stronger foothold, and I see the same thing happening with the Concord, only on a larger scale. And you're part of it. I can't…"

"Are you saying this is over?" he asked, his voice a whisper.

She nodded. "It's over, Tom. I'm sorry. It was fun, though."

"Fun." His finger tapped the desk. "Take care of yourself. I wish it didn't have to end like this, but it's obvious you've made your mind up."

She was about to speak again when he tapped the projection closed. He instantly regretted the rash decision, but he had to clear his mind for the impending Ugna attack.

He slammed a palm onto the desk. "Damn it!"

The door opened to reveal Rene Bouchard in uniform, her head tilting to the side as she appraised him. "Are you okay, Baldwin?"

Tom stood, crossing the room. "Don't you ever knock?"

She raised her hands in front of her chest. "It's my ship, Admiral. I thought you'd want to hear that the fleet's been spotted. We're set to intercept them in twenty minutes."

He stared at her, trying to calm himself after the difficult discussion he'd just had with Aimie. It wasn't like he was going to marry her and have kids right away, but they'd mentioned moving in together. It was going to be a big step for him. Instead, he was on someone else's starship, waiting to encounter the damned Ugna. How could they have been so blind?

"Tell me something, Rene."

She smiled, her expression easing some of the tension in his shoulders. She could always do that to him. "Anything, Baldwin."

"Did we do something wrong? Was there ever a solution to this without the Ugna's assistance?" he asked.

"We were in shambles. Our fleet was broken up, spread far too thin under poor leadership. We had to glue ourselves back together, and the only way to stop the Assembly and return to fight the Statu was with their help," Rene assured him, and Tom nodded along.

"I have a feeling they knew exactly what they were doing," he told her. "They had a hand in everything. They were playing puppeteer with Prime Pha'n, and their fingers were all over Admiral Hudson, and probably Admiral Keen before him. You don't pull off something like this on a whim. Damn it. Fayle has always known, and it took her this long to say anything."

"Fayle could be lying too. Setting us up again," Rene suggested as they walked from his room, heading toward the elevators.

"I don't think so, but I've been struggling to read women lately, so I'm probably wrong."

They entered the elevator, and Rene turned to him. "Was that the good Doctor Aimie Gaad you were talking with?" she asked, mischief in her tone.

"It was."

"How about we have dinner when this is over… talk about it? Like old times," Rene said, grinning at him.

Tom was caught off-guard but could only shrug. "If we're alive after today, I'd be happy to."

The doors opened, and they entered the bridge. It was

a flurry of activity, and Commander Kan Shu pointed to his own seat, offering it to Tom. Kan took the helm position, and Lieutenant Commander Asha Bertol sat along the edge of the bridge, manning the weapons systems.

Hans remained in Engineering, where Tom would have ordered Reeve to maintain shields and thruster power control during battle. He watched over their processes, and within ten seconds was pleased with what he saw. Rene was a great captain, and her crew was a testament to that.

Conner Douglas was seated beside Kan Shu, and he smiled nervously at Tom. Yin Shu's AI walked from behind him, stopping at his chair when he arrived at it. "Hello, Admiral."

"Shu, good to see you," Tom told her. "I trust we're prepared for this?"

"The fighters are manned, the shields are at full capacity, and weapons are charged. We are as ready as we can be," the projection informed them.

They were an hour out from Aruto, with a few surprises waiting for the incoming fleet, but it had been Tom's idea to parley first. See if it was possible to divert the attack before it began.

"Captain, we have visual," Kan said, and the viewscreen zoomed on the mirror ship. It looked exactly like *Shu* and *Constantine*, and Tom was shocked the Ugna had the ability to create such a magnificent piece of machinery.

"Reach out to them. Request communication," Rene ordered.

The response came quickly. The screen flashed, showing an image of a bridge far different than theirs. The seats were rough, the computers nothing like the advanced ones Tom saw around him on this bridge. They'd built the flagships to resemble the Concord's on the outside, but had probably kept them hollow inside. It was a respectable

Lineage

trick.

It did have a crew, but Tom was surprised to see they weren't all Zilph'i or Ugna. A man stood, his size and thick dreads identifying him as a Tekol. Nothing about him seemed Ugna, but it was apparent once he spoke that he was with them.

"We've been wondering when someone would stand against us," the man said. "And from the looks of it, we have the pleasure of coming to blows with the very face of the Concord. The High Elder will be pleased."

Tom bristled, trying to keep him calm. "We don't need to fight. Is there no other eventuality we can discuss?" he asked the man, who only smiled wider.

"There will be no negotiating. I have been tasked with destroying Aruto, and I will do just that," he said.

Tom was happy they didn't have any of the Ugna cruisers with them, because Hans in Engineering didn't know their weaknesses like he did the Concord replica a few kilometers from their position.

"Then we have nothing further to speak about." Tom watched as Kan powered off their communication. "*Be steadfast, be vigilant, be strong. The Vastness welcomes all.*" He whispered the Code phrase as the alarms sounded.

The battle was upon them.

"This is quite the facility. It has evidence of Ugna technology mixed with that of the Zilph'i," Ven said as they walked through the manufacturing station's programming center.

"I don't fully understand what you're describing, but these methods came from the Invaders. Earth had space travel, but nothing like this yet. The Invaders brought with them promises of greatness and riches, and I'm told our divided world grasped at the chance to be included in something larger than humanity." Cass led Reeve and Ven to the edge of the room, the lights flickering on at their arrival. "Instead, we lost ourselves and gave up everything to the newcomers."

Reeve found she liked the girl. She was thoughtful and had a brilliant mind. She was a little surprised that these Invaders had abandoned a human woman alone here to do all the work by herself, but if they were anything like the Ugna she'd met, they probably couldn't anticipate anyone going against their wishes. They were arrogant to a fault.

"These Protectors, do you have their schematics?" Ven asked, and took a seat beside Reeve as she made herself familiar with the software. It was written in Standard, making it a breeze to navigate.

Cass pointed to the files, guiding Reeve to the blueprints, and within minutes, she was working on their plan for revenge.

"What we need to do is create a virus that'll disengage the drives," Reeve told them.

"What if we go a step further?" Cass asked.

Ven turned to face her, his eyes piercing. "What do you propose?"

"They've forwarded the plans from Earth, asking me to prepare for the modifications. We could create a trigger within this jump drive that would change their trajectory, and destroy the Bentom afterwards," she suggested.

Reeve considered this. "Why not just obliterate the star drive when they activate it?" she asked the woman.

"If they explode here, the Invaders will know that they've failed and were likely sabotaged. If the ships depart and make the jumps, the ones remaining behind will have

Lineage

no idea that the outgoing vessels were obliterated. At least, not for some time." Cass paled as she said it, and Reeve understood why. She was talking about killing hundreds, maybe thousands of people, even if they were the Invaders.

Reeve peered at Ven and waited for his advice. "I say we do what Cass suggests," he replied after a tense moment.

"Okay. Let's get to work," Reeve said.

A few hours later, they had the processes laid out, the drones and robotic arms prepared for the incoming modifications. Reeve's eyes felt like they were crossing by the time they were done, but she was confident they were one step closer to success.

Bootsteps rang out behind them, and she glanced over her shoulder to find Treena arriving. "How's it coming along?"

Reeve stood, stretching her aching back. "We're set. The only issue we have is Cass." The woman had taken a quick break, with the promise of returning with some water. Ven had joined her, getting a tour of the main plant.

"How do you mean?" Treena asked.

Reeve kept her voice low. "If we take her, the Invaders will be suspicious."

"What do you propose?"

"She has to stay. We'll promise to bring her later," Reeve said.

"And the moon?" the captain asked.

"I don't know… we should really return home after this. Tell Baldwin what's going on," Reeve said.

Treena stared at her, eyes unblinking for a few seconds. "What if we have it look like an accident happened? Cass was making a last-minute change on the space dock arms. Repairs in preparation for the incoming fleet. She was lost in an airlock malfunction."

Reeve grinned at the captain, appreciating the woman's idea. "It could work. But what about your superior? We'd better add him in too, since they aren't aware he died over a year ago."

Cass returned with Ven, and they discussed the plan. She obviously didn't like the idea of staying behind as the alternative. An hour later, the work was done, the fake footage of Cass's accident loaded into the system. Reeve did the overlay herself, and was sure no one would catch the flaws. The Invaders would arrive to find the plant ready for the modifications and Cass gone: dead from a mistake as she prepared for the Protectors' arrival.

They departed from the station, leaving untraceable video surveillance linked to *Constantine* so they could keep a watchful eye on the progression. Reeve was proud of their efforts today and could only hope their arrival at the moon would go as smoothly. Saturn hung in the viewscreen in the distance, a regal world with beautiful rings.

She found Harry in the boiler room where she'd left him and checked how far they were from their next destination. If they pushed the drive, they could arrive in an hour. She had a feeling that time was of the essence.

The answer had come fast. The president had only kept them waiting for an hour before advising them that Earth would be assisting the mission as requested. The Protector was beautiful, and the president himself rode in *Asteri,* the lead vessel in the twenty-ship procession from Earth to some remote hidden station near a ring-world named Saturn.

The president made Lark uncomfortable. He was

human but clearly had powerful Ugna abilities, which brought so many questions to mind. Could someone be gifted the abilities? Were the Ugna able to reprogram one's brain, to train a mind to control objects with no more than your thoughts?

He had free rein and walked through the straightforward corridors to his destination. Prophet was sleeping, and she'd been less than forthcoming about being an Ugna after his discovery. He shouldn't have been so shocked. The woman was an enigma, but the mere fact that she was Callalay meant he hadn't even considered that she was one of *them*. Things were changing, and if the Ugna had infiltrated each of the Founders, that made it impossible to determine who was an Ugna and who wasn't. Nothing about Prophet had given her away.

The president had requested a meeting with Lark. Alone.

Lark was nervous. He was having second thoughts about joining forces with these Invaders and Earthlings. The humans looked like him, but he knew next to nothing about their species. He felt like a fraud.

When he'd been working under the Assembly, acting as the face of a movement, he'd truly seen himself as a revolutionary. He'd wanted to spark change within the Concord, to make a difference and topple the autocratic nightmare that was leading their partners. Lark was quite aware that each person was the protagonist of their own story, and the entire time he'd worked to build up the Assembly, he'd seen himself as exactly that: a hero. A champion for the people.

But with the Concord's recent changes and improvements, he realized that perhaps he wasn't the man for the job after all. Maybe a peaceful method would have been best. Thomas Baldwin had worked his way up from the inside and managed to do more for the Concord than Lark had ever been able to. Leave it to his old buddy Tom to beat him at that too.

Now he was being asked to work with the Ugna, pretending to be the highest-ranking admiral, and convincing this Ugna human president to return with him to the Concord to fend off the Founders and allow the High Elder to claim the top title. From the outside, Lark knew it was wrong. Did he have a choice any longer? He felt like he was in too deep, his body buried in the sand, and if he wasn't careful, his head would be covered soon too.

"There you are," the president said, walking up behind Lark as he stared through the large open room's viewer of space. The feed showed them passing a planet, this one distant but unmistakeably red.

"I'm here," Lark said, smirking. His mouth suddenly went dry, and he searched the room for something to drink. The space was comfortable, loungers and built-in cushioned seating lining the walls, with tablets and computers near the opposite end.

"This is our library. Of course, it's nothing like the old archaic ones of the past, with physical books. Have you ever seen one?" Gordon Basher asked him. The man was in the same uniform as before, but he was more casual in it this time. His shoulders didn't seem so tense, his expression softer.

"I've seen books. My father-in-law used to prefer them. He kept journals and hand-wrote notations in them," Lark said, taking a seat on a dark blue couch. Basher sat across from him, a table separating them.

From nowhere, a woman appeared, walking softly across the open floor with cloth shoes on. She was human, her hair cut short, styled to the side. "Can I get you anything?" she asked.

Lineage

"Tuscan red. Two glasses," Basher said.

Lark had no idea what that was, but he was anticipating the refreshment.

Basher continued. "Cursive is a lost art. No one needs to do that any longer, just as no one needs to paint or play music. To sculpt wonders with bare hands is unnecessary, because we have drones to do these things for us. We have computers to create the loveliest tunes, things the human mind could never have imagined. But you know what?" he asked as the woman returned, pouring the beverages and leaving the bottle after she'd handed them each a glass.

"What?" Lark asked.

"We still need to make art, to compose music, to sculpt with our hands, because if we don't, we lose what it means to be human," Basher said.

"Are you human?" Lark asked, taking a sip. The beverage was much like Vina, but smoother, lighter.

The older man laughed, his face growing friendlier with the expression. "I am *very* human. The Invaders, or Ugna as you call them, have been generous with us, Admiral Keen. We were a troubled people. Our vanity blinded any chance of success. We needed someone to come in and show us the error of our ways, because we were on the wrong track."

Lark had so many questions. "What happened? Why did people stay behind?"

"You say this Concord has humans, correct?" the president asked, and Lark nodded, taking another drink. It was making his head warm and fuzzy, and he set it down. "We went through a dark time, from what the records show. There isn't much on record. Strife and nuclear war. I imagine some fled, while others didn't have the resources to. Humans are resilient, Admiral, as I'm sure you're aware. We'll adapt to any reality, and survive, just as we did when the Invaders touched down."

Lark was beginning to understand the picture a little better now. "The Invaders offered you unity and technology. That gave you an excuse to control the people, didn't it?"

Basher frowned at him. "Are you suggesting that we did nothing? The Invaders would have stolen our world. They sought a home, and we had one they were compatible with. If we'd denied them, we'd have died."

Lark could see the man's point, but within a few minutes of being on Earth, he'd glimpsed the fear in the people's eyes and the cocksure attitude of the Invaders. This was no mutually beneficial relationship. "And now? So many years later, does this remain the case?"

Basher smiled, taking a drink. "I think you misjudge your relationship with me, Admiral. I'm not here to be judged by you or your Concord. We've been summoned to assist you and have accepted this role. Are you asking me to negate the terms?"

Lark stared at the man. This was his chance to tell the man they'd been wrong to come. He might not be allowed to leave, but so be it. He could find a way to keep Prophet quiet about the Concord's location, and the High Elder could go to the Vastness. But when he closed his eyes, he saw Seda's beautiful face, his daughter Luci's bright smile, and he lost all sense of himself.

"That's not what I meant. I'm hoping that we can work together, President Basher, and create a strong bond. The Concord will be delighted to have you in her ranks, and the Ugna are glad to have a powerful ally coming to their aid in a time of need. This is an important time in human history, and that of numerous other advanced races. I'm thrilled that you've agreed to join us. The Vastness welcomes all."

Lineage

Lark grabbed the glass, trying to make sure his hand didn't shake as he took another swallow of the red drink.

"Good. Now, tell me about the Concord, and what is this Vastness you speak of?" Basher leaned forward, and Lark began to recite the carefully practiced speech provided to him by this mission's benefactor, High Elder Wylen.

SEVENTEEN

Stepping onto the moon was a surreal moment in Brandon's life. It had been over twelve years since he'd last visited, making a supply delivery to the surface. He'd managed to speak with his brother then, if only for a few minutes. So many years ago, Clark had been too thin, his eyes sallow, his skin gray. That was the moment when Brandon had risked everything. Clark had listened to his plan to head to Mars without emotion, and by the end, his older brother thought he was kidding. He kept shaking his head, his expression reminding Brandon of the disappointment in their father's eyes when they were kids.

Brandon had left the moon shortly after, his brother saying he was done with the president and was happy to be far away, working on the frontier. That was what they were calling the newest outpost on the moon, and it was as apt a name as any. Except the same rules and laws imposed by the Invaders on Earth were here as well, meaning Clark was no freer here than at home.

"This is strange," Carl said, his voice muffled by the layered mask. His friend took the lead, exiting the designated shuttle pad, passing through a security checkpoint.

Brandon's heart raced as he spotted one of the Invaders: her long legs, her bald head, those piercing pink eyes. There was no one else in line, and Brandon fought to

Lineage

keep his composure. They weren't doing anything wrong. Their IDs labeled them as new workers for the crater project, and Brandon stepped to the lectern the woman stood behind.

"Welcome to Luna Seven." She didn't even glance up as she used a handheld device to scan their tags. "Enjoy your stay."

She said it with a sneer, knowing they were there to be worked like dogs in the fields, digging ditches and creating more space for agriculture. Carl paused as if he was going to comment, and Brandon lightly shoved him forward, whispering when they were past the security desk. "Not worth it."

Carl grunted but walked faster. "That was too easy."

"When's the last time anyone tried to sneak *onto* the moon? They're overconfident, and I can't blame them." Brandon stopped as they exited the building. The city had grown so much, he couldn't recognize any of it. The atmospheric bubble covered the moon, and he guessed the Invaders had terraforming technology they were utilizing. He'd heard rumors of it, but now he was beginning to believe them.

"This place is amazing," Carl whispered. "Imagine if we didn't have this oppression hanging over our heads, and we were able to live here."

Brandon let out a light laugh. "You do remember what Earth is like? The majestic mountains, the green grass?"

"Only in the A-Class zones. Most of it is scorched, remember?" Carl reminded him.

"You think the moon looks good because you've been living on Mars for a decade. Anything seems like paradise compared to our old rickety domes," Brandon said.

"Good point. Let's go find your brother. He didn't help you ten years ago, so what's to say he'll help now?"

Carl asked for the third time today.

"Trust me, he'll help," Brandon said with an assuredness he didn't feel.

The streets were wide, and Brandon moved to the side as a giant rover drove by, three trailers tethered behind it, kicking up dust in its wake. The main complex of buildings was a couple of kilometers away, and that was where they headed, walking along the edge of the road.

Brandon kept assuming they'd be stopped, and he observed a few drones hovering high above. Their ID tags must have been quality enough, because they weren't pestered by anyone—robotic, human, or Invader—by the time they arrived at the first of the residential compounds.

"Where do we start?" Carl asked, and Brandon stared at the beige multi-plex.

"Everything's too different. We're going to have to ask someone," he said, and Carl nodded, pointing to a masked woman near the entrance.

They strode across the promenade, happy to see a human face. So far, the place had felt barren, unused, and Brandon had begun to think things had progressed even worse than he'd expected.

"Hi. We're new, looking for a man named Clark. Clark Barrett."

All he could see were her bright blue eyes. They filled with tears at the mention of his brother's name. "Who are you?" the woman asked.

Carl stepped in front of him. "Lady, do you know where we can find him?"

She pointed over her shoulder, toward the edge of the city. "About five kilometers that direction."

"There's nothing out there," Brandon told her.

She nodded in response. "That's right. Nothing but a graveyard. Clark's been dead for three years."

Lineage

Brandon's chin dropped to his chest, and the air from his lungs froze in place. His brother was dead, along with his access into the president's palace.

"Who are you?" she asked again.

Brandon decided there was no need to lie. "I'm Brandon, his brother."

She pulled her mask off, rushing over to him. He caught a glimpse of her face, recognizing the young girl from his past. "Elya. Is that you?"

Her muffled cries into his shoulder answered the question.

"Who is this?" Carl asked, glancing around to make sure no one was watching.

"Friend. Her father worked in manufacturing for the Invaders," Brandon said.

"He did. He's dead too. Cassandra's still working near Saturn, or we think she is," Elya said, breaking her embrace.

Brandon had always respected their father. He'd helped them steal the freighter that had taken them to Mars and had assisted their initial supply needs.

"Tell me everything that's happened. We want to help." Brandon let Elya guide them into the building, out of sight from the hovering drones.

"And you're sure this uniform will pass muster?" Treena asked Cass, and the woman pursed her lips, running a finger over the front of the cloth.

"This is incredible. You did this based on a sketch in under a half hour." Cass was clearly impressed.

"The trick will be convincing Ven to wear it." Treena

laughed, and Ven entered the printing room, stopping a few feet short with his hands behind his back.

"You wanted to see me, Captain?"

"We're going to extract Cass's family from the moon, and to do that, we need to have a figure of authority with us."

Ven's gaze drifted to the red uniform. "And you would like me to play that role?"

"Yes. You'll play the Invader." Treena saw a flicker of something in his eyes, but he nodded along, silently agreeing to the terms. "Good. Grab Brax and meet us at *Cleo*." She held the garment out to him, and he took it, turning to stare at her from the room's exit.

"Are you coming to the surface with us, Captain?" he asked.

"I'm joining you, yes."

"That's not a good idea, Captain."

Treena walked toward him, Cass staying behind. "I know it's unorthodox, but I want to see what we're up against firsthand. These are humans, Ven. Technically, humans are Founders, which puts them under Concord protection. If they're being mistreated or enslaved, it's my responsibility as a Concord captain to help, if possible."

"There are too many of them," Ven said.

"Perhaps, but we know for a fact these Invaders are coming for us. How else did they receive Nek drive blueprints? This is all calculated, and I'll not let anything happen to the people of Earth." Treena spoke quietly, and Ven leaned in slightly.

"Captain, I understand your hesitation at leaving to return home, but if these Invaders are conspiring with someone within the Concord, we have to warn Nolix. The Prime must learn what's happening. I fear it's more important than the lives of the humans of Earth."

Lineage

"Be that as it may, we have to help them," she said firmly.

"But these humans are technically not part of our Concord, no matter which way you view it," Ven said, making good points.

"Meet me in ten minutes, and tell Brax to be prepared for an extraction," Treena said, not wanting to continue this argument in front of Cass.

"Yes, Captain." Ven departed, and Treena left Cass there while she darted through the corridor before taking the elevator to Deck One.

She found Reeve in her usual position, working over a console, with Harry at her side.

"Captain," Harry said, walking away.

"Reeve, where are we on the ship's identifications?" Treena asked.

"Cass's information was accurate. I've tweaked *Cleo* to read as one of the Invaders' private-issued vessels. Her records at the manufacturing station were a little old, so we're hoping nothing's changed in the past couple of years in their labeling system. I chose an Invader from their capital city. It's in a region known as New Europe, an island country." Reeve brought up the string of information, which was currently linked to *Cleo*'s computer system, and Treena grinned at her, patting the woman on the arm.

"Good work. Now we need find her family," Treena said.

Reeve spun slowly in the chair, turning to face her. "Why are we bothering? Can't you see how much of a risk we're taking?"

"What would you have me do?" Treena asked. "She helped us at Saturn. Without her, we couldn't have set the trap. And we made a promise."

"We could have destroyed the entire station," Reeve

suggested.

"They would have rebuilt or found another place to make the modifications. We're giving ourselves a real shot at being prepared for a war," Treena told her.

"That's if these Invaders are acting of their own volition. But the mere fact that they have Nek drive schematics at all tells us someone's working with them. It has to be the Ugna." Reeve's expression was unusually serious.

"I think you're right."

Reeve threw her arms up dramatically. "We don't know much. Someone directed us to Planet X for a reason. It's apparent the Ugna are a very old race, and that they brought in a million of their own people in a colony ship that once hit Earth. This tells me a lot."

Treena had almost forgotten that Reeve had been with Ven when the Ugna had killed the incoming Vusuls. She'd borne witness to their destructive potential and was probably right to fear them and their motives.

"Just make sure *Cleo* is clear, and I'll consider your suggestions." Treena departed. It was time to locate and obtain Cass's family. Then she had a decision to make, and it was already gnawing at her mind.

She rushed to the bridge, and the moment she entered it, she wondered if Ven was right. She glanced at Commander Pol Teller, and realized that if she left *Constantine*, she'd be putting the old man in charge.

Brax and Ven waited near *Cleo*'s hangar entrance above them, and Treena's chief of security stared at her, as if awaiting an important decision. Cass was with them, a frown over her forehead. She was ready to find her family. They were right. She was making rash decisions.

Her place was on *Constantine*. "Good luck, crew. *Be steadfast, be vigilant, be strong. The Vastness welcomes all.*"

Brax nodded once, and Ven brushed a crease from his

red uniform. He looked so different in the garb, surer of himself, and they departed.

Treena sat in the captain's chair, hoping it was the right decision, and Teller surprised her once again. His assistant was nowhere in sight, and she was glad.

"You're a good captain." His eyes sparkled as he said that.

"Time will tell." She sank into the seat, watching *Cleo* depart from her perch atop *Constantine*.

The Ugna-created version of the Concord flagship didn't seem quite as fast as *Shu,* but the weapons systems were state-of-the-art. It was a good thing Tom had a surprise or two in store for them.

"Captain, the Stickers are nearly ready." Hans' voice carried from the speaker. He was working endlessly on the devices in Engineering, and Tom sat up straighter as the image hit the viewscreen.

Four of the gadgets sat on the floor, and the drones were putting on the final touches, welding and soldering joints hurriedly.

Rene glanced at him, raising her eyebrows. "Stickers? You know these were banned after the War, right?"

Tom shrugged. "*Rules can be bent in times of need, so long as nothing is broken as a result.*"

"I never liked that one. It gives too much room for interpretation," she said.

"Do you not want to use them?" he asked.

"We'll use them, Baldwin. We'll use them."

Conner Douglas perked up at his console. "Captain, they've deployed their fighters."

"Tell Lieutenant Fehu to do the same," Rene ordered, and Tom watched as a dozen dots emerged near *Shu* on the radar. He missed the rush of flying one himself and wished his own personal fighter hadn't crash-landed when he'd been fighting the Statu and their Tubers.

Instead of coming to face *Shu*'s attack, the fighters from the Ugna vessel gave them a wide berth and attempted to move past them, tilting in Aruto's direction.

"Captain, the enemy is trying to breach our barricade," Commander Kan Shu advised.

"Then stop them," Rene ordered. The fighters were already past *Shu*, and Conner aimed at them, using the flagship's targeting system.

"These guys are slippery. They're blocking my tracking," Conner said.

Tom considered how that was possible. "I think they have Ugna pilots. They must be using their telekinesis to thwart the sensors," he muttered.

"Then we do this old school. Fehu," she called into the comm system.

"Go ahead, Captain." Fehu's voice was garbled, and it was clear she was racing toward an enemy in her lead fighter.

"They've managed to evade our trackers. Meaning you're going to have to do this another way."

"Got it, Captain. Switching to manual," she said, and Tom heard her relay the message to the other fighters.

The giant mirror of *Shu* finally began firing at them, and Tom grimaced as their shields took the brunt of the blows. Their vessel shook briefly, but Conner was already on it, sending an array of pulse blasts against the enemy as Kan guided *Shu* from the incoming Ugna.

Ven said the Vusuls had been within twenty kilometers when the Ugna were able to attack, and that was their range currently. The closer the enemy came, the farther Kan moved *Shu* away. As long as they were out of range, Tom hoped they were safe. Not to mention, there were far fewer Ugna here than had been near Driun F49. They hadn't been expecting opposition, and definitely not from *Shu* and Admiral Thomas Baldwin.

"Hans, where are we with the Stickers?" Rene asked, jabbing her finger hard against the console screen.

"Almost ready. Another ten minutes. We're calibrating now," he said.

One of their fighters caught an enemy ship, and they watched as the Ugna was destroyed by a well-trained trigger finger. Conner let out a cheer, but it was too premature to celebrate a minor victory. A planet stood waiting for an attack, and the entire Concord was in disarray.

The next encounter didn't go so smoothly. The Ugna ended the Concord fighter, and Conner's voice caught in his throat.

The assault on their shields ended momentarily, and Thomas watched as Conner increased his own attack. "Shield reading?" Rene asked.

Lieutenant Commander Asha Bertol answered. "Captain, they're scanning at seventy percent, and we're at sixty-three."

"Damn it. We need those Stickers."

"For someone that didn't want to use them, you're thanking me now," Tom told her.

"I'll thank you when we've won… Admiral," Rene said through gritting teeth.

More fighters faced off as they sped toward Aruto, and another two from each side were ruined within the next five minutes.

"They're kicking the star drive on," Kan warned.

Tom stood, not wanting to allow this vessel anywhere

near Aruto. They were a Founder; their reluctance to even partake in the Concord was high, and their loyalty was hanging by a thread. Tom had to protect them, prove the alliance was strong. They couldn't lose the Callalay, and he already respected and admired President Bertol.

"Hans, deploy the Sticker," he ordered the chief engineer.

"It's..." the man started to say through the speaker.

"Don't hesitate. Just do what I say. Target the rear shield generator," Tom ordered.

"Baldwin, this is my ship!" Rene barked, but he didn't care. This was their only chance before the star drive activated. Even if they could stop the enemy, the Ugna would be able to fire at Aruto from orbit, doing far more damage than was acceptable.

"Rene, trust me," he whispered, barely loud enough over the ringing klaxons for her to hear.

She gave him a curt nod, and he continued. "Hans, are we prepared?"

"Deploying the Sticker. Targeting the rear shield generator."

They watched the device onscreen, with the remote camera placed on its hull. It raced from *Shu* with computer-controlled precision, and quick pulses from its thrusters caused it to avoid the coming attack from the enemy flagship. The Tekol captain sensed the imminent threat, because he focused on the small device, giving Conner the ability to go on the offensive.

"Conner, the bow shield generator. Aim for it!" Tom shouted. His pulse remained steady, a bead of sweat pushed from his forehead. Rene stood beside him, watching as Conner sent everything they had against their adversary.

"Second Sticker deployed," Hans said, and Tom

Lineage

grinned, even though the first one was finally targeted and destroyed before doing its job. "Third Sticker deployed."

Hans must have understood Tom's motivation, because each of them went in a different direction, heading toward the positions on the ship that would require the most shield power to protect.

"Captain, their star drive is off," Kan shouted.

"You knew they'd have to divert their energy to the shields," Rene said.

Tom stayed silent as the second Sticker found its target. It blinked a few times and exploded, sending an electromagnetic pulse out instead of a giant detonation. The shields flickered, and the third Sticker entered, landing on the ship's hull.

Tom wanted to win, but he also wanted the prize. The Sticker did what it was intended to, and the entire vessel went dark. The alarms continued to ring out, but any incoming fire ceased.

"Captain, two of their fighters broke through our defenses and have changed course for Aruto," Lieutenant Fehu said from the cockpit of her own fighter.

"Track them down!" Rene said, but Tom wasn't overly concerned about two lone single-manned ships against what the president had waiting for any incoming enemies.

Tom watched as they neared the enemy ship that looked exactly like *Shu*. If they had the technology to sabotage a vessel so large, that meant the Stickers might eventually land in the Ugna's or some other opponents' grip. They'd kept the devices handy since Yollox, not wanting to give anyone the means to disable the Concord fleet ships. Tom was grateful to use them, but also regretted reactivating the old technology.

"Captain, I'm receiving a message," Kan said, and Tom was surprised when a familiar voice echoed through the speakers.

"Do not go any nearer to that ship, Captain Bouchard," Fayle said.

"Fayle, what in the Vastness are you doing here? Is this a trap?" Rene asked.

Tom was standing and staggered to the side, an immense pain growing in his temple. The other crew members began doing the same. Asha Bertol cried out, falling to the floor, and Tom saw blood.

"Kan, move us from them!" Tom shouted, and the young Callalay commander obeyed. He pounded the console, using the star drive to shoot them a few thousand kilometers away. Tom instantly felt better, and he used Conner's seat to right himself, holding it to remain steady. "Is everyone okay?"

There were scattered murmurs in response, but the crew appeared unharmed, despite the vicious attack on their minds. So this was what the Vusuls had faced, but they hadn't been lucky enough to avoid death.

"Get me Fayle," Tom barked, and her image emerged on the screen. She looked tired, her skin a pallid eggshell.

"Admiral," she said.

"Don't 'Admiral' me. What are you doing?" he asked.

"I was leaving. We have important business to attend to," Fayle said, straight-faced.

"Who are *we*?"

Someone moved closer from the shadows of the shuttle's cockpit.

"Jalin?" Tom asked.

"That is correct, Baldwin. You've done well, but there are far more moving pieces than you are aware of," Admiral Benitor said.

The shuttle flew toward the giant replica flagship. "What are you playing at? I'd recommend leaving them

Lineage

alone, unless you want one hell of a headache," Tom quipped.

Elder Fayle shook her head slowly. "If I do this, you cannot fear my position any longer, understand?"

"Do what?" Rene asked, arms crossed at her chest.

"I'll take their ship. We're going to need all the defenses we can get soon, and this is a great asset," Fayle said.

The hair on Tom's arms rose up at her words. "Fine. You bring me that ship, and I'll trust you. But by the end of today, I want to know exactly what's happening. If you want me to have faith in you… both"—he glanced at Benitor—"I want the same courtesy in return."

Fayle looked at her peer, who nodded in response. "Very well, Baldwin. You've earned that."

The shuttle was growing closer, and he heard Fayle advise the ship's captain of who she was, and that she was entering the hangar. It didn't seem like she was going to face any resistance. "*Until we meet in the Vastness*," he whispered, and the screen went dark.

Rene bumped into him gently. "She could be playing both sides."

"I fully expect her to," he told her.

"And we're okay with that?"

"As long as she's really on ours… yes." Tom wondered how Fayle could possibly take over the entire ship so easily.

EIGHTEEN

*V*en felt uneasy in the red uniform, pretending to be one of the local Invaders. *Cleo* had been tweaked to match the colorings of Earth's vessels, and Reeve had done a wonderful job duplicating the ID codes from the Invaders' fleet. No one had questioned them as the expedition ship landed on the moon.

Not one person had asked them to stop as they walked through security, the Ugna woman at the desk nodding in deference to Ven despite him lacking any sort of rank on his garb. He'd reached out as they'd passed her, but he'd felt nothing but emptiness from her emotions. Either she was dead inside or she was adept at barricading her mood internally.

"I don't like it," Brax said, his voice muffled by the mask over his face. He wore a dark hood, and so did Cassandra. There was an atmosphere, allowing them to breathe, as well as a gravitational generator. He'd witnessed them in action a few times over his life, but mostly on video feeds at the Academy. It wasn't something often used in the Concord.

The entire place was dusty, and he spotted a plume of dirt rising into the air a couple of kilometers to his left. The rover looked to be heading toward the giant crater where the locals were growing food. It was no small feat to

Lineage

develop a lifeless rock like this moon, and he was impressed with the Invaders' dedication to their mission.

He supposed taking over the human race and turning them into slaves was just the tip of the iceberg for these cousins of his. There weren't many people out and about, but the few they spotted as they entered the town wore masks and headgear like Brax and Cass, making Ven the only one out of place. His red uniform was a beacon amidst the grays and browns of the landscape, and each human they passed glanced at him, some with trepidation, others with contempt. He couldn't blame them, not after hearing how oppressed they were as a result of the Invaders.

Cass was a kind soul, a smart woman, and despite the risk and dangers, he was glad to see one of the colonies the humans lived on. He glanced up, admiring the gorgeous blue sphere in the distance. Cass had told them tales of a distant war, a near world-ending event that had left their people in ruin. These were the descendants of those survivors, the ones that hadn't departed with the initial outgoing group of humans that eventually settled on Earon and became a Founder of the Concord.

It was impressive that they'd managed to survive their plight, and countless years later, it had been taken from them by these Ugna. He wondered if the Invaders were aware of the Concord, or if they were only another piece on High Elder Wylen's game board.

"Follow me," Cass told them, guiding their group to the edge of the uneven street. A few drones hovered overhead, and Ven assumed they were security. His gaze caught a larger craft lifting in the distance, and he saw it was hauling a massive hunk of rock under it.

"What's that?" he asked Cass.

"They use pieces of the moon to build the structures. They're very proficient. The Invaders are as resourceful as they are repressive." Cass walked ahead, and Brax trailed after her, his gun concealed beneath his robes.

Ven wore an earpiece, and the message from *Constantine* came through with some heavy interference. "There's a vessel approaching. It's one of the Protectors, and it appears to be sending a lander to the surface." It was Darl, and he sounded concerned.

Brax would have heard the same communication, and he grunted, waving Ven forward. He leaned in, his voice gravelly. "Ven, we have to hurry. That might be someone coming to check on us. The moment they get a visual on *Cleo*, they'll see it's not one of theirs."

"Then we hurry," Ven said, loud enough for Cass to hear him. "Where are they?"

She shook her head. "It's been four years since I was able to visit. So much has changed." She scanned the area, her eyes crinkling as she pointed to a building's peak a kilometer away. "There. That was where my sister worked. She operates on the energy fields, ensuring the solar panels are in order and that the atmospheric pressure remains steady."

"Smart family," Brax said, making Cass grin beneath her mask. It reached her eyes.

Ven tensed as they neared the workplace. There were five armed human soldiers stalking around the complex, and Cass raised a hand, motioning for them to hide in the shadows. "This isn't good. They know we're here."

"We need to leave," Brax suggested.

"We can't. You promised you'd help extract my family," she pleaded.

Ven watched the soldiers combing the streets. "I don't think they are searching for us."

"What do you mean?" Brax asked.

Ven pointed further down the street. There were more

Lineage

armed humans, moving from a residential apartment block. It was utilitarian, bland stone and few windows. "We just arrived. They seek someone from that direction."

Brax's hand instantly reached for his gun, but Ven caught his wrist, stopping him.

"Let's find out what this is about. It might be a good distraction for our plan." Ven started forward, staying in the alley between the buildings. He suddenly wished he'd dressed in a mask and robe too, instead of standing out like a flame in the desert. He had an idea. "Follow my lead."

"You're not seriously going to walk up to them, are you?" Cass asked.

"I will merely ask what is occurring. You two, sneak off to your sister's workplace," Ven advised.

Brax grabbed hold of him by the shoulders. "Stay vigilant."

"Until we meet in the Vastness," Ven replied.

Ven stayed where he was while his two counterparts jogged off, and he stepped from the shadows, stepping in the middle of the stone walkway. A soldier instantly recognized Ven's uniform and assumed he was one of the Invaders.

"Sir, we've managed to track them to this quadrant. They stole a rover, and we have reason to believe they killed the Invader sent with it." The male soldier was tall, standing nearly as high as Ven.

Ven tried not to act surprised. So there was a fugitive human. It would be a good distraction, although it also meant there were a lot of active soldiers. He needed to divert their attention elsewhere. "These humans. How would they ever manage to defeat one of the Invaders?"

"We haven't been given that information, sir. But we do know one thing," the man said, his face contorted in anger.

"What?" Ven asked.

"Dissenters. The group that went missing a decade ago. I guess they were hiding out on Mars, and they've returned. But they aren't going to get very far without a ship." The guy laughed gruffly as a female soldier arrived. She glanced at Ven nervously and pointed toward the farmland.

"Plant called it in. A group sighted near the crater," she said.

"Move out, soldiers!" the lead man said. "You coming, sir? I'm sure you have a few questions for them."

Ven nodded, beginning to follow behind the regiment. He peered at the building Brax had left for and hoped his friend could find Cass's family, and quickly.

---

*B*randon watched through the window as the soldiers ran by, continuing as they headed for the false lead. Elya breathed a sigh of relief, meeting his gaze. She was older than he'd remembered, but he had been gone an entire decade. He was sure his own face was barely recognizable.

"It worked," Carl muttered. "Brandon, I've tried to reach Kristen and Jun."

Brandon's stomach sank. "And?"

"They aren't responding."

"They've taken over your vessel," Elya said. "How else did they know to search for you?"

"We took too long!" Brandon slammed a hand against the wall. "How do we solve this?"

Carl glowered. "Better yet, how do we save our friends?"

Shame flushed Brandon. He couldn't leave Kristen

Lineage

behind. He could only imagine what the Invaders would do to the recently captured human Dissenters.

"You don't…" Elya averted her eyes, looking to the ground.

"There has to be a way," Carl said.

"There isn't."

Something buzzed in Elya's pocket and she pulled a tablet free, tapping the screen. "Someone's at the plant." The woman smiled widely and pulled her mask over her mouth and nose, rushing for the door.

"Someone?" Brandon asked.

"She's here… she found Jason." Elya was a speed racer, darting through the hall and down the stone steps. Brandon chased after her, Carl at his heels, and a minute later, they were pressing through the apartment's main exit, cautiously scanning around. Elya checked her tablet, which was linked into the surveillance drones. "Coast is clear. Two soldiers." She pointed through the alley to their left. "We go right."

"Elya, who is it?" Brandon asked, and she slowed enough for him to hear the answer.

"Cassandra. My sister, and she wants to take me with her."

Brandon's mind raced a mile a minute as they crossed the few blocks, ending at Elya's workplace.

They crept around the corner of an outbuilding, Carl holding a gun as if expecting trouble around every bend.

"Elya," a voice said, and Brandon relaxed when he spotted Cass.

The sisters embraced, and Brandon noticed the huge man behind the mechanic.

"Hi. I'm Brax, and I'm here to extract you."

233

*E*lder Fayle guided the shuttle through the energy field onto the strange replica vessel. She'd known about the manufacturing facility nearby, Obilina Six, but hadn't pressed High Elder Wylen on it. She'd tried to bring it up once, and he'd threatened her in the same mild manner he always had. With Wylen it was "blindly do my bidding, or you and everything you love will die."

For years, she'd obliged, but since arriving at Driun F49, she couldn't continue on that path any longer. He'd been working on this for ages, as had his predecessors, but Fayle also had her own plans, which involved getting her people to a colony and out of hiding. But now was the time to thwart the next stage of Wylen's mission.

The Concord could not fall. Instead of being the enemy, Fayle wanted to go in the other direction. To save the Concord from Wylen, while keeping their planet and standing within the Concord. The first step had been convincing Jalin Benitor of her motivations, and that had allowed *Shu* to be sent to defend Aruto. To ensure they didn't let Aruto be destroyed as the High Elder wanted, Fayle had to have Baldwin involved.

From the past year, Fayle had been confident Thomas Baldwin was the most capable human she'd ever met. Tom had a skill of making others around him better. Whether he was an officer, captaining his own ship, or hitching a ride on *Shu*, people stepped up when he was near. It was impressive, and she wished she could have seen him grow up as an Ugna. There were techniques to force it into someone, contrary to what they'd told the Concord, but it was impossible to know who would eventually grow to become great.

Ven Ittix had that potential. She'd seen it in the boy the

Lineage

moment she'd met him so many years ago. He'd never comprehended how high she ranked within the Ugna hierarchy, and Fayle was glad for it. Their village had been one of the most remote and rudimentary, modeled after the old world.

As the shuttle's engines turned off, Elder Fayle stood, her knees protesting at the action. Her back was beginning to stoop, her neck in a state of perpetual aching. She couldn't kid herself any longer. Even though the En'or extended their lives, she was far too old to be traipsing around stopping centuries-old diabolic schemes like this.

"Are you ready, Elder?" First Officer Hanli said, offering her arm. This one was astute. She could tell Fayle was suffering and wanted to assist her. That was good, because where they were about to go, Hanli would need to be strong at her side.

"I am always prepared, Hanli. The better question is, are you ready?" Fayle turned to face the young woman, and her eyes flickered with uncertainty. Hanli's expression changed, her masseter muscles clenching tightly along her jaw.

"I would do anything for my people, Elder Fayle." She lowered her voice. "I'd do anything for you."

Fayle patted the back of the woman's hand three times and moved for the exit. "Then stay close." She took a deep breath, sealing her eyes shut. This was it. The En'or vials were in her deep pockets one second; the next, they hovered in front of the pair of Ugna women. "Don't use it yet. We want the element of surprise."

Hanli nodded, reaching for one of the vials. She tucked it inside her gray jumpsuit and clicked a gun onto her wide black belt.

Admiral Benitor had watched all of this without expression, and she rose finally, staying at least six feet from them. "Take care. *To rule absolute is an atrocity, to rule with care is a kingdom that will endure.*"

Fayle smiled at the old adage and pursed her lips. It was time to go.

She exited the shuttle first, leaving Hanli to trail behind her. She'd been expecting to be welcomed, but not by the sole captain himself.

"Greetings, Elder," the Tekol man said.

Fayle grinned in return. "You did well to scare them off. I apologize for intruding during such a battle, but the High Elder thought we might be of assistance." Emergency lights lit the hangar, one in each corner, casting strange shadows of the captain over the floor.

"It appears you're right on time. They've been more effort than we were told to expect. We had no idea the Concord would be present with one of their flagships."

I did, Fayle thought. Jalin was the reason Tom had been sent, knowing what they'd be facing. Their relationship had started out rocky, but soon they'd become fast friends, especially after she'd spilled the entire Ugna plan to the head admiral.

Fayle had also managed to utilize someone's assistance in reprogramming the Nek drive on *Constantine*. She wished she could have seen Starling's face when they'd found the Ugna village. Ven was with them, and she knew for a fact he would recognize it.

She'd expected *Constantine* to use the Nek drive to return to Concord space immediately, and it worried her thinking they may have actually traveled to Earth. If they were caught, the Invaders would use them as an example.

"Follow me, Elder."

"Captain Gunale, how many crew members do you have?" Fayle asked as they walked toward the hangar's exit.

"Basically a skeleton crew. Twenty-three. As you know,

Lineage

the ship is mostly empty rooms built on the flagship schematics, but only engineering and the weapons systems are built to spec," Gunale told her.

Twenty-three. That should be simple enough. This man worked for High Elder Wylen, as did so many others, and Fayle couldn't let herself feel remorse for what they were about to do. This was war. The Ugna could not win. Not with everything at stake. Sacrifice your own kind so that the rest can survive. It was an ancient problem, as old as the cosmos itself.

Fayle smiled at the man, and he turned to press the hangar door open. Fayle gave Hanli the signal, and they each pressed the vials to their skin. The En'or shot in, streaming through their blood. Fayle's eyes felt like they'd exploded, her fingertips alive again. Her aches melted away, and her cumbersome concerns for life dwindled like flames on a doused fire.

She didn't need Hanli, not yet.

Fayle floated from the ground, her eyes burning with power. A sickening sound emerged from Captain Gunale's throat, and he sank to the ground, dead.

"Hide him," Fayle ordered, and she could see that Hanli was in a similar euphoric state. Normally the death of an Ugna would affect them deeply, but they were one with the Vastness, swimming in the current of the universe.

Gunale's body lifted as Hanli used her telekinesis to move him to the edge of the room. She opened a locker, shoving the corpse inside. The door closed loudly, and Hanli's eyes snapped toward Fayle apologetically.

"There are twenty-two more, and we are only two Ugna. Remain vigilant." Elder Fayle stepped into the hall, her feet landing softly. She had one kill today, and she wished that would be enough.

She moved for the elevator. There were at least four

on Deck One. "Come, child. We have work to do."

Hanli strode beside her as they entered Engineering, and Fayle's hand grasped the woman's forearm, sapping her strength as the four crew members died within seconds. Their bodies crumbled to the floor, and Fayle counted down.

Eighteen to go.

They returned to the elevator, seeking the next encounter.

―――――

Brax wasn't sure how they could pull this off, but he was willing to try. His captain had asked them to free Cass's family, and this group of people was all that she had left.

"You're from Mars?" Brax asked the two men.

One had dark skin, his eyes light brown, and he glanced around nervously. The other was shorter, his hair slightly gray along the edges. He was the one that answered. "Name's Brandon. We were living out in the old colony on Mars, before they discovered us and tried to destroy us."

Brax didn't know anything about an old colony, but he supposed any human here would. "And you fought?"

"We did," the other man said. "I'm Carl."

"I'm Brax. Brax Daak," he said.

"Where you from, Brax Daak? I've never heard a name like that before," Cass's sister said.

They were in the back room, a utility shed behind the power plant, and Brax was glad for the dim lighting. He slid the mask off and removed the head covering, revealing himself to them.

"He's not human," Cassandra said pointedly.

"I can see that," Brandon said. "If you don't mind me

asking, what are you?"

Brax was aware that these humans had only ever seen the Ugna Invaders, and no other aliens. While Tekol were similar to humans within the Concord, they were distinct enough for it to be obvious to these people.

"It doesn't matter, Brandon. If we're leaving this moon, now's the time," Brax said.

"We can't abandon our friends," Carl said firmly.

Brax considered this. "Your ship has been compromised, correct?"

Brandon nodded. "They boarded it. They were waiting for us, but we've sent them on a wild goose chase."

Brax had no idea what a goose was, but he continued. "My friend is with them. I can communicate with him and keep tabs on the soldier's position."

Elya showed him her tablet, and he squinted, seeing the aerial view of the gardens. The crater was far wider than Brax had initially assumed. The people resembled small specks as they walked the perimeter. Brax thought he could see Ven's red uniform from the drone feed.

"We have an escape route, in the dock, but I doubt I can return without Ven." Brax leaned against the wall, tapping his toe on the floor, trying to find a solid option.

"I have it," Cass said.

Brax waited, and when she didn't elaborate, he impatiently waved his hand. "Spit it out."

"We need to separate Ven from the soldiers. Elya, do you still have friends at the gardens?" Cass asked.

"Sure. I can send Terry a message, but he's not going to like being thrown in a cell again," Elya said.

"Are we going to be able to help our people?" Brandon asked, stepping closer to Brax. "Wherever you come from, is it far away?"

Brax nodded.

"Then you can return, help us..." Carl started toward him too, and Brax stepped back.

"Look. My captain will do what she can, but we have to go home, and soon. There's a lot at play, and we don't have time to stop a tyranny." Brax instantly regretted it, but he kept talking. "But the Concord will not let this pass without justice. Humans are a Founder of our alliance, a cornerstone to our entire Concord. And because of that, we will do everything in our power to help Earth become free once again."

This seemed to ease the tensions, and the two men smiled at one another. They clasped hands, and briefly hugged. "Clark would be so stoked to see this. An alien from the Concord, promising us aid. Where do we sign up?" Brandon asked Brax.

"Looks like you already have." He pressed his earpiece and explained the scenario to the captain and Ven.

Treena's command was quick and concise. "Bring *Cleo* home and take the others with you. Ven, use your authority to make this happen, and be quick about it. I'm growing nervous out here. We can only remain unseen for so long."

"Yes, Captain," Brax said, ending the call. "Ven, you hear that? There's about to be a commotion out at the crater. My advice? Move out as soon as the smoke rises."

"Smoke?" Ven asked.

"It's a figure of speech," Brax said. The truth was, he had no clue what kind of distraction this Terry would have in store for the soldiers. "Time to go. Elya, make the call."

NINETEEN

Ven checked his tablet, finding Brax's position. They were advancing to the landing pad, and he still hadn't seen a distraction from the human contact at the fields.

The crater was deep, at least two kilometers at the lowest point, and giant machines floated into it. It looked like most of the humans living here were inside the crater at this time. It was the work shift, and there had to be over four hundred active employees around the crater.

The soldiers had spread out, but so far, their targets had been elusive.

"Sir, what would you have us…?" Plant started to ask, but halted as a detonation hit the side of the fields. Rocks erupted, sending a small avalanche over the crater's hillside. Plant turned, rushing toward the catastrophe. He muttered something about being underpaid, and Ven listened as the man barked out a series of orders over a communication device in his hand.

Ven froze, waiting for them to forget he was even there. He didn't move for another two minutes, but eventually, he let loose. It was time to act. He'd been avoiding using his Ugna skills, mostly out of principle. He did feel stronger than ever, and despite the urgings from his peers on Driun F49, he hadn't consumed En'or in a long time. It didn't matter. He was flush with strength.

Ven ran. Gravity was light, and he pushed off with each bound, sending himself farther and farther ahead with the leaps. He covered a few kilometers' distance in the matter of a minute and saw he was going to beat Brax to the docks.

"Ven, another vessel is arriving. A Protector. You have about ten minutes before they're within range," Lieutenant Darl told him through his earpiece.

He had to act quickly. The woman behind the moon city's security desk rose as he entered, and Ven used a palm to wipe off dust, trying to keep his expression unimpressed. "Where is the recently acquired craft?"

"Sir?"

"The one with the detainees. I have been instructed by the president to bring them with me," Ven said, keeping his voice low and commanding.

"Are you... I don't see any record of such a request," she said, fiddling with her console.

"Stop it!" his voice boomed. "Do you dare question my motives?"

She hesitated, staring up from the console before speaking. "No, sir. It's only that..."

"I do not have time for this." He used his mind to open the door and ran for the exit.

"Bay Five. They're in Bay Five."

Ven recalled that *Cleo* was in Bay Four, and he strode through the halls, not bothering to pause at the soldiers stationed outside the Invader ship. It was typical Ugna in design, familiar, yet different enough to make him stare.

"Where are the detainees?" Ven asked.

"They're on board. The senior administrator is coming. She's instructed us to hold them until they arrive." The soldier looked at a device on his arm. "Which should be in the next ten minutes."

Ven nodded. "Change of plans. She's asked me to

Lineage

bring them to her."

The man flushed and shook his head. "Sir, this is the senior administrator. She's not going to be happy…"

Ven shoved the man backwards, sending him against the wall with nothing but the pressure of the air. "Do you think I am a fool?" Ven asked, using his best accusing tone. He was starting to enjoy playing a tough character, but only hoped his hasty plan worked.

"No, sir…"

"Bring them out! I'm taking them in my private craft. These people are terrorists and will be dealt with covertly. Do you think we want them ushered around in Invader vessels, causing more human tongues to wag than usual?" Ven barked.

The man paled and glanced at his partner, a tall woman who'd been silent until now. She stalked toward the stolen ship, and Ven followed her.

The crew members were tied up in the cargo hold, under twenty of them in total. Ven felt their devastation at being caught, their dreams shattering at their capture. He played along. "To your feet, humans. Dissent is not permitted, and you will be tried for your actions."

A woman, who he assumed to be their leader, stepped up to Ven and locked gazes with him, unafraid. "Since when does the president try anyone? He murders, that's what he does. He's killed our futures, all of us. But what would an Invader know about that? Nothing." She walked past him, hitting his shoulder with hers, and the others exited after her.

Ven smiled inwardly. He liked their spirit, never giving up on their ideologies despite terrible circumstances. He couldn't throw in the towel yet either, not on his people. There were too many good Ugna.

The soldiers began following him through the corridor

to Bay Four, but he held a hand up, stopping them. "You stay here. Clear the ship. Make sure they have not set any traps. The last thing we need is for the moon dock to be blown up because of incompetence."

The man's eyes went wide, and he jogged off, going for the ship's ramp.

"We are heading to Bay Four," Ven called to the lead woman, and she stopped at the door.

"Why would you move us now?" she asked, and the others parted the corridor, allowing Ven through.

He leaned closer and even passed her a grin. "Because that's where Brandon and Carl are waiting with the others."

The lady's face went slack, and she broke into a run, finding *Cleo*'s door hinged open. Ven saw Cass with a woman that looked similar to her, along with the two men the soldiers had been searching for across the barren city.

Brax peeked over their heads from the pilot's seat. "Everyone in. This is going to be a tight fit, but we can make room."

Ven waited while the refugees entered the expedition ship, and he climbed in last, sealing the doors shut.

"It seems we're out of time," Brax told him. "The Protector is here."

"How did she do it?" Rene asked Tom as they stared out the expedition vessel's viewscreen. Hans sat between them, his fingers tapping nervously on the dash.

"Elder Fayle has her own distinct means." Tom recalled the first time they'd stepped foot on Driun F49, when the tree creatures had ambushed them. She'd killed the beasts within seconds. He also remembered how Ven

Lineage

had been so adamant that the Ugna preached against violence of any kind. Now he understood their teachings.

The Ugna's leadership was trained to kill. To rule with impunity. The acolytes, the children, the young impressionable minds, were taught to be kind, placating, and moral. When push came to shove, and the Ugna made the move to take over the Concord, they would have a million people that trusted their leaders could never harm another soul. They prayed to the Vastness, meditated on their actions, and consumed unlawful substances to gain an advantage. The Elders, along with this creepy High Elder Wylen, were drug dealers and dictators at the same time.

Tom only wished someone had seen it before it was too late.

"Hans, we need you to recharge the drive and bring it to working order. We must return to Aruto at once and continue to Nolix," Rene said.

"I wish we had a Nek drive too," Tom said quietly.

"We'll be at the capital soon enough. The Prime is a smart man. He'll dissuade any imminent attacks. The people of the Concord will understand," Rene said.

Tom watched her over Hans' mostly bald head. She was worked up. He could see it in the whiteness of her knuckles, the way the left side of her lips twitched, and the fact that her brows were permanently set in a frown.

"The people of the Concord are agitated. They think ships like *Shu* and *Constantine* are harassing helpless planets. They'll act before thinking, because that's the kind of partners we've curated over the years. If the leadership was bullying anyone in Concord space, I'd join the revolt, but we have to convince them it wasn't us," Rene said in a rush.

"Easier said than done. Not to mention, they'll blame us for allowing the Ugna in as a partner when the truth is revealed. We'll see repercussions for years," Tom said.

"But we have to survive first and deal with the lumps after."

The other flagship grew larger in their screen. Tom's plan had worked, and now he trusted that Elder Fayle was actually on their side. He'd fought hard to keep Rene on board *Shu*, but she wouldn't have any of it. He was glad to have her along. Something had changed in their relationship, and spending time with the robust captain had become more... interesting.

They entered the hangar, the back-up generator keeping life support and airlocks in check. The Stickers were good, but these newest designs were built to prevent loss of basic needs.

Hans stood impatiently, trying to climb over Tom, who obliged him by sliding from the seat. The moment they exited the ship, he saw Fayle. Someone stood beside her, and he recognized her as First Officer Hanli, the same woman Ven had been spending a lot of time with.

"Good to see you, Admiral," a voice said from beside him, and Tom glanced over to the parked shuttle.

"Admiral Benitor, likewise," Tom said, but it was Rene who left the formalities at the door.

"Benitor, what in the Vastness is going on?" Rene crossed the handful of steps in a flurry. Tom thought she was about to physically assault the old Callalay woman, but she reined herself in, towering in front of her.

"Bouchard, you're out of turn," Jalin said.

"I don't think so. You up and vanish from Ridele, and don't tell anyone? You leave the Prime high and dry, the very same man you fought to put in the most important seat in the Concord? You send Tom with *Shu* on a basic diplomatic mission, only so we could be side-swiped by this mess!" Rene's finger hovered near Jalin's chest.

Benitor's mouth opened, but it was Elder Fayle who

responded to the accusations. "It was my fault, Captain. We conspired to this together. I realized I had no allies within the Concord, none that would protect my people when they learned the truth."

"What about Tom?" Rene asked, but Tom knew why Fayle hadn't come to him.

"I was already digging up dirt on the Ugna. I haven't trusted them since day one, and Fayle knew it," Tom admitted.

Fayle nodded, and Tom noted that Hanli was propping her up. They were both exhausted, ready to drop to their knees.

"How many Ugna did you kill?" Tom asked.

"Too many," Fayle said. It was evident that her heart ached for the Ugna she'd killed for the sake of the Concord.

Hans stood to the side, and Tom glanced at him. "Is it safe in Engineering?"

Hanli nodded. "The bodies have been cleared."

"Good. Hans, would you get started?" Tom asked, and the engineer grabbed his heavy pack. A drone followed him from inside, carrying a charger with it. When Hans was out of the hangar, their group moved closer to one another. It was dark in the room, and Tom squinted as Jalin finally spoke.

"Tom was on the right track, but when Fayle came to me the last time, we knew we needed to expedite things. Wylen is no fool, and he was using the time properly. With Baldwin out of a flagship, and the capable crew of *Constantine* gone on a long journey, he made his move," Benitor said.

"It doesn't excuse Fayle for waiting to share that information," Rene complained.

Tom instantly recognized the flicker in the Callalay

admiral's eyes. "You knew," he whispered.

Benitor nodded. "Fayle advised me of their plan some time ago."

"Then why did you give them Driun F49?" Tom asked, outraged.

"Because it was better to know where they were, especially with what they were planning. They were always going to attack us, Baldwin. Always. Think about it. Wouldn't you rather have the enemy where you can see them and deal with them appropriately?" Benitor asked.

He tried to consider her reasoning, but it fell flat. "What about these manufacturing plants? How did you let them create a damned space fleet that looks like ours?"

Fayle's knees gave out, and Tom rushed to her aid, catching her before she hit the ground. "I wasn't included in those plans. Wylen evidently didn't trust me with everything."

"For good reason," Rene murmured.

They moved the spent Ugna women to the expedition vessel, settling them onto the rear bench. "You mentioned *Constantine*. Is she in danger?" Tom asked.

Elder Fayle nodded. "I disrupted them."

Rene was still fuming, and it was clear in her tone. "You what? You sabotaged them?"

"Nothing like that. Ven had to see it. The first Ugna village. It's thousands of years old. I believed they'd shout foul play and return."

"Why didn't you tell us instead?" Tom asked. "We could have stopped this before it started."

Fayle shook her head. "There is no stopping Wylen, not when he gathers his forces of Ugna aboard his colony vessel. He will destroy anything and everything if he doesn't get his way."

"What's at Earth?" Rene's voice lowered, stayed quiet.

Fayle met her eyes, then stared at Tom. Her eyelids grew heavy. She was wearing out. "We are. Wylen sent someone there to bring reinforcements. I suspect they'll return with reinforcements within a month."

"The Ugna are at Earth?" Tom almost laughed at the incredulous idea. "I thought it was a human world."

"It is. The Ugna own them."

Tom's heart rate picked up. "Starling might be in big trouble."

"Captain Starling can take care of herself, Thomas." Fayle's words were accurate, but he still worried about his old ship and crew.

The hangar buzzed, and Tom peered out the expedition vessel's open doors, seeing the lights flick on. "Looks like Hans worked his magic. A month? Who did they send to recruit these Ugna?" Tom asked, but his gut answered for him. "You have to be kidding me."

"Who else?" Benitor told them. "I guess Lark Keen continues to be a thorn in the Concord's side."

Asteri arrived at Saturn slightly ahead of schedule. Lark guessed the president was impatient to begin the modifications. In the end, only nineteen Protectors had made the trip, with one being called to the moon colony for an unknown reason. He'd asked, but the crew members weren't very forthcoming with a stranger.

"What do you think? Smoother than you'd expected?" Prophet found him near the courtyard. The Protectors were impressive vessels, far more advanced than the old fleet ships the Assembly had procured from Earon Station. He did think *Constantine* still had the upper hand compared with *Asteri*, but it was irrelevant. When these nineteen battle-ready Invader crafts skipped to the Concord, ready to join Wylen's impressive fleet, there would be no stopping their combined forces.

The Ugna would take control, Lark would be given a big important title, and more importantly, his wife and daughter would once again be by his side.

"Keen?" Prophet nudged him with an elbow, and he forced a smile.

"I'd say you can take some of the credit. Who are you, really?" he asked. He'd seen how easily she'd dispatched his crew, and how dispassionate she seemed about everything, like nothing mattered beyond the moment she lived in.

"I grew up near Beacon on Aruto and was removed from my home when I was seven years old." Her eyes were dark, and she ran a hand over the ridges on her forehead, taking a seat on a hard bench across from him. The courtyard didn't have the lush advancements of Baldwin's ship, but it was pleasant and bright, and gentle instrumental music played through hidden speakers.

"That's how they do it, right? The Ugna? They find kids with telekinesis and bring them in?" Keen asked. Honestly, he wasn't overly familiar with the Ugna. Up until a couple of years ago, they'd been as big a mystery as anything within the Concord.

"Yes. But with the other races, I've always wondered." She leaned her elbows onto her knees, resting her chin on her hands.

"Wondered what?"

"How. Why does it happen?"

"Would you have preferred to stay with your family?" Keen asked. Saying the word reminded him of all he'd given up on accepting this mission.

Lineage

"I'm not sure. I don't remember them. Just the odd thing, like the smell of my kitchen when mother was cooking, or the scent of my father as he returned from his day in the fields. We were simple folk. People who'd be scared to lose a child to this illness, and also people who could use the money the Ugna offered in exchange."

"They paid for you?" Keen asked.

"They always do."

He couldn't imagine parents giving away their kids, but knew the Ugna were persuasive if necessary. "Have you ever returned home?"

"To Aruto? No. Nothing there for me."

"You became an assassin for the High Elder. You must have a long tale to tell," Keen said.

She acted shocked at his accusation but didn't deny it. "It's not as complicated as you might assume. I showed aptitude. He brought me to a secret planet, tucked away a couple of months from the Border. No one knew where we hid."

"A planet? What's it called?" Lark was no fool. His back might end up against a wall, and he needed all the small details he could gather while he had a chance.

"Tebas. Nothing special, but they terraformed it to a Class Zero-Nine."

Terraformed. That was interesting. He filed the name away and tried to keep her talking. "And then what?"

"He took me under his wing after a few years. Not many acolytes gained his attention, and I thought I was special."

"Weren't you?"

"I suppose. But I was nothing more than a tool. Which I'm okay with," Prophet said.

"I guess we aren't that different, you and me. I was convinced of a path when I was a youth, and chose it rather than following along with my best friend into the Concord ranks. There's been no turning back." Lark smiled at her, despite the weight on his shoulders. Something about this felt wrong, but he was in no position to change anything.

"It's astounding, Keen."

"What's that?"

"That a single decision can determine the rest of your life. One choice, and everything changes. I know we make them constantly, hundreds a day, but there comes a time when you're asked something and you know, deep down, that it's the road that will either propel you to excellence or spark your demise."

"And yours… which one is it?" Lark asked.

Prophet blinked and stared at him before shrugging. "I can't say yet. I guess time will tell." She rose, pointing at the viewscreen. "We're decelerating. We've made it to Saturn."

Lark didn't stand; he only watched her depart and sank into his seat. If his one choice had been following Seda's father's advice to join the Assembly twenty years ago, he wondered if it was possible to make another decision that could push him in the opposite direction. One he could be proud of.

Lark stood, stretching his legs before striding through the corridors leading to the bridge. He thought about Prophet's words, and how she felt like she was nothing more than a tool for the High Elder.

He was no man's puppet.

"Where are they?" Treena asked herself, pacing the bridge.

Lineage

"Would you sit down, Captain?" Pol Teller asked. "You're making me dizzy!"

Treena grimaced, catching the man's assistant staring at her. She took his advice and seated herself. The probe feeds showed the Protector arriving in the moon's orbit, and finally, after a few breathless moments, *Cleo* began its escape.

"Captain, Brax here. We've begun our ascent. We'll move for rendezvous," the lieutenant commander said through the speakers.

"Reeve, are we ready for the jump?" Treena asked, targeting Engineering.

Reeve's voice sounded tinny through the speaker. "We have course set for Nolix, deep system."

Everything was working out fine. They'd discovered the Ugna on Earth, managed to sabotage the Nek modifications on the Protectors, and had more intel into what Earth really held. They'd sent dozens of information-gathering probes to Earth but hadn't been able to comb through the data yet. There would be ample time for that once they returned home.

Treena couldn't wait to meet with Baldwin and tell him about their discoveries in Sol. She wished they'd been able to investigate Earth firsthand, but things were escalating. Whoever had come here to share the Nek schematics with these Invaders hadn't done so unselfishly. Treena felt that an attack on the Concord was imminent, but with their trap, she was confident they'd at least delay it.

Pol leaned toward her, his breath stale. "You know, Captain, we could head to Earth. Deliver some news." His bushy white eyebrows bobbed under his wrinkled forehead.

"Are you suggesting we attack Earth?"

"Take this on the offensive. These buggers are all over

this place. It's been infested with them. I say we eradicate the lot, so we don't have to concern ourselves with them later," he told her quietly.

Treena hoped the others weren't listening in. She glanced behind Teller, and saw his aide was trembling. "Are you out of your mind, Commander?" She said his title with distaste.

"Listen up, Captain. We're trained in the Concord to do what is necessary. You think allowing this scum to survive is going to be a good thing for our people? You believe they'll let it go when they discover it was us behind losing twenty solid warships?" He seemed to be waiting for a response she wasn't offering. "Didn't think so. They're going to come at us hot and heavy, and that's why I say we nuke the buggers now and be done with it. They didn't build these ships for show, you know that, right?"

Teller spoke with more fervor and passion than she'd ever heard from the man. Perhaps he was onto something. There was a reason Admiral Benitor had sent this man to her side, and it wasn't for the company. Treena hated his thought process but had to consider it. His logic was sound, but there were too many innocent lives on Earth, and she told him as much.

"You have no idea how many there are. The girl didn't know, did she?" he asked, inferring Cassandra.

"Cass hadn't been to Earth in a decade. But she estimated millions," Treena told him.

He grunted contemptuously. "Estimated. The girl has no idea what's even there. She grew up in some desert in the middle of nowhere. All she knows is what the buggers told her."

Another solid point.

"Captain, the Protector has targeted *Cleo*. They've set course, heading in our direction. And by all accounts, their shields have been raised, their energy readouts suggesting their weapons systems are online," Lieutenant Darl said.

She wished Brax and Ven were on the bridge with her. "Reeve, activate the star drive. This is going to be a close one."

"So you won't fight? We could beat that ship, I'm sure of it," Teller said.

"Our information is too valuable, but I appreciate you speaking up. You're a good commander." Treena meant it. His reasoning for suggesting they attack Earth on their own terms was sound, and one that was engrained into them at the Academy, but that didn't involve killing innocent people in the crossfire. Not to mention that humans were Founders. Had there been any innocents, she wouldn't have pulled the trigger. Not like that. She'd give them a fair fight in the end, if they made it that far.

Cleo pushed her limits, racing toward *Constantine*, and Treena glanced at the ship's namesake, his AI projection a couple of meters to her right. "Con, go to them if your Link is in range. Tell Brax to dock in motion. We need to move."

"Done." The AI flickered and vanished.

Darl glanced at her. "They'll be in firing range of us in forty-seven seconds."

"They're already in range of Brax. Focus on defending *Cleo*. Reeve, once you see your brother has docked, activate the Nek drive and send us home." Treena released the communication with Engineering and watched the expedition ship near them through the viewscreen.

TWENTY

*V*en felt the power of the Ugna in the Protector closing in on them. The Invaders' ship was faster than their expedition vessel, and far better armed. The first blast struck their shields, shaking the craft as Brax clenched his teeth, forcing *Cleo* toward its dock above the bridge.

"Come on, give me a few more minutes," Brax said.

The group of survivors from the moon filled the entire hold of the ship, and their leader, the man named Brandon, rushed up behind Ven. "Can I help in any way?"

"Not unless you know how to use a targeted pulse beam," Brax said.

"Sounds easy enough," Brandon said, taking the third seat, a fold-down chair connected to the pulser's controls.

"I don't have time to teach you, but you'll figure it out," Brax told him.

Ven closed his eyes, sensing the Invaders reaching out to assault the ship. Their minds were merging, using a different form of attack than he'd ever seen the Ugna attempt. Ven threw his own shield up, encapsulating the entire expedition ship within his canopy. Another shot struck their shields, but they were close to *Constantine*.

"Come on, Darl. Stop moving so much," Brax whispered, and Ven opened his eyes, letting his mind protect the others. His barriers were battered by the Invaders

Lineage

aboard the adversarial Protector, but Ven held them at bay.

Another blast, and *Cleo* jarred lower, nearly sending her into *Constantine*'s hull. Their flagship was huge on the viewscreen, and Ven held his breath as Brax tugged on the yoke, throwing them upwards along the edge of the larger vessel's shields.

"Almost there…"

"I think I have it!" Brandon shouted, and Ven tried staying in his meditative state. Shots fired from *Cleo*, but Ven could tell they went wide of the target. It didn't dissuade Brandon from aiming again. A few more attempts, and he was striking the Protector's shields.

Constantine was moving quickly, and the familiar lights danced around Ven's vision. They were the same ones he'd seen since saving Brax's life in the Nek shuttle… when Ven had died.

And been brought to life by Elder Fayle.

The dots grew in size as he continued fighting off the Invaders' mental assault, streaking by his vision in wide loops. He felt like he could step into the Vastness, if he so chose.

"Ven, what are you doing, buddy?" Brax asked, but Ven was standing, staring at the viewscreen.

The lights went faster, in a circular and hypnotic pattern, and he waved a hand in front of his face.

"Brax, hurry." Ven observed Constantine was there with them. The AI projection stood solemnly.

"Con, what are you doing?" Brax asked.

"*Constantine* has to go to keep from being struck. You need to dock on the fly. Would you like me to take over?" Constantine asked, and Ven heard Brax shift in his seat.

"I'll shift to automatic controls, if you think you can latch on better than I can," Brax told the AI, and the young version of Admiral Baldwin's grandfather laughed.

"That won't be a problem," he told them.

Ven continued to feel the pressure building from the Invaders, and he could sense over a hundred of the enemy piled onto the Protector.

He couldn't let them harm *Constantine* or these people on *Cleo*. These humans had been through too much and were about to be given a chance at freedom within the Concord. It was up to Ven to protect them. The lights danced excruciatingly fast, a constant whirlwind of the Vastness. Was he dying? Was this the end?

He shouted, sending forth all his anger toward the Protector, and everyone in *Cleo* went silent. He was empty, devoid of any emotion, of any telekinetic energy. It was as if his batteries had been diffused of power. A few seconds later, Ven felt them docking, and he blinked his eyes open.

Brax was at his side, holding Ven by the shoulders. "Ven, did you do that?"

Ven was unsure what he meant. He was tired. He plopped into his seat.

Brax crouched near him. "Ven, are you okay?"

Captain Starling's voice carried into the expedition speakers. "Brax, are we a go?"

Ven watched as the lieutenant commander tapped the button. "Make the jump!"

There was a brief delay, long enough for Ven to see through the viewscreen at the spot the Protector had been. It was torn in four quarters, floating lifelessly.

He began to climb out of the seat, wondering how he'd managed to destroy it with his mind, when the jump hit.

One second, they were in the Sol system; the next, they were somewhere near Nolix. It was all Ven saw before blackness filled his eyes, and he fell to the floor.

Lineage

"Thomas Baldwin, Captain, Admiral, helmsman." Tom sat at the lone console of the Ugna-made vessel, controlling it by himself. The trip to Aruto had been quick, and they'd been relieved to see that President Bertol's defenses had managed to handle the remaining Ugna fighters with few losses.

The subsequent journey to Ridele would take nearly a week, and Tom didn't think they had that much time. Hans lingered in the boiler room, and as Tom slowed the giant craft, he wished there was a faster way to access the capital.

"Admiral, you're never going to believe this." *Shu*'s chief engineer entered the bridge with a smile on his face.

"What is it?" Tom asked.

Shu slowed, and Tom watched as the president's private vessel took the lead, leaving Aruto. She was joining them at Ridele. She thought they could use the word of a Founder's leader to defend the Concord in a time of internal strife. A couple of days had passed since the aggressive protesters began filing into Nolix, and Tom hoped calmer heads prevailed.

"Hans, are you going to tell me?" Tom asked, and the man came to sit nearby. The entire bridge was a hollow unfinished version of the real ones. It was an open rounded space, with exposed wires and temporary flooring. The vessel worked exactly as the others, without the interior expenses. It was strange piloting a craft with none of the features he'd grown accustomed to.

"Engineering. There's a half-finished Nek shuttle waiting to be used," he said.

"You have to be kidding me," Tom said. These things were popping up everywhere.

"I'm not."

"How long before it's operational?" Tom could use a miracle, and jumping to Ridele before things grew worse was imperative.

"If Kan Shu helps, I believe we could have her done by tomorrow, Admiral."

"Make it so," Tom said. He slapped the communication button, getting Rene on the viewscreen.

"Admiral, are you prepared for our journey?" she asked, a slight coyness to her voice.

"We have a development," he said, noticing Benitor on *Shu*'s bridge.

"Do tell," Rene said.

"Hans has discovered an unfinished Nek shuttle. He's requesting that the commander assist its completion." He saw Kan receive a nod, meaning the Callalay man would be arriving within minutes. "I'll return to *Shu* for the evening. We should discuss the plan."

"Very well. Come aboard, Admiral." The screen went blank, and Tom shrugged, nodding to Hans.

"Do your best. We're relying on you. All of us." Tom clapped the older man on the shoulder and started for the hangar.

An hour later, he found himself in the meeting room with Rene, Admiral Benitor, Elder Fayle, and President Bertol. He felt himself oddly outnumbered and wished Kan had stuck around.

"You think that's such a good idea, Baldwin?" Rene asked.

"I do. Us returning in a Nek drive is the only thing that makes sense. We can't wait a week. It might be too late," Tom said again.

"This is ill news. If the Ugna have access to Nek drives, we're out of our element," Benitor said.

"Not necessarily. We have the technology too, not to

Lineage

mention we hold the supply. I'll make sure the Prime increases mining operations and defenses at the Tingor Belt, and..." Tom saw the doubt in the admiral's eyes.

"If they have the blueprints..." Benitor started, and Fayle finished.

"They've used them to return to Sol. That's what they were after," she said. "Meaning our timeline is sooner than we'd hoped. I thought they were taking the long journey there, as *Constantine* was supposed to."

"If Keen jumped to Sol, they might already be working on mods for their fleet. We could have company within a week or two," Tom said, wiping his beading brow. Things were going from bad to worse.

"Which makes it all the more imperative that we use this shuttle as soon as it's prepared," President Bertol said.

"There's no way you're coming on the shuttle, President," Rene told her firmly.

"Excuse me, Captain, but I don't think that choice is yours. These are dire times, and the people need to hear my side of the story," Bertol said.

"She's right. The Nek drive could be erratic, making it extremely dangerous." Rene grinned as he backed her.

"But you're going on it, correct?" Bertol asked him, then aimed her stare at Elder Fayle. "And her? She's going? I presume Admiral Benitor is also..."

"Enough," Benitor said stiffly. "You will join us. Hans and Commander Shu will confirm we're in for a safe ride."

"I'll ensure Kan is prepared to lead *Shu* to Nolix," Rene started, but stopped when the admiral shook her head.

"I'm afraid you won't be coming, Captain Bouchard. We need you to lead the fleet to Nolix. There may be opposition along the way," Benitor advised her, and Rene's lips pursed.

"From what I've heard, there are at least three flagship

replicas and over forty fighters. We must remain vigilant. They can sneak in to Nolix with ease, and I suspect they are already near, ready to assist the growing collection of partners as they storm the capital's system. Add in the Ugna fleet of a hundred…"

"I thought they had half of that!" Tom bellowed, standing up in shock. All eyes fell on him, and he took his seat again. "I guess I shouldn't be so surprised that the Ugna lied about that too. That you, Elder Fayle, lied to my face."

"I was telling the truth at that time. We did only have forty vessels when we went after the Assembly. Wylen brought the other sixty with him. These are trying times for people, and we're about to meet a foe unlike any other," Fayle told them.

"With the ability to melt our brains through our shields? We already had a taste of that and didn't take kindly to it. We need to prevent these types of attacks," Tom said.

Fayle met his gaze. "There might be. Believe me, much testing has been done by the Ugna on this matter. They've determined it's nearly impossible to cut someone's power off, but even I'm not strong enough. You need someone who can cut the flow, but to do something so powerful, you must be in contact with the Vastness."

Rene guffawed and slapped a hand over her mouth. "Honestly. This sounds like a bunch of rubbish. We're dealing with a telekinetic killer race. This is absurd. You make it sound like we need a magic hero to save the day. This is the Concord. We fight with our minds and our technology, not with the waving of our hands."

"Believe what you will, Captain Bouchard, but there *is* one that can help us. One I kept safe all these years." Fayle returned her gaze to Tom. "One I placed right in Admiral

Lineage

Baldwin's capable hands."

"Ven Ittix." Tom mouthed the name, and she nodded. "You didn't place him there. The Concord did."

"Thomas, must you think so little of me? Of course it was my doing. I had Admiral Hudson's ear. He was a surprisingly cheap man to buy off. When I started to comprehend what was coming, I had Ven placed into the Academy. When High Elder Wylen found out, I made an excuse, saying it would only help our chances of acceptance into the Concord. That Ven was weak in ability but solid of mind, and he would make the ideal candidate to connect with a flagship crew. When I mentioned your name and lineage, he was only too happy to agree.

"Wylen has no idea the power my Ven holds within him. His death and resurrection confirmed it. Ven Ittix will be our savior and leader when the dust settles. Surely even the Concord can agree to those terms," Fayle said.

"What are you proposing?" Benitor asked, assessing the Elder.

"This war will be arduous. We need to unite the partners against the coming forces, but when word escapes on Driun F49 about the truth behind the Ugna, our people will be split in half. I want amnesty for those that fight alongside the Concord.

"We keep Driun F49 and continue to be partners on a probationary calendar. I will retire from my position. You can imprison me, or kill me to make a show of it, but I do demand one thing."

Tom expected what was coming, and he waited for it along with the rest of them.

"Ven Ittix will become our new High Elder," she finished.

Admiral Benitor set her hand on Tom's arm. "We have the power to make this deal, and I don't see any other choice. But I'll cede to you in this case, Admiral Baldwin. You know Executive Lieutenant Ittix better than anyone. Will this be a good move on our behalf, and on the behalf of the loyal Ugna?"

"The better question is whether Ven will want the role or not. I know him well, or at least as well as anyone can. He's been cautious with his heritage, because he's become aware there's an entire underground world he doesn't approve of. This deep-rooted deception will taint his view of you, Fayle, as well as your people. He might abandon you and choose to continue with us." Tom drummed his fingers on the desk. "But he cares so much. If he feels there's no other choice, and it's for the good of the people, he'll take the role, albeit with hesitation."

"Do we have a deal?" Fayle asked.

This was a big moment, an agreement the Prime should be making about the future of the Concord. Tom was backed into a corner, but without the aid of a loyal faction within the Ugna, this war was going to be difficult to win. They needed to show strength for the partners, to have a common enemy, and Wylen and his soldiers would become that adversary. "It's a deal, Fayle, but remember this."

"What?"

"If you betray us, I won't stop until every last Ugna has been dealt with and banned from ever returning to the Concord. Including Ven Ittix," he told her. He clenched his jaw, waiting for a barbed reply.

"I have no concern about that. I've laid my eggs in your nest, Admiral."

"If there's nothing else, we have a shuttle to prepare." Benitor rose, heading for the room's exit. "Gather your things. Baldwin, Elder Fayle, President Bertol. We depart first thing tomorrow."

Lineage

The others filed out of the room, leaving Rene and Tom alone. He deflated as soon as the door closed. "That was intense. Do you trust her?"

Rene shrugged, tilting her head to the side. "I suppose. What choice do we have? The Concord is about to engage in a civil war, and we're at the epicenter of the first battle. And to think, things had finally started to smooth out since the overhaul a couple of years ago."

Tom gulped his glass of water and suddenly felt thirsty for something stronger. "Is there anything to drink?"

"How about you join me in my quarters?" Rene said.

"Is that a good idea?" he asked.

"Oh, Tommy, always with the dirty mind. Can't two peers enjoy a drink in the captain's quarters once in a while? I'm sure you and Starling did the same."

"First of all, Treena and I have never slept together, and second..." He lost his train of thought as she walked away, heading for the doors.

"It's a drink, Baldwin. Are you coming?" she asked, a smirk on her lips.

He followed her, and they entered her suite within a few minutes.

"Aimie and I are through," he said as soon as the door closed.

"Is that so?" she asked. "What happened?"

"We're on different pages."

"How about that drink?" Rene asked, and Tom appraised her. She was smart, capable, a great leader, and extremely easy on the eyes. He imagined they'd have come to this moment a lot sooner if they'd spent more time together over the last few years. Working on different postings meant you rarely encountered anyone but your own crew, and being in a position of power meant Tom didn't often have the chance to explore relationships.

"Why are you looking at me like that?" she asked, pouring brown liquid into a squat glass.

Instead of answering, he stepped over and kissed her. Tomorrow, he was charging into the pit, but tonight was another story.

Rene set the glass down and led him into her bedroom.

---

*I*t worked! The doors opened, and Ven and Brax raced onto the bridge, a human stranger behind them. He stopped at the edge of the room, watching with interest.

"Are you two okay?" Treena asked her crew members.

"We're fine. We have the humans on *Cleo*, and we need someone to escort them to Doctor Nee for examinations. Make sure they aren't carrying anything harmful to us," Brax said. The two officers in their positions rose, and Treena asked them to take the humans to the medical bay.

Treena walked across the bridge, standing behind Ven's seat. "I need an update."

"We're near Lionar, meaning the mining station is the closest Tekol outpost," Ven said.

"Probes deployed, Captain," Brax said.

"Get me Ridele. See if Baldwin's there," Treena said, and Darl went to work.

"Admiral West here." The man's image appeared on the viewscreen.

"Admiral West, we'd like to speak with Admiral Baldwin." Treena cracked her knuckles. Baldwin had been away on a mission, but it was possible they'd returned early.

"I'm sorry, Captain. Baldwin's not available." West seemed pleased about that.

"What about Admiral Benitor?" she asked.

Lineage

"I'm afraid Benitor is… missing."

"Missing?" Something was wrong. "Patch me to the Prime, West."

"The Prime? Starling, aren't you supposed to be gone for the next four months?" he asked, frowning.

The call was muted, and Brax turned toward her. "Captain, there are over one hundred vessels approaching Nolix." He put the image on the viewer, and she stepped forward, seeing various crafts. She recognized a Greblok Defender, as well as an Eganian Trader.

"What in the Vastness is going on?" she asked.

"Captain, it appears as though the Prime is available after all," Ven said as he flipped the view back to Ridele's head office.

"West, how many times have I told you? I want word as soon as *Shu* or *Constantine* touches base with us," Prime Xune said.

Treena hardly recognized the man. It was as if he'd aged a decade in the past few weeks. "Prime Xune, what's happening at Nolix?" she asked.

"We're under attack," he told her.

She stiffened. "From inside? Why are those Concord ships coming for Nolix?"

"Someone's been posing as the Concord. They built fake ships and have confronted four of our partners over the last week or so. They recently went for Aruto," the Prime said.

"Isn't that where Admiral Baldwin is?" Treena asked nervously.

"It is, and a good thing too. They've managed to defeat the enemy and are returning to Ridele," he told her.

"Who's infiltrating us from the inside? Is it the Assembly?" she asked.

He shook his head, his eyes narrowing to slits. "We

think the Assembly is dead. But we've been fools…"

"The Ugna," she said softly.

"That's right. High Elder Wylen is behind this."

Ven's attention snapped to the viewscreen. "What is happening?" he asked.

"They've lied to us. The Ugna came to take over. They're creating dissent within the ranks and have turned our own people against us," Prime Xune said.

"There's more to it." Treena placed her hands on her hips and told him of their discovery in Sol: about these Invaders and the Nek modifications they were attempting to make to their Protector vessels. She also advised him of their trap, which would cripple their efforts.

"You may have bought us some time, but we have a crisis on our hands. I've been trying to parley with the incoming force, but they don't trust me. And with Baldwin gone, I fear the attack is coming soon." Xune glanced behind him, where Admiral West was hovering. "If we don't talk some sense into this force in the next few hours, they'll come for us, and blood will be drawn."

"Captain, the probes are showing incoming," Brax said. "Twenty vessels. Ugna."

"How long until they arrive?" Treena asked.

"Four hours."

Prime Xune blinked too many times and leaned over to the camera. "Move to Nolix. We need all the defense we can muster. War is upon us, Captain. Until we meet in the Vastness," he said, ending the communication.

Treena glanced at her crew, seeing concern spread across their faces. "You heard the man. Bring us to Nolix and set us up between Ridele and the fleet. Send Lieutenant Basker and the other pilots out in the fighters. This is not a drill. We defend our capital at any cost."

She returned to her seat and looked at Pol Teller. Her

commander was smiling. "What are you so happy about?"

"We're about to kick some asses. That's always been my favorite part of the job."

TWENTY-ONE

Tom awoke to the sound of the buzzer, the room pitch black. He felt the heat of Rene Bouchard beside him, and he smiled in the dark. Last night had been something. His relationship with Aimie Gaad had awoken something dormant inside, and after being with Rene, he felt alive again. Right in time to head into a fight.

He shook her gently, and she kicked a leg out of the blankets. "Time to go?"

The lights came on as he commanded the computer, and she squinted at him as he climbed out of the bed. He tugged a blanket along, and she grabbed it, pulling it free.

He chuckled. "What was this?" he asked.

She sat up, staring at him. "It was fun. As for what it meant, I'll let you decide."

He grinned and stalked to the bathroom for a quick shower. Three minutes later, he was dressed and heading for the door, where Rene stood in a robe, waiting for him.

She kissed him softly, but the hug she gave him afterwards said it all. She was worried.

"I know you wish you were coming, but Benitor's right. Your crew needs you," he told her, fully aware it would do little to appease her wishes to join the shuttle jump.

"Be careful. Do your thing, Baldwin. The people do love you. You don't see it because your nose is in a console

Lineage

when you're not on the bridge, but the Concord fully trusts Thomas Baldwin. Use that now. Save our people and set us up to win this coming war," Rene said, giving him the bolster of confidence he needed.

"Thanks, Rene. See you at Ridele," he said, and with that, he was off, straight for the hangar.

An hour later, he watched as Kan and Hans put the final scans on the shuttle as they tested it, using a robot pilot from *Shu*.

"And?" he asked, leaning over Hans as he worked on the keyboard.

"It checks out. It's a good thing I had those weeks with your chief engineer, Reeve Daak," Hans said.

"She's no longer *my* chief engineer, but she is a damned good crew member," Tom reminded him.

"Can you program the coordinates for us, Hans?" Admiral Benitor ordered, and Tom stepped aside as the shuttle returned into the hangar, passing through the blue energy field.

"Already done, Admiral." The ship landed, and the doors automatically opened.

It was time to head home. Tom said his goodbyes to Kan and Hans, waiting by the shuttle's entrance while President Bertol walked on, followed by Elder Fayle, then Admiral Benitor.

He was the last on board and closed the doors, taking the pilot's seat. "I guess I'll do the honors."

Once they were outside the Ugna-replicated flagship, he moved toward Aruto. There was quite the amassed fleet gathered, prepared to make the trek to Nolix. With two flagships and twenty Callalay cruisers, they were quite the force. He only hoped a week wouldn't be too long.

Tom guided the shuttle farther from the fleet, making sure they were in the clear before going over the directions

Kan had given him a few minutes ago. "Let's see if I have this right." He flipped the switch, and the rear of the shuttle glowed brightly as the Nek drive kicked into gear.

He saw the fear in the Callalay president's eyes, and he tried to ease her worries. "We've started to use this technology. It's new, but the engineer that tweaked the process is a good friend of mine, and she's brilliant. *Constantine* had been fitted with the same tech, making it the largest Nek drive-capable vessel in the known universe.

"We're totally safe in this shuttle," he promised her and the others, wishing that assurance covered his own lingering doubts. If this failed and destroyed them, the chances that the Concord prevailed in the coming war decreased. So many things hinged on Tom being able to convince the partners of their innocence, as well as Benitor taking control of their fleet to prepare for the attack on Driun F49.

Elder Fayle had to gather her forces, separating the Ugna in their own civil war. This shuttle needed to make the jump without complication.

As Tom returned his attention to the controls, he heard Elder Fayle chanting behind him. She floated against her buckles, repeating the mantra over and over. He'd seen Ven meditate enough times to not be disturbed by the sight.

The dash light blinked, advising him the Nek drive was charged, and Tom took a deep breath, slowly exhaling. He confirmed the destination for the fourth time and hit the button.

---

*T*reena took a good tally on the approaching vessels and calmed. The Concord imposed limitations on their partners' spaceship weapons systems for a reason. Not only did they not want rogue wars over turf breaking out within their Border, but they didn't want an upheaval like the one coming for Nolix at this moment.

"Anything out of place, Brax?" she asked.

"I say hit the big one first. It's clearly the leader," Commander Teller said. He was standing with Missy at his side, aiding him.

"We aren't fighting any of them. They're misguided." Treena frowned as she searched for the one he was indicating. She finally spotted the greatest of the makeshift fleet, a Finos cruiser. "How do you know that's the leader?"

Teller grunted. "They're subcontracted as a Border patrol along the far reaches closest to Earon when the Concord can't make the run. Which means…"

Brax finished for him. "It means they're allowed regulation weapons, making them our biggest threat."

Treena was once again impressed with the knowledge Teller gave them. That didn't mean she had to agree with him and attack anyone. Not yet.

There were over a hundred various craft congregated nearby, carving a thousand-kilometer-wide stretch as they slowly made for the Concord's capital.

"Prime Xune, are you there?" she asked, seeing his image emerge on the viewscreen.

"They refuse to listen. The battle is coming," he said. "I've sent what we have to assist our defense, but I fear we're thin on real defenders."

Treena knew exactly what they had on hand. An old cruise ship named after a Tekol leader from two centuries ago—*Gutam*—as well as the recently re-established *Andron*, along with another dozen skimmers and cruisers. It might be enough against the current grouping of vessels, but once the twenty Ugna arrived, that was a different story. They needed to change the script before the reinforcements came.

"Let me try," Treena said. "Which vessel have you contacted?"

"The lead one. I assumed they were in charge." Xune looked frustrated.

"That's the mistake. Ven, hit up the Finos cruiser," Teller said, and Xune shrugged.

"Until we meet in the Vastness," he said, the communication ending.

There will be no meeting in the Vastness today, not if I can help it. Treena calmed herself as the image of a Finos woman landed on the viewscreen. Her skin was dark orange, the color of autumn leaves back home on Earon. She wore her hair short and spiky; a black vest and pants rounded out her appearance.

"The illustrious *Constantine*." She smiled, her teeth white and pointy. "I should have expected the poster-ship would arrive to defend the Prime. Do you really think it's good to continue this ruse? The Concord is attacking its own, and we're going to cut the head off the leader."

"You'll have to forgive me. I'm Captain Treena Starling. Who are you?" Treena remained stoic.

"Captain Edgalo Vulons."

"And, Captain Vulons, did you receive your information from the Ugna, by chance?" Treena asked her.

"What do they have to do with this? You have one on your bridge. I see him right there. Do you not trust them?"

Treena wished she'd asked Ven to stand aside, but it was too late. "They're creating a disruption, a distraction from within. We're fighting a war, but you're facing the wrong direction."

"Is that so? And what do you say about the recent

Lineage

attacks on our own soil? You think the Ugna were behind those? They were Concord fleet ships, killing innocent people on partners' home worlds. You are part of the problem, Captain Starling. Prepare to engage." The call ended, and Treena kicked out, striking the corner of Ven's helm desk, her boot crushing into the plastic casing.

"Sorry. They're fools!" Treena shouted. "How can they not see this?"

"Because the Concord *is* corrupt. The people are nervous. It wasn't so long ago the Zilph'i were talking about leaving. The Callalay have been all but locked down, and we've essentially given the Ugna the perfect planet to colonize. I'd question their motivations too, if I were on the other side," Brax told her.

"What do we do?" she asked, not wanting to fight these people. They should be working together, not wasting time and lives on misguided communication.

"We blast that damned Finos cruiser." Teller grimaced, and she could tell he didn't really want to. He was doing as trained. Strike hard, strike first, and the others might disperse. Would it work?

"Brax, target the cruiser…" The first blast took Treena by surprise, and it had come from below them. The next hit rapidly, and she cursed herself. "We've been suckers. I was relying on the sanctity of the Concord's regulations, but if this fleet assumed the Concord was pulling a fast one on them, they don't believe in the rules any longer."

"They've updated the weapons," Brax said.

"That's right." Treena took her captain's chair and watched as another five pulses hit their shields, which held without issue.

Andron and *Gutam* flanked them, and Treena imagined this going into an all-out war. Teller might be right. The only move might be striking first before this angry mob went for Nolix and Ridele. There were billions of lives on the planet, and it was up to her to ensure their safety.

"Brax, we're done being friendly. How long until the Ugna arrive?" she asked.

"An hour and a half," Brax advised her.

"Hopefully, we have some juice left in the tank." Another blast hit them, this time a sizeable cannon pulse from the Finos vessel. "Brax, on your mark..."

The blast struck the shuttle's shields, sending their compact craft reeling. Tom was able to recover, pulling out of the spin toward Nolix.

"What in the Vastness was that?" President Bertol asked.

"We're in the middle of a dogfight." Tom tried to get hold of the situation. He saw his beloved *Constantine* on one side, along with an unfamiliar ship, and his grandfather's old one, *Andron*.

On the other side were over a hundred opponents—vastly outgunned, but what they lacked in weapons, they made up for with numbers. Out of habit, he checked the long-range radar, seeing twenty additional sleek vessels coming in hot, their formation perfect. The shuttle's system recognized them. "Ugna," he whispered.

"Thomas, you have to do something," Elder Fayle said with far less panic than should have been expected.

He thought about the issues while attempting to maneuver the shuttle out of harm's way. "Admiral, connect me with Ridele. I need to tap into their network so my message hits them at the same time!" Tom cranked the direction, the pulse striking the rear shields. Alarms rang out around him, and he silenced them with the push of a button.

"I have you patched," Benitor said. At least she knew how to use the equipment.

"Am I linked? Will the entire fleet see this?" he asked, and she paused, a long ten seconds of breathless flying, while he waited for her response.

"And... you're good. They will each bear witness," Benitor told him.

Nolix was a busy planet, with almost ten times the trade traffic of any other Concord world. To ensure safety and disaster mitigation, they had the ability to talk to every vessel within range at once, to save trouble. It wasn't used often, but today it might save some lives.

He saw the blinking light near the shuttle's panoramic viewer and focused on it, sitting up in his seat. "People of the Concord, stop this. I am Admiral Thomas Baldwin, and I need to tell you something of the utmost importance."

He saw the bridge of *Constantine* appear in the lower corner of the screen and noticed Captain Starling raising a finger to make Brax stop firing.

More shots were fired, and Tom frowned, speaking faster. "I repeat. There is no reason to fight our own. Please, cease fire, and I'll reveal everything we know."

"Thomas, there's an incoming from the Finos cruiser," Benitor told him. "Would you like it onscreen?"

Tom nodded, adding, "Make sure this is shared with everyone too."

The woman stalked toward the camera, her face stoic. "I am Captain Edgalo Vulons. How can we trust you? You might be involved in the conspiracy."

Tom only smiled, shaking his head. "Well met, Captain. I've spent my entire life working to make the Concord a formidable alliance. When I was given *Constantine*, I fought the Statu. I defeated the Assembly from attempting a hostile takeover, and I returned to finish off the Statu threat. I helped bring the new Prime to his seat and saved the Bacal people from their destruction.

"I stand before you today, swearing on the Flame of Life and the Vastness that I am not lying to you. The Concord is strong. The flagships you're suggesting attacked our partners were none other than fakes built by a wayward Ugna leader. High Elder Wylen has planned this for a lifetime, and he seeks to disrupt us, to weaken our capital to make his invasion easier.

"He's a coward, hiding in the shadows while he uses trickery to win a secret battle, but we aren't going to let him win. We're here to tell you that the Concord stands united. I stand with you, Captain Edgalo Vulons." Tom waited, seeing her expression soften.

"There are twenty Ugna ships coming now," she told him.

"Then we're running out of time." At least all one hundred spaceships were no longer firing. They were watching their viewscreens with great interest. "There will be a war, but we can't have it on our soil. I'm asking you to join us, to change our focus on the incoming fleet, because it will be the only way we can turn the tides in our favor. The Ugna want everything. They're powerful and have advanced measures to deal with an enemy. Will you join us?"

Vulons shifted on her feet, backing away a few steps. "Why do you think the Ugna were behind this?"

President Bertol moved behind him and answered, "I am President Bertol of Aruto, the leader of the Callalay, a Concord Founder. We encountered them only a day ago, and Thomas Baldwin stopped the Ugna. We now have that replica in our possession."

Tom took over. "And it's heading toward Nolix with

Shu as we speak. It'll arrive in a week. I'd be happy to give you a tour of it then."

"We don't have a week, Admiral," Vulons sneered. "We have under an hour."

"Then you'll need to make a decision. This is our biggest threat in some time, Captain. Remember that. Remember why you signed up to run Border patrol with your Finos cruiser when we didn't have a large enough fleet to do so. We need to be united, because the Ugna have waged a war, and I intend to give them one." Tom sat back, setting his hands on his lap. This was it. This woman was clearly in charge of their group, and he hoped he'd been able to convince her.

"Very well. What's your plan?" she asked, and Tom grinned.

"Thank you. The Ugna will think you're with them. Let's ensure they keep believing that. Continue the fight, but lower your pulses to twenty percent, and make sure your weapons officers' aim is inferior for the next while," Tom ordered.

"You want us to keep fighting?" Captain Vulons asked, her sharp teeth showing as she smiled.

"That's right. When the Ugna arrive, we don't give them a chance to recover. Understand?" Tom asked.

"I see what you're suggesting. It will be done." The Finos captain's image disappeared, and Tom cut the all-play communication.

"Admiral Benitor, can you connect me to *Constantine*?" Tom was enjoying bossing the old Callalay admiral around for a change of pace.

"They may not be fooled so easily, Baldwin," Elder Fayle warned him.

"I don't expect them to, but I do have a favor to ask of you, Fayle," Tom said.

"What is it?"

"Does Wylen have any idea you've betrayed him?" Tom asked.

She shook her head. "I've kept my tracks very light. There is no trail."

"I need you to return to your new home. Take the shuttle, escape during the battle. Set course for Driun F49 and plead your case to your people while staying covert. If we're going to stop him, we need someone on the inside," he told her.

Fayle didn't speak, and her fear was almost palpable. "I do not think that is such a great idea."

"Admiral Baldwin," Treena said.

Tom checked to make sure their conversation was private. "Captain, good to see you in one piece."

"You did a great job, and nice timing. I was about to lay waste to that fleet," she said, her voice wavering. That wouldn't have been an easy decision for Starling.

"We don't have long. What do we know?" he asked her promptly.

"Earth. We've been close. The Ugna rule the planet. They've taken over and enslaved the humans. We escaped and set a trap. Someone has gone there with Nek drive schematics, but we managed to deceive them. The moment they try to make the jump to the Concord, they're going to find a nice surprise," Treena said.

Tom checked the clock. Thirty minutes until the Ugna were in firing range. "I know who delivered the plans."

"Who?" Treena asked.

Tom watched the crew through his screen. Ven Ittix was there, and he thought about Fayle's words. He was powerful. Something special. The future leader of the Ugna at Driun F49, and he had no idea. This wasn't the time to speak up about it.

"My old nemesis."

"Lark Keen?" She almost jumped as she said it. "That son of a…"

"He's a piece of work, and we know for a fact that Wylen was behind his prison transport break," Tom advised them. "Will your trap kill them?"

She shook her head. "We wanted to buy time. There was no secure manner of arranging that, not one that the pre-flight run analysis wouldn't discover. We had to do what we were able to while being discreet."

"Will it work?" Tom asked.

"We think so. We'll have time to discuss it after, but for now, we have a looming battle on our hands." Treena looked confident as a captain, and Tom's gaze lingered on the old man beside her. Teller seemed to be good at keeping quiet, and he wondered how her experience had been with the ex-captain.

"Very well. Let's prepare for a fight." Tom drew up the plans, sending them to Ridele and the fleet.

TWENTY-TWO

*I*t was time. One advantage of using an android body was the lack of nerves. It wasn't the same, with none of the physical trepidation that came along with the emotion. The Ugna were close, expecting the battle to be raging over Nolix. Tom had been right about one thing. They were cowards, tricking others into doing their dirty work, but not anymore.

Brax continued to fire at the ragtag group of vessels gathered there, but none of the shots held much power, and he was sure to miss more often than hit, just as they were doing. She only hoped the approaching Ugna didn't notice in the heat of the moment.

"Captain, they're close," Ven said. "I can sense them, but it doesn't feel as it did with the Vusuls. They are confident, not worried enough to attempt a mass kill."

"Good. Let's hope the buggers stay assured," Teller said, making Treena laugh.

Teller had tweaked Tom's idea a bit, and the Admiral had gone for it. Treena prayed to the Vastness that it worked.

The twenty ships broke formation, as Ven had suggested they would, splitting into four groups as they were instructed from a young age. He hadn't trained with them, but in his time on Driun F49, he'd grilled Hanli about their fleet any chance he'd gotten, and apparently, it had worked.

"Good job, Ven," she told him.

Five ships flew to the far edge of the assembled partners: another five to the near side, five above, five below. They were more susceptible to an attack, but from their point of view, they were stronger to pen in the one hundred ships and destroy them before they could escape. Their plan banked on the fact that the Ugna would be deceived.

"Brax, select your targets. *Andron*, take your two," Treena ordered.

"On your mark, Captain," Brax said, and she waited until the Ugna began firing toward *Constantine*.

The bridge doors opened, and Tom ran through, followed by Admiral Benitor and President Bertol. Treena had never met her, only seen pictures, and she snapped her attention to the viewscreen again, not wanting the distraction.

"Did I miss anything?" Tom asked, rushing to her side.

"Not yet. Brax, fire!" She called the command, and they watched as his shots hit their targets, destroying two freight haulers from Yollox. *Andron* aimed at two others, these farther out near the Ugna, on top of the fleet. They also exploded quickly, sending a sign.

In order to make the battle seem real, they'd emptied out four ships, with the promise of compensating the owners later. Evacuating them had been a close call, but in the end, it made their fight seem in full swing.

The moment the ships were destroyed, the entire fleet started firing—only not at the Concord vessels, like the Ugna were doing. They didn't see it coming for a second. *Constantine* targeted the left side, *Andron* the top, and *Gutam* the right. The other ninety-five struck with a ferocity that shocked Treena.

The first Ugna vessel was destroyed within moments, and another followed a second later. But the Ugna were no fools, and once they saw the deception, they altered their attack, focusing on the Finos cruiser first. But it was too late.

Treena watched as two freighters were destroyed in the crossfire, and she closed her eyes for a moment at the loss of life. When she opened them, Ven was guiding *Constantine* in the direction of the last cluster of Ugna ships. One of them was attempting to flee, and Treena shouted at Brax, "Don't let them escape!"

There was no mercy given. The Ugna had broken the Code, and there was no turning back.

Brax chased the ship, the Finos cruiser flying along beside them. Both Concord allies fired until the sleek Ugna vessel was destroyed, and everything went silent in the vicinity of Nolix.

Only then did she turn to Tom. "Welcome home, Admiral."

Ven waited for *Shu* and the second flagship to dock before allowing himself to think of the next steps. He hadn't had a chance to speak with Elder Fayle, and he hated that. He had so many questions for her that couldn't be answered now. If Wylen learned about her transgressions, she would be dead within moments.

The expedition ship was scheduled to arrive at the main landing pad near the Concord's head office in twenty minutes, and Ven paced behind the glass windows, anxious for her arrival. First Officer Hanli had been with Fayle. She would have some details. Admiral Baldwin appeared to

Lineage

know more than he was letting on, but he promised Ven it was good news, and that everything would be solved.

Ven didn't believe that. He'd seen the Invaders near Earth. They were going to attempt to come to Wylen's aid, and he feared if that occurred, the population of the Concord would end up slaves like the humans of Earth.

Earth. He felt the need to return, to help the people, and he had been glad when Baldwin agreed that they would eventually do just that. After all, they were Founders of the Concord, even if they didn't know it.

He tried not to think about what he'd managed to do to that Protector chasing them in Sol. It had felt beyond his control, but he'd tapped into a river of the eternal Vastness. Was he a monster? Was he worse than Wylen? No man should have that ability, and he'd managed that without the use of En'or. He really wished he could speak with Elder Fayle about what was happening to him. Once they'd made the jump, the colors and dancing lights had stopped instantly. Even now, he felt good, strong and clear-headed.

The expedition ship lowered, and a thrill ran through him when Hanli stepped off. Her hair glowed in the sunlight atop the high rise facing the massively populated city of Ridele. She was beautiful.

He found himself pushing through the doors, stepping onto the roof's landing pad, and striding toward her. Hanli smiled as she saw him, and he continued until he was close enough to embrace her. He took her in his arms, spinning around before letting her down.

"Ven Ittix, what has gotten into you?" she asked, unable to hide a light laugh at his actions.

"I am happy to see you, Hanli." He glanced around, finding Captain Rene Bouchard and Commander Kan Shu filing out. "We have a lot to discuss. Would you accompany me for dinner?"

She nodded. "We do. The Ugna are about to have their biggest challenge yet, and we need you to lead us down the right path."

"Me?" he asked.

"Come. Let us dine. I have much to say."

It was strange to return to his condo overlooking the city, and Tom already missed the comfort of the executive crew quarters on *Shu*. The city looked the same as always, like nothing had happened only a week earlier.

Nolix wasn't out of the woods yet, but they had time to regroup and make a plan against High Elder Wylen. Fayle should be on Driun F49, but Tom hadn't received a message from her yet, making him worried about her well-being.

The buildings reflected the bright sunlight, and he tapped the tint level higher as he observed the skyline. Maybe the city wasn't so bad, but what was here for him? With Aimie gone... He should have checked on her. Asked if she was all right.

He crossed the living room, tapping his tablet to life. He found her contact information and tried to reach her. He needed some closure.

Her face appeared, and he found himself smiling despite the circumstances. "Aimie."

"Tom," she said softly.

He recognized the art behind her, and he squinted. "Are you at home?"

She nodded, giving him a grin. "I couldn't leave. Not without speaking to you first."

"I've been here a week," he told her.

Lineage

"I know. I was… trying to figure things out."

"And have you?" he asked, seeing another call was incoming.

"I have… I don't think I should go. I made a mistake ending things with you," she admitted.

The other communication was from Rene. He'd scarcely heard Aimie.

"Tom, are you listening? I think we should talk."

"Head office is attempting to reach me. Let me get back to you, okay?" he asked.

"Come over when you're done. I need to see you," she told him, and he ended the call, swiping Rene's icon.

"Baldwin. What are you doing for dinner?" she asked cheerfully.

"You made it! With my ship too, I see." He laughed.

"Your ship? I highly doubt that. Admirals don't have postings, haven't you heard?" she jabbed.

"Desperate times… et cetera." He thought about Aimie's invitation and her sad tone. It was the polar opposite of Rene's friendly banter.

"What do you say? Know a place we can have a few drinks and eat something good?" she asked.

"Sure. I'll ping you the details. See you in an hour?" he asked, and she smiled again, small dimples showing.

"It's a date." Her image vanished, and Tom slumped into his chair.

Aimie had asked him over, saying she made a mistake, and Rene wanted a date. Sometimes Tom felt like fighting an enemy was easier than navigating relationships. The outcome was always the same. There was one winner. With a relationship, the goal was to have both parties winning, at least until it inevitably went sideways.

He took one last look over the cityscape and decided he'd take a shower. Maybe he'd have a better idea of who he was going to move on with.

EPILOGUE

A month. The modifications had lasted a solid month, but only because the past week had been spent running test programs. The Invaders took this stuff very seriously, but Lark knew the High Elder trusted them to return to Driun F49 as soon as possible.

His own future depended on it. Luci's and Seda's, too.

"Are we ready yet?" he asked Prophet, and she nodded.

"It appears that we're going to make the jump," Prophet told him.

The station outside of Saturn had started feeling cramped, and he was glad to return to the Protector. They wound their way to the bridge, and the Invaders hesitantly let him in. President Basher was present, and their ship was going to be the first to depart.

The bridge was half the size of *Constantine*'s, but it was laid out well, making the available space feel like more than enough room.

The crew was primarily composed of Invaders, while much of the ship's crew were human. They always had their eyes averted, and they seemed to have a million unasked questions for Keen when they saw him walking through the halls in his Concord admiral's uniform.

"Course is set," the captain, a lanky pale Ugna, told the president. "We are prepared to make the trip to Driun, sir."

"Good." Basher glanced at Keen and waved him over. "Come here, Admiral. I look forward to assisting your cause."

Keen almost laughed at the words he chose, because nothing about this was *his* cause. But he stayed in character and smiled at the man. "And we appreciate it. You will be rewarded."

"Nonsense. We're allies, and I'm eager to build our relationship." The president turned to face the viewscreen. "Captain, hit it."

Keen pressed his eyes closed as they activated the Nek drive, and he heard the ship's alarms chiming loudly before he braved to open them again.

"What happened?" the president asked.

The captain leaned over his first officer, checking the console. Lark stared out the viewscreen, seeing nothing resembling Driun F49.

"Sir, we're not at the proper coordinates," the captain said.

"Then where are we?" the president asked.

"We can't tell. But our scans indicate we're far from any known space," he answered.

"Reprogram it. There must have been a glitch. Get us to Driun!" The president stood, his posture full of venom, his voice echoing with rage.

The captain slowly turned, his pale pink eyes watering. "I can't. The star drive is dead."

Keen's shoulders slumped as he peered in Prophet's direction.

"I think we've been sabotaged," she said quietly.

Lark had to agree, and wasn't sure if that was such a bad thing.

Lineage

*H*er shirt clung to her skin as she fell to the chair in exhaustion. Every time Treena thought about giving up, she pictured the Ugna coming for them and continued pushing herself. Her body was like the Concord, in a strange sense. She'd once been strong, powerful, and content. Then she'd been assaulted, her allies killed, but she'd survived. Now she was rebuilding, just as their alliance would.

The lights near the entrance flicked on, and she glanced over at the doors, seeing none other than Conner Douglas moving toward her. He tended to have a swagger when he walked, but today, he seemed slower, a little withdrawn as he approached her.

She was inside the R-Emergence offices in Ridele and was grateful for her continued access, despite the fact that Aimie Gaad had opted out and disappeared to some other world. Treena couldn't blame her, not after the threat of an internal attack on Nolix. Then there was the whole Tom break up to deal with, along with the fact that her company was built on blackmailing and extortion.

"Conner, come for a run?" she asked from her seated position.

He stared at her, a smile reaching his eyes. "I don't think so. But I do have something important to ask you."

She patted the chair next to hers, and he obliged. "What is it?"

"I love working with Rene, I do, but this is going to be one intense battle we're about to face. I… I'd like to join the crew of *Constantine*." He averted his gaze, fidgeting with his hands.

"But I have a full bridge crew, Conner. You know that. And *Shu* is going to be an integral part of our success too," Treena reminded him. She thought there might be another reason; a more personal one she didn't want to discuss presently. She was still too unsure of herself, lacking confidence in this healing body, to allow someone like Conner into her life.

"I thought you were going to say that. Are you keeping Commander Teller on staff?" he asked.

She nodded absently. "I am. He's a good officer, and he brings an old but wise mind with him. He has a knack for war, and I'm afraid we need that."

"Please don't tell Captain Bouchard about my request. I... Maybe when this is over, and the Ugna have been dealt with? Then we can work collectively?" His hand landed on top of hers, and a spark coursed through her. When was the last time anyone had touched her skin while she was out of her android body?

"I'll consider it. In the meantime, what do you say we go find something to eat? I just need to freshen up," she said.

Conner perked right up. "You're coming as you?"

His question was innocent, and Treena laughed. "I'd like to get used to it. Does it bother you if I leave my android at home?"

"Quite the opposite. I'm glad you're feeling better about things. I think you're... I think you can pull it off." He smirked and moved for the exit, while she veered off to the showers.

She entered, seeing her reflection in the mirror. She was filling out. She was strong, and she would be ready for the upcoming war.

Treena let the water cleanse her worries: her trip to Sol, her fear of what was to come. She pictured Felix when she closed her eyes, water pouring over her face, and he smiled, telling her it was time. Time to move on. Time to take ownership of who she was. Time to be happy.

Lineage

"What are we supposed to be doing?" Carl asked, pacing the room.

"What do you mean? We're waiting," Jun told him. She was most comfortable in this big city. Brandon was the opposite. After years on their small Mars colony, Ridele was something from a dream, or a nightmare.

All the noise, the people. The aliens. He felt so sheltered after being told there were no other races outside of the Invaders and humans.

"Do you think they'll really help us?" Kristen asked.

Brandon nodded. "Sure they will. Because we have something they want."

Val stood, moving for the door to their suite. The Concord had been kind enough to give them the entire top floor of a skyscraper, and Brandon felt like a king relaxing amidst this opulence. Part of him was appreciating the luxuries, despite his trepidation at being in such a populated area.

"Ven Ittix," Brandon said as the man entered the room. He was just like the Invaders, but now he wore his Concord uniform, his yellow collar denoting his rank on *Constantine*. They'd been fed so much information over the last month, it was hard to keep it straight.

"Hello. Admiral Baldwin suggested you had something that might prove beneficial to us," Ven said, entering the room. A man was right behind him: white hair, light green skin, his eyes slotted and yellow. He wore gloves over his hands, and he smiled handsomely at the gathered humans.

"I'm Doctor Nee."

Brandon stuck his palm out, and the doctor stared at

it. He took the glove and shook hands with him.

"You don't shake hands here?" Brandon asked.

"Not many risk contact with a Kwant," Nee said with mirth in his voice.

"What's a Kwant?" Carl asked.

"It's my race. Our skin is poisonous to the touch. But don't worry, the glove protects you."

Brandon let go and peered at his palm before wiping it on his pants leg. "Executive Lieutenant, can we help you with something?"

Ven nodded and stepped further into their suite. "I heard something when going over your transcripts. You had an Invader on the rover, and you stopped him from using his powers. How?"

Brandon glanced at Val. She was the expert, and she lifted her arm. "I'll tell you how we do it, but we need something in return first."

He saw Ven and Nee share a look, and the Concord Ugna's lips closed tightly before he nodded once. "What do you seek?"

"Earth. When this is over, we need your help to free our people." Val had practiced this, but her voice still cracked.

"I would say that is a fair trade," Ven told them.

"Do you have the power to ensure the bargain is completed?" Brandon asked, suddenly wary. It was difficult to put your trust in someone that resembled your oppressors.

"I do not, but I have already been informed we will be assisting your race," Ven advised them.

"Good. Val, please give them the sample," Brandon said, and the woman left the room, returning with the vial in her grip. She hesitantly passed it to Doctor Nee.

"Inject them with this, and it cuts them off for at least a half hour per two cc's."

Lineage

"Thank you. This might aid our cause." Ven moved for the door.

Brandon darted ahead, blocking his exit. "I want to help. When will the battle begin?"

Ven met his stare. "It's already begun. A long time ago. But we may be seeking new crew for the replica vessel we're fitting. I'll speak to Admiral Baldwin."

"This Baldwin. Is he the real deal?" Kristen asked the Ugna.

"The real deal?"

"Yes. Is he a good man?"

"Of that I am sure. He is the best man I know," Ven said.

"Same here," the doctor agreed.

"Good." Brandon stepped aside, letting them leave. The thought of joining a crew in this strife was enough to energize him, and from the grins on his friends' faces, they were thrilled at the idea too.

Elder Fayle strode through the underground corridor, wishing the lights were brighter. She nearly tripped on a jutting rock and caught herself on the damp wall. Water dripped from the ceiling, splashing on her forehead as she waited near the hidden doorway.

It finally slid open, revealing a far different interior than surrounded her now. A group of ten Ugna soldiers waited inside and rushed her into the room, shutting the door behind her.

"Elder. We've been awaiting you," Gar Ellix told her. He was broad-shouldered, physically stronger than any Ugna she'd ever met. The perfect man to lead their revolt.

"I assume you have eyes on the High Elder?" she asked.

"We lost contact with Roe two days ago," he advised her.

Elder Fayle stiffened. "Do you think she was found out?" If they were going to win this internal war, they needed to track Wylen's position at all times.

"She is strong, her barriers tight. I don't suspect she was discovered, but Wylen is on the move. The remaining fleet has departed Driun F49," Gar said.

"When?" Fayle wiped her brow.

"Shortly ago."

"Do we know where they go?" Fayle asked him.

"It appears as though they're proceeding to Tebas." Gar crossed his thick arms and turned his head to the side, as if speaking the very name of the secret Ugna training grounds caused him pain.

"Tebas. It leaves the manufacturing plants at Obilina Six free for attack. Gather the forces. Send word to our network. Today, we break our thousand-year oath of the Ugna and fend for ourselves." Elder Fayle glanced around the room, seeing screens along the walls, chairs lining desks, and twenty eyes staring at her, their owners standing proudly at her words.

"Very well. We are honored to be the first to see you as you now are, High Elder Fayle," Gar said, though Fayle guessed the title would be short-lived. Ven Ittix would wear the crown soon enough, but she'd keep it warm for him.

"Come. There is much to do." She walked past Gar and took a seat at one of the consoles, sending a message to her contacts throughout the cities above on the surface of Driun F49.

Today, they were separatists, and she could only hope

that enough followed her into the coming war against her own people.

"No word from Fayle?" Admiral Benitor asked, and Tom shook his head.

"Nothing." Their informal group consisted of Bouchard, Prime Xune, Benitor, Starling, and himself.

"We have to assume these Invaders have failed their jump to Driun by now," Treena said. "We ought to go on the offensive."

"We've gathered the forces near Earon and will continue to do so in groups. But we need information from the Ugna camp before we do anything, so we're sure what we're up against. Fayle was our best chance," Tom said.

"You might have sent her to her death, Baldwin," Admiral Benitor accused without malice.

"True." He ran a hand through his hair, hoping that it wasn't. His tablet chimed, and he checked it from its resting position near the door. It was a coded message from an anonymous sender.

"It's her." He brought it to the table and sat down, scrolling to the proper notification.

"What does it say?" Prime Xune asked.

"Parley at Earon. Instructions to follow." Tom read it again, this time in his head.

"I don't think that's her," Benitor said.

Tom skimmed over it. "Neither do I."

"Do we respond?" the Prime asked.

Tom shrugged. "I wouldn't."

"We're about to face a terrible foe, one that would seek to destroy us from the inside. We're working on finding out the location of their manufacturing plant, and that's target one. We have five vessels being outfitted with Nek drives, which will allow us quick access to Driun F49 when the time is right," Admiral Benitor said.

"Remember, Fayle wants a peaceful outcome. She says the Ugna will side with her."

"If she lives," Xune said.

Tom nodded once. "Are we done for today?" He had a date and didn't want to be late again.

"We're done." The Prime left first, followed by Benitor.

"You kids have fun," Treena said, exiting after the admiral.

When it was just Rene and Tom in the meeting room, he turned to Rene. "It's going to be a gruesome war."

"We already won the first three battles: Treena's trap in Sol, our win near Aruto, and the blindside at Nolix. We're five steps ahead," she told him, walking across the room to settle her hands on his chest.

"We can't turn cocky," Tom told her. "This Wylen is all in. He's not going to stop until he wins or we kill him."

"Then we settle on the latter," Rene agreed.

"You said you wanted to talk to me about something?" he asked. Her earlier message had been confusing, but with Rene, that wasn't a shock.

"I do." She kissed him, their lips pressing together, then she broke the embrace. "You remember that first night we had together… before you skipped town with a shuttle full of other women."

He laughed at her description of him piloting some of the most powerful women in the Concord in a Nek-modified shuttle. "Sure. I recall it distinctly." He leaned in for another kiss, but she held a finger up, touching it to his lips.

"Tom. I know this is going to be a trying time we have

Lineage

ahead of us, but there's something you need to hear."

"What is it?"

"I'm pregnant."

He stared at her, disbelief racing through his mind. "Are you messing with me?"

Rene's cheeks flushed, matching her red hair, and he trusted she wasn't. "Just what we need. Another Baldwin running around."

Tom knew what he had to do. He pulled her close, hugging her tight. "This changes everything."

THE END

ABOUT THE AUTHOR

Nathan Hystad is an author from Sherwood Park, Alberta, Canada.

Keep up to date with his new releases by signing up for his newsletter at www.nathanhystad.com

Sign up at www.shelfspacescifi.com as well for amazing deals and new releases from today's best indie science fiction authors.

Printed in Great Britain
by Amazon